PUFFI

A PUFFIN BEDTI

NEVER MEDDL

With tales of dragons and dolls, ghosts and Green Grobblops, princes and princesses, birthday cakes and disappearing lunches, Forgetful Fred and Father Christmas, *Story Chest* is a wonderful mêlée of stories with something for all tastes.

There's a story about Francis who cut off all his sister's hair; a story about a Queen who held a 'Super Rumble Jumble Sale'; a boring bear who turned out to be far from boring; a dragon who cheated . . . There are old favourites such as Galldora alongside new stories published for the first time in this collection. There are stories by well-known children's writers such as Gene Kemp, Dorothy Edwards and Ursula Moray Williams alongside stories by brand-new authors.

Delightfully illustrated by Glenys Ambrus and Caroline Sharpe, this book will provide hours of fun and amusement whether read aloud or read alone.

Barbara Ireson is a story writer herself and a highly acclaimed anthologist of many books of stories and poetry, including another Bedtime Story Chest, *The Runaway Shoes and Other Stories* and the classic *Young Puffin Book of Verse*.

A PUFFIN BEDTIME STORY CHEST

NEVER MEDDLE WITH MAGIC

and other stories

Chosen by Barbara Ireson

Illustrated by Glenys Ambrus
and Caroline Sharpe

PUFFIN BOOKS

PUFFIN BOOKS

Published by the Penguin Group
27 Wrights Lane, London W8 5TZ, England
Viking Penguin Inc., 40 West 23rd Street, New York, New York 10010, USA
Penguin Books Australia Ltd, Ringwood, Victoria, Australia
Penguin Books Canada Ltd, 2801 John Street, Markham, Ontario, Canada L3R 1B4
Penguin Books (NZ) Ltd, 182–190 Wairau Road, Auckland 10, New Zealand

Penguin Books Ltd, Registered Offices: Harmondsworth, Middlesex, England

This collection first published as *Story Chest: 100 Bedtime Stories* by
Viking Kestrel 1986
Published in Puffin Books (containing the first 50 stories) 1988
3 5 7 9 10 8 6 4

Made and printed in Great Britain by
Richard Clay Ltd, Bungay, Suffolk
Typeset in Photina

CONTENTS

CONTENTS

THE KIDNAPPING OF
CLARISSA
MONTGOMERY

'You'll only have to stay here till your rich guardian pays the ransom,' said the kidnapper, whose name was Humphrey. He felt rather sorry for poor little Clarissa. She hadn't said anything since they'd grabbed her from the luxurious grounds of her mansion that afternoon. 'I think the poor little kid's in shock,' Humphrey said worriedly to Spud, who had masterminded the abduction. Spud didn't care if she was in shock, neither did Milligan.

'Just sit tight and don't cause any trouble, kid,' Spud snarled; 'Soon as the old man pays the fifty thousand, you'll be sent back.'

Clarissa finally spoke. 'Fifty thousand?' she said.

'I'm sure he'll manage to find it,' said kind-hearted Humphrey reassuringly. 'You'll be out of here in no time.'

Clarissa looked at him coldly. 'You're all mad,' she said. 'You could have got a whole lot more than fifty thousand. My guardian is loaded.'

'She's in shock,' Humphrey thought, and made her a cup of cocoa with his own hands. He'd fixed up a corner of the barn quite nicely with a toffee apple in a saucer. He was fond of little kids.

Spud was setting up a poker game. Clarissa watched silently.

'You don't have to be scared of those gorillas,' Humphrey whispered. 'They're really harmless.'

'I'm not scared of anything,' Clarissa said, and drew closer to the table.

'Beat it,' growled Spud, but Clarissa looked at his card, then went round the table and inspected Humphrey's and Milligan's. 'Get rid of the red queen and keep the clubs,' she said to Humphrey, and he did, and won.

'Scat, kid,' said Spud, but Clarissa sat down at the table.

'I want to play, too,' she said.

'Go back to your cocoa,' Spud ordered, but Clarissa opened her mouth and let out a high-pitched wailing yell. It went on and on, unbearable in the galvanized-iron roofed barn, and Spud, Milligan and Humphrey covered their ears.

'Maybe she'll stop if we let her play,' suggested Humphrey, and dealt out a hand to Clarissa. She stopped screeching and picked up her cards. Then she proceeded, without any trouble at all, to win ten games and fifty dollars.

'It's not very nice, if you ask me,' Spud said disgustedly. 'Little girls shouldn't know how to cheat at poker.'

Clarissa pocketed her winnings and went to bed. She slept very well. In the morning she woke up early. Humphrey, Spud and Milligan were dozing fitfully in uncomfortable chairs. Clarissa made herself a substantial breakfast, then examined the barn.

'Get away from that door!' Spud said, waking up.

'I've seen play forts in council parks better defended than this old barn,' Clarissa scoffed. 'The police could have this place surrounded and you wouldn't even know. No wonder you only asked for fifty thousand. It's all you're worth.'

Spud was so indignant that he bit his pre-breakfast cigar in two. 'What became of all the food?' he demanded angrily.

'I had it for my breakfast, of course,' Clarissa said.

So Humphrey, Spud and Milligan had to make do with discussing the plans for collecting the ransom money instead. Clarissa listened. 'It won't work,' she jeered. 'Just how do you expect Humphrey to reach the hollow tree in the park past a whole lot of detectives all lying in wait? It's too corny, collecting ransom money from a hollow tree.'

'And what would you suggest then, Miss Smarty?' Spud asked.

'Some place where they can't set up an ambush, of course. Tell them to put the money in a briefcase in a plastic bag and drop it off the pier. One of you could get in wearing scuba gear. It's a much better plan than your old hollow tree. I'll draft a new anonymous letter to my rich guardian.' Clarissa began cutting letters from Spud's newspaper, even though he hadn't read the racing page yet. She pasted the letters to a sheet of paper, and even Spud had to admit that it looked much more professional than theirs. And she'd doubled the ransom money, too.

'But none of us can scuba dive,' Humphrey pointed out.

'I can,' said Clarissa crushingly. 'I'll collect the money. But only if you give me a share.'

'That's only right,' said Humphrey. 'If she picks it up, she should be given something.'

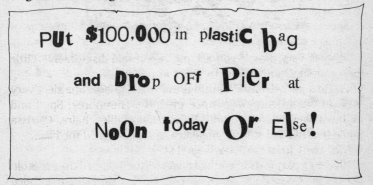

PUt $100,000 in plastiC bag and DRop OFf PieR at NoOn tOday Or Else!

'Ninety-five per cent,' said Clarissa. 'Or I won't go at all. Anyhow, you wouldn't have any ransom money in the first place, if it wasn't for me.'

'If it wasn't for you, we wouldn't be sitting in this draughty old barn with nothing to eat for breakfast but a toffee apple,' said Spud. 'I wish we'd concentrated on stealing your rich guardian's valuable oil paintings instead.'

'You'd never get near them. They're fitted with electronic alarms.'

'I stole the Mona Lisa once,' Spud said boastfully.

'And you only got as far as the front door before they caught you. I read about it in the papers. The only way you could steal my guardian's paintings is if I came along and showed you the secret panel where you can cut off the alarm circuit. So there.'

Spud sourly began a round of poker while Humphrey went out to deliver the ransom note. Clarissa won another ten games. Spud thought with pleasure that after tonight they'd be rid of her. 'Soon as we pick up that briefcase, we'll drop you off at your mansion,' he said.

'First we'll come back here and count the money,' contradicted Clarissa. 'Don't you know you can't trust anyone? You're the most hopeless gang leader I ever met. And you'll have to make plans about leaving the country, too. You'll need to learn a foreign language, but that's no problem. This afternoon you can all study French verbs. I'll supervise. That's after you clean up the getaway car. I'm not going anywhere to pick up ransom money in a car as dirty as that.'

She nagged so much that Spud, Humphrey and Milligan went out in the cold and cleaned the car. Clarissa sat at the window and made sure they did a thorough job. Spud, Milligan and Humphrey consoled themselves with thinking of all the goodies they'd buy once they got their hands on the ransom money. 'A farm in France,' Spud said. 'I always wanted one of those.'

'I bet you don't know anything about farming, or France,' said Clarissa. 'It might be a good idea if I came along to advise you. I always give my guardian advice on real estate and money investment and I practically run his affairs for him. I don't know what he'd do without me.'

Milligan, Spud and even Humphrey eyed her with distaste. They were getting fed up with the draughty barn, the waiting and the French verbs, and most of all they were fed up with Clarissa and her organizing.

It was almost a relief when the time came to collect the ransom money. They drove to the waterfront, and Clarissa put on the scuba suit and galloped confidently into the sea.

'She might swim to the pier and just pop up and give the alarm,' said Humphrey nervously. 'Let's get out of here.'

'Not without our share of the money,' said Spud. 'I haven't put up with that kid all day for nothing.'

'We won't have to put up with her much longer,' said Milligan thankfully. 'Soon as we sort out the ransom money, we can drop her off at her mansion, and good riddance. Then it's off to the south of France for us.'

'That guardian's welcome to her,' said Spud. 'We should give the poor old fellow a few thousand dollars back. I feel sorry for him, having to put up with her till she's grown up and married.'

'No one would marry her,' said Milligan with conviction. 'Not even if they were bribed with all of the Montgomery fortune.'

They watched the water anxiously, but no police boat bristling with armed constables skimmed into sight. And after fifteen minutes Clarissa emerged, carrying a weighted briefcase in a plastic bag. Milligan, Spud and Humphrey tried to grab it from her, but Clarissa put it in the getaway car and sat on it. 'Don't be so greedy,' she said. 'You're making as much noise as kids in a sandpit. You'll just have to wait till we get back to the barn.'

On the way back the three gangsters were quite civil to Clarissa. They were all thinking that very soon they could drop her off at her mansion and never have to listen to her again or be ordered about.

Spud had the first try at the locked briefcase, and failed. Milligan failed, too, and then Humphrey had a turn, with his skilful hands that had foiled every bank safe in town. But even he couldn't get the combination lock open.

'What a lot of butterfingers!' said Clarissa, and turned the little numbered cylinder and the lid flew open.

But the briefcase wasn't full of bank notes at all. There wasn't anything but the bricks that had served to weigh it down in the water. And one short typed note. Spud snatched it up and read it aloud, and his eyes rounded with horror and disbelief.

> DO NOT WANT CLARISSA BACK,
> SHE IS TOO IRRITATING.
> AND BOSSY. YOU CAN KEEP HER.
> GLAD TO GET RID OF HER,
> REGARDS, ALGERNON MONTGOMERY,
> MILLIONAIRE.

All the kidnappers turned pale and sat down.

'Why are you all sitting down wasting time?' Clarissa demanded, frowning. 'We have an oil painting job to plan. And now that I'm in charge of this gang, I expect much better work from all of you.'

ROBIN KLEIN

IN THE MIDDLE OF
THE NIGHT

In the middle of the night a fly woke Charlie. At first he lay listening, half-asleep, while it swooped about the room. Sometimes it was far; sometimes it was near – that was what had woken him; and occasionally it was very near indeed. It was very, very near when the buzzing stopped: the fly had alighted on his face. He jerked his head up; the fly buzzed off. Now he was really awake.

The fly buzzed widely about the room, but it was thinking of Charlie all the time. It swooped nearer and nearer. Nearer . . .

Charlie pulled his head down under the bedclothes. All of him under the bedclothes, he was completely protected; but he could hear nothing except his heartbeats and his breathing. He was overwhelmed by the smell of warm bedding, warm pyjamas, warm himself. He was going to suffocate. So he rose suddenly up out of the bedclothes; and the fly was waiting for him. It dashed at him. He beat at it with his hands. At the same time he appealed to his younger brother, Wilson, in the next bed: 'Wilson, there's a fly!'

Wilson, unstirring, slept on.

Now Charlie and the fly were pitting their wits against each other: Charlie pouncing on the air where he thought the fly must be; the fly sliding under his guard towards his face. Again and again the fly reached Charlie; again and again, almost simultaneously, Charlie dislodged him. Once he hit the fly – or, at least, hit where the fly had been a second before, on the side of his head; the blow was so hard that his head sang with it afterwards.

Then suddenly the fight was over; no more buzzing. His blows – or rather, one of them – must have told.

He laid his head back on the pillow, thinking of going to sleep again. But he was also thinking of the fly, and now he noticed a tickling in the ear he turned to the pillow.

It must be – it *was* – the fly.

He rose in such panic that the waking of Wilson really seemed to him a possible thing, and useful. He shook him repeatedly: 'Wilson – Wilson, I tell you, there's a fly in my ear!'

Wilson groaned, turned over very slowly like a seal in water, and slept on.

The tickling in Charlie's ear continued. He could just imagine the fly struggling in some passageway too narrow for its wing-span. He longed to put his finger into his ear and rattle it round, like a stick in a rabbit-hole, but he was afraid of driving the fly deeper into his ear.

Wilson slept on.

Charlie stood in the middle of the bedroom floor, quivering and trying to think. He needed to see down his ear, or to get someone else to see down it. Wilson wouldn't do; perhaps Margaret would.

Margaret's room was next door. Charlie turned on the light as he entered: Margaret's bed was empty. He was startled, and then thought that she must have gone to the lavatory. But there was no light from there. He listened carefully: there was no sound from anywhere, except for the usual snuffling moans from the hall, where Floss slept and dreamt of dog-biscuits. The empty bed was mystifying; but Charlie had his ear to worry about. It sounded as if there were a pigeon inside it now.

Wilson asleep; Margaret vanished; that left Alison. But Alison was bossy, just because she was the eldest; and, anyway, she would probably only wake Mum. He might as well wake Mum himself.

Down the passage and through the door always left ajar. 'Mum,' he said. She woke, or at least half-woke, at once: 'Who is it? Who? Who? What's the matter? What? –'

'I've a fly in my ear.'

'You can't have.'

'It flew in.'

She switched on the bedside light, and, as she did so, Dad plunged beneath the bedclothes with an exclamation and lay still again.

Charlie knelt at his mother's side of the bed and she looked into his ear. 'There's nothing.'

'Something crackles.'

'It's wax in your ear.'

'It tickles.'

'There's no fly there. Go back to bed and stop imagining things.'

His father's arm came up from below the bedclothes. The hand waved about, settled on the bedside light and clicked it out. There was an upheaval of bedclothes and a comfortable grunt.

'Good night,' said Mum from the darkness. She was already allowing herself to sink back into sleep again.

'Good night,' Charlie said sadly. Then an idea occurred to him. He repeated his good night loudly and added some coughing, to cover the fact that he was closing the bedroom door behind him – the door that Mum kept open so that she could listen for her children. They had outgrown all that kind of attention, except possibly for Wilson. Charlie had shut the door against Mum's hearing because he intended to slip downstairs for a drink of water – well, for a drink and perhaps a snack. That fly-business had woken him up and also weakened him: he needed something.

He crept downstairs, trusting to Floss's good sense not to make a row. He turned the foot of the staircase towards the kitchen, and there had not been the faintest whimper from her, far less a bark. He was passing the dog-basket when he had the most unnerving sensation of something being wrong there – something unusual, at least. He could not have said whether he had heard something or smelt something – he could certainly have seen nothing in the blackness: perhaps some extra sense warned him.

'Floss?' he whispered, and there was the usual little scrabble and snuffle. He held out his fingers low down for Floss to lick. As she did not do so at once, he moved them towards her, met some obstruction –

'Don't poke your fingers in my eyes!' a voice said, very low-toned and cross. Charlie's first, confused thought was that Floss had spoken: the voice was familiar – but then a voice from Floss should *not* be familiar; it should be strangely new to him –

He took an uncertain little step towards the voice, tripped over the obstruction, which was quite wrong in shape and size to be Floss, and sat down. Two things now happened. Floss, apparently having climbed over the obstruction, reached his lap and began to lick his face. At the same time a human hand fumbled over his face, among the slappings of Floss's tongue, and settled over his mouth. 'Don't make a row! Keep quiet!' said the same voice. Charlie's mind cleared: he knew, although without understanding, that he was sitting on the floor in the dark with Floss on his knee and Margaret beside him.

Her hand came off his mouth.

'What are you doing here, anyway, Charlie?'

'I like that! What about you? There was a fly in my ear.'

'Go on!'

'There was.'

'Why does that make you come downstairs?'

'I wanted a drink of water.'

'There's water in the bathroom.'

'Well, I'm a bit hungry.'

'If Mum catches you . . .'

'Look here,' Charlie said, 'you tell me what you're doing down here.'

Margaret sighed. 'Just sitting with Floss.'

'You can't come down and just sit with Floss in the middle of the night.'

'Yes, I can. I keep her company. Only at weekends, of course. No one seemed to realize what it was like for her when those puppies went. She just couldn't get to sleep for loneliness.'

'But the last puppy went weeks ago. You haven't been keeping Floss company every Saturday night since then.'

'Why not?'

Charlie gave up. 'I'm going to get my food and drink,' he said. He went into the kitchen, followed by Margaret, followed by Floss.

They all had a quick drink of water. Then Charlie and Margaret looked into the larder: the remains of a joint; a very large quantity of mashed potato; most of a loaf; eggs; butter; cheese . . .

'I suppose it'll have to be just bread and butter and a bit of cheese,' said Charlie. 'Else Mum might notice.'

'Something hot,' said Margaret. 'I'm cold from sitting in the hall comforting Floss. I need hot cocoa, I think.' 'She poured some milk into a saucepan and put it on the hot plate. Then she began a search for the tin of cocoa. Charlie, standing by the cooker, was already absorbed in the making of a rough cheese sandwich.

The milk in the pan began to steam. Given time, it rose in the saucepan, peered over the top, and boiled over on to the hot plate, where it sizzled loudly. Margaret rushed back and pulled the saucepan to one side. 'Well, really, Charlie! Now there's that awful smell! It'll still be here in the morning, too.'

'Set the fan going,' Charlie suggested.

The fan drew the smell from the cooker up and away through a pipe to the outside. It also made a loud roaring noise. Not loud enough to reach their parents, who slept on the other side of the house – that was all that Charlie and Margaret thought of.

Alison's bedroom, however, was immediately above the kitchen. Charlie was eating his bread and cheese, Margaret was drinking her cocoa, when the kitchen door opened and there stood Alison. Only Floss was pleased to see her.

'Well!' she said.

Charlie muttered something about a fly in his ear, but Margaret said nothing. Alison had caught them red-handed. She would call Mum downstairs, that was obvious. There would be an awful row.

Alison stood there. She liked commanding a situation.

Then, instead of taking a step backwards to call up the stairs to Mum, she took a step forward into the kitchen. 'What are you having, anyway?' she asked. She glanced with scorn at Charlie's poor piece of bread and cheese and at Margaret's cocoa. She moved over to the larder, flung open the door, and looked searchingly inside. In such a way must Napoleon have viewed a battlefield before victory.

Her gaze fell upon the bowl of mashed potato. 'I shall make potato-cakes,' said Alison.

They watched while she brought the mashed potato to the kitchen table. She switched on the oven, fetched her other ingredients, and began mixing.

'Mum'll notice if you take much of that potato,' said Margaret.

But Alison thought big. 'She may notice if some potato is missing,' she agreed. 'But if there's none at all, and if the bowl it was in is washed and dried and stacked away with the others, then she's going to think she must have made a mistake. There just can never have been any mashed potato.'

Alison rolled out her mixture and cut it into cakes; then she set the cakes on a baking-tin and put it in the oven.

Now she did the washing up. Throughout the time they were in the kitchen, Alison washed up and put away as she went along. She wanted no one's help. She was very methodical, and she did

11

everything herself to be sure that nothing was left undone. In the morning there must be no trace left of the cooking in the middle of the night.

'And now,' said Alison, 'I think we should fetch Wilson.'

The other two were aghast at the idea; but Alison was firm in her reasons. 'It's better if we're all in this together, Wilson as well. Then if the worst comes to the worst, it won't be just us three caught out, with Wilson hanging on to Mum's apron-strings, smiling innocence. We'll all be for it together; and Mum'll be softer with us if we've got Wilson.'

They saw that at once. But Margaret still objected: 'Wilson will tell. He just always tells everything. He can't help it.'

Alison said, 'He always tells everything. Right: we'll give him something *to* tell, and then see if Mum believes him. We'll do an entertainment for him. Get an umbrella from the hall and Wilson's sou'wester and a blanket or a rug or something. Go on.'

They would not obey Alison's orders until they had heard her plan; then they did. They fetched the umbrella and the hat, and lastly they fetched Wilson, still sound asleep, slung between them in his eiderdown. They propped him in a chair at the kitchen table, where he still slept.

By now the potato-cakes were done. Alison took them out of the oven and set them on the table before Wilson. She buttered them, handing them in turn to Charlie and Margaret and helping herself. One was set aside to cool for Floss.

The smell of fresh-cooked buttery potato-cake woke Wilson, as was to be expected. First his nose sipped the air, then his eyes opened, his gaze settled on the potato-cakes.

'Like one?' Alison asked.

Wilson opened his mouth wide and Alison put a potato-cake inside, whole.

'They're paradise-cakes,' Alison said.

'Potato-cakes?' said Wilson, recognizing the taste.

'No, paradise-cakes, Wilson,' and then, stepping aside, she gave him a clear view of Charlie's and Margaret's entertainment, with the umbrella and the sou'wester hat and his eiderdown. 'Look, Wilson, look.'

Wilson watched with wide-open eyes, and into his wide-open

mouth Alison put, one by one, the potato-cakes that were his share.

But, as they had foreseen, Wilson did not stay awake for very long. When there were no more potato-cakes, he yawned, drowsed, and suddenly was deeply asleep. Charlie and Margaret put him back into his eiderdown and took him upstairs to bed again. They came down to return the umbrella and the sou'wester to their proper places, and to see Floss back into her basket. Alison, last out of the kitchen, made sure that everything was in its place.

The next morning Mum was down first. On Sunday she always cooked a proper breakfast for anyone there in time. Dad was always there in time; but this morning Mum was still looking for a bowl of mashed potato when he appeared.

'I can't think where it's gone,' she said. 'I can't think.'

'I'll have the bacon and eggs without the potato,' said Dad; and he did. While he ate, Mum went back to searching.

Wilson came down, and was sent upstairs again to put on a dressing-gown. On his return he said that Charlie was still asleep and there was no sound from the girls' rooms either. He said he thought they were tired out. He went on talking while he ate his breakfast. Dad was reading the paper and Mum had gone back to poking about in the larder for the bowl of mashed potato, but Wilson liked talking even if no one would listen.

When Mum came out of the larder for a moment, still without her potato, Wilson was saying: '... and Charlie sat in an umbrella-boat on an eiderdown-sea, and Margaret pretended to be a sea-serpent, and Alison gave us paradise-cakes to eat. Floss had one too, but it was too hot for her. What are paradise-cakes? Dad, what's a paradise-cake?'

'Don't know,' said Dad, reading.

'Mum, what's a paradise-cake?'

'Oh, Wilson, don't bother so when I'm looking for something
... When did you eat this cake, anyway?'

'I told you. Charlie sat in his umbrella-boat on an eiderdown-
sea and Margaret was a sea-serpent and Alison –'

'Wilson,' said his mother, 'you've been dreaming.'

'No, really – really!' Wilson cried.

But his mother paid no further attention. 'I give up,' she said.
'That mashed potato: it must have been last week-end ...' She
went out of the kitchen to call the others: 'Charlie! Margaret!
Alison!'

Wilson, in the kitchen, said to his father, 'I wasn't dreaming.
And Charlie said there was a fly in his ear.'

Dad had been quarter-listening; now he put down his paper.
'What?'

'Charlie had a fly in his ear.'

Dad stared at Wilson. 'And what did you say that Alison fed
you with?'

'Paradise-cakes. She'd just made them, I think, in the middle of
the night.'

'What were they like?'

'Lovely. Hot, with butter. Lovely.'

'But were they – well, could they have had any mashed potato
in them, for instance?'

In the hall Mum was finishing her calling: 'Charlie! Margaret!
Alison! I warn you now!'

'I don't know about that,' Wilson said. 'They were paradise-
cakes. They tasted a bit like the potato-cakes Mum makes, but
Alison said they weren't. She specially said they were paradise-
cakes.'

Dad nodded. 'You've finished your breakfast. Go up and get
dressed, and you can take this' — he took a coin from his pocket –
'straight off to the sweetshop. Go on.'

Mum met Wilson at the kitchen door: 'Where's he off to in such
a hurry?'

'I gave him something to buy sweets with,' said Dad. 'I wanted
a quiet breakfast. He talks too much.'

PHILIPPA PEARCE

14

A BUNCH OF
FLOWERS

It was my Mum's birthday and I decided to buy her a present like every year since last year (before that I was too little).

I took all the money out of my moneybox and luckily there was a lot because quite by chance Mum had given me some the day before. I knew what I was going to get her for a present: an enormous huge bunch of flowers to put in the big blue vase in the sitting-room.

I could hardly wait for school to be over so I could go and buy my present. I kept my hand in my pocket all the time at school so as not to lose my money, even when we were playing football at break – but since I wasn't in goal that didn't matter. Alec is our goalie. 'Why are you running about with one hand in your pocket?' he asked me. I explained that I was going to buy my Mum some flowers, and he said personally he'd rather have something to eat, like a cake or some sweets or sausage rolls, but since the present wasn't for him I took no notice and I got a ball past him into the goal. We won 44–32.

When we came out of school Alec went along to the flower shop with me, eating half the chocolate roll he'd saved from the grammar lesson. We went into the shop and I put all my money on the counter and told the lady I wanted an enormous huge bunch of flowers for my Mum, only no begonias because we had plenty of those in our garden, so it wasn't worth buying any more. 'We want something nice,' said Alec, and he went and stuck his nose into the flowers in the window to see how they smelt. The lady counted my money, and she said she was afraid she couldn't give me a *very* enormous bunch of flowers. I was very sad, so the lady looked at me and thought for a moment, and then she told me I was a dear little boy and she patted me on the head and said she'd fix it. She picked out all sorts of flowers, and she put in a lot of green leaves. Alec liked them, because he said they looked like nice fresh vegetables. It was a big bunch, really fantastic; the

15

lady wrapped it up in crackly transparent paper and told me to be careful how I carried it. So now I had my big bunch of flowers and Alec had finished smelling the others in the window, and I said thank you to the lady and we went out.

I was feeling very pleased with my flowers when we met Geoffrey, Matthew and Rufus from school. 'Hey, look at Nicholas!' said Geoffrey. 'He looks a right twit with that bunch of flowers!' 'You're jolly lucky I'm carrying these flowers or I'd thump you!' I said. 'Give them to me,' said Alec. 'I don't mind holding them while you thump Geoffrey.' So I gave Alec my bunch of flowers, and Geoffrey thumped me. We had our fight, and then I said time was getting on, so we stopped. However, I had to wait a bit longer, because Matthew said, 'Just look at Alec – now *he* looks a right twit holding a bunch of flowers!' So Alec hit him over the head with the bunch of flowers. 'My flowers!' I shouted. 'You'll hurt my flowers!' I was right, too. Alec went on hitting Matthew with the bunch and the flowers were flying all over the place because the paper was torn, and Matthew was shouting, 'Doesn't hurt, yah boo, doesn't hurt!'

By the time Alec stopped Matthew's head was covered with

greenery and Alec was right, he did look like something you could cook for Sunday lunch. I started picking up my flowers and I told my friends they were beastly. 'That's right!' said Rufus. 'You shouldn't have gone and done that to Nicholas's flowers!' 'Nobody asked you!' said Geoffrey, and they started thumping each other. Alec had gone home, because the sight of Matthew's head made him feel hungry and he didn't want to be late for dinner.

I went off with my flowers. Some of them were missing, and there was no more greenery or paper left, but it was still a nice bunch. Then, a little further on, I met Eddie.

'Hi,' said Eddie, 'have a game of marbles?' 'I can't,' I said. 'I've got to get home and give my Mum these flowers.' But Eddie said it was still quite early. And I like playing marbles – I'm good at marbles, I just take aim and wham! I nearly always win. So I put my flowers down on the pavement and I started playing with Eddie, and it's great playing marbles with Eddie because he often loses. The trouble is he doesn't like losing and he said I was cheating and I told him he was lying, so he shoved me and I sat down on top of my bunch of flowers and it didn't do them any good. 'I'm going to tell Mum what you did to her flowers,' I said to Eddie, and Eddie was very upset. He helped me pick out the least squashed ones. I like Eddie, he's O.K.

I started off again. My bunch wasn't very big any more, but the flowers I did have left were all right; one of them was just a bit squashed, but the other two were fine. Then I saw Jeremy on his bike.

I decided I wasn't going to fight him, because if I went on fighting all my friends I met in the street I soon wouldn't have any flowers at all left to give Mum. Anyway, it's none of their business if I want to give my Mum some flowers. I've got a perfect right to give her flowers, and personally I think they're just jealous because Mum would be very pleased with me and give me something nice for pudding and tell me what a kind boy I am, so why do they all want to gang up on me anyway?

'Hi, Nicholas!' said Jeremy. 'Right twit yourself!' I shouted back. 'So what's the matter with my bunch of flowers, then?' Jeremy got off his bike and looked at me in surprise and said, 'What bunch of flowers?' 'This bunch of flowers!' I said, and I threw the flowers

17

in his face. I don't think Jeremy was expecting to get a faceful of flowers, and anyway he didn't like it. He threw the flowers into the road and they landed on the roof of a passing car and drove off with the car. 'My flowers!' I shouted. 'My Mum's flowers!' 'Don't worry!' said Jeremy. 'I'll follow the car on my bike.' Jeremy's O.K, but he doesn't pedal very fast, specially not uphill, even if he says he *is* in training to win the Milk Race when he's grown up. When he came back he said he hadn't been able to catch up with the car, there was a lot of traffic and it had got away from him, but he did bring me back one flower which had fallen off its roof. Unfortunately it was the squashed one.

Jeremy rode off very fast – it's downhill all the way to his house – and I went home with my crumpled flower. I had a sort of a big lump in my throat. Like when I bring home my mark book with my monthly report and it's got all noughts in it.

I opened the door and I said, 'Happy birthday, Mum,' and then I burst into tears. Mum looked at the flower; she seemed a bit surprised. Then she put her arms round me and hugged me lots and lots of times, and she said it was the nicest bunch of flowers she'd ever had, and she put the flower in the big blue vase in the sitting-room.

I don't care what you say, my Mum is O.K!

RENÉ GOSCINNY

THE DRAGON WHO CHEATED

The kingdom of Urgburg-under-Ug was as pleasant a little place as you could wish to find. In fact, it was a great deal more pleasant than most people would dream of wishing to find. It was beautiful sunshiny summer all the year except on the 15th March when there was always a slight snowstorm.

But owing to a special arrangement that had something to do with leap years and that kind of thing, the 15th March occurred only twice in ten years in Urgburg-under-Ug.

Then again, the King and Queen of Urgburg-under-Ug were two exceedingly charming people, and about the only law that was ever enforced in the kingdom was one which said that no one was to be unhappy.

There was a special force of joyous policemen employed particularly to see that this law was not disobeyed. If anyone fell over and hurt himself, or dropped down a grating a penny that he was going to buy sweets with or anything like that, these joyous policemen would make funny faces and give them new pennies which the King secretly provided himself. That will just show you how nice it was in the kingdom of Urgburg.

There were only two things wrong with the kingdom of Urgburg-under-Ug.

One of them was its name which was slightly difficult to say and definitely difficult to spell, but that didn't matter very much because nobody minded whether it was pronounced properly or not except the Urgburg Broadcasting Company, and they knew how to pronounce it.

But there was a dragon in Urgburg, and a very unpleasant dragon at that. It arrived quite suddenly from goodness knows where and started stamping on places and burning things up with its fiery breath, and kicking things down with its spiky feet.

'This dragon business is most distressing,' said the King, who had gathered all his ministers together to discuss what should be done. 'What can we do to release the kingdom from such a monster?'

'Perfectly simple, my dear Gilbert,' said the Queen, who wasn't supposed to be at the conference at all. 'All you have to do is to issue a proclamation and say that you offer half the kingdom and the hand of the Princess in marriage to whoever shall slay the dragon.'

'But, my dear Agnes,' protested the King, 'you know perfectly well we haven't a princess.'

'Neither we have,' said the Queen; 'I was forgetting.'

She put her thumb in her mouth because it helped her to think, then remembering there was company present, if you can count ministers and chancellors as company, she hurriedly took it out again, and said, 'Well, we can still offer half the kingdom and there'd be sure to be plenty of nice strong dragon-slaying sort of people who would be willing to do a spot of work for a prize like that.'

'That's right enough,' said the King; 'they might even be more willing to slay the dragon for half the kingdom alone than if they thought they had to marry a princess as well. I don't suppose all dragon-slaying people are very used to princesses, and it might put them out a bit. You know what I mean – having to turn half a kingdom into a little kingdom of its own and be majestic sort of majesties themselves, so that the Princess should not feel homesick.'

'That's what I think,' put in the Prime Minister. 'I know a man who has a sister who used to know a friend who once heard of a dragon-slaying sort of man who slew a dragon to win half a kingdom and a princess, and he used to say –'

'Now never mind what he used to say,' broke in the Queen

20

hurriedly, guessing that whatever it was it would take a long time to tell because she used to say things like that to her friends and it used to take her ages. 'Let's think out the proclamation.'

'Certainly, my dear,' said the King, licking his pencil which was copying-ink, only he had forgotten, and it made his tongue all purple. 'Let me see, how does this sound? "Wanted, superior dragon-slayer" . . .'

'No, no,' said the Queen, 'don't say "superior". It doesn't matter what sort of a dragon-slayer he is so long as he slays the dragon.'

'Pardon me, Majesties,' put in the Lord High Marshal of Heralds, who knew all about proclamations because he used to be a herald in another kingdom before he came to Urgburg, and had shouted many a one round the streets. 'Pardon me, but if I might make so bold as to say so, proclamations ought to start with "Oyez".'

'Oyez,' said the King.

'Oh! no,' said the Queen, 'that is much too old-fashioned. We must be up-to-date.'

'Dragons are rather old-fashioned,' put in the Prime Minister, who had not quite forgiven the Queen for stopping him from telling them about the man that his friend's sister's acquaintance had heard of, and thought this was a chance to get his own back. But by this time the King, who had been writing away like anything on the back of an old piece of paper for several minutes, suddenly said, 'Listen to this. "Oyez, oyez – wanted, dragon-slayer to slay dragon" – that doesn't sound quite right, but I can't think of any other way of saying it – "half kingdom reward, no princess, no questions asked."'

At this, there was a tremendous babble of voices, as everybody started talking at once and saying how they thought the proclamation ought to go, and the noise became so loud that the King had to go outside and have a cannon or two let off to get silence.

'Now, I'll tell you what we'll do,' said the Queen; 'everyone is to go away and write out in nice clear handwriting their own idea of a proclamation. Then we shall all meet again here at this time tomorrow and there'll be a small prize for the one whose proclamation is considered the best.'

Everybody applauded this idea except the King, who guessed that he would have to pay for the little present, but before he could say anything, the tea bell rang, and everybody streamed out, headed by the Queen, who was rather good at that sort of thing.

Next day, at the appointed time, the proclamations were read out.

The Lord Chancellor had written his in rhyme, because he liked to think he was rather a poet, although nobody else could bear to think it.

> *'Oyez, oyez, and be it known*
> *A dragon-slayer's needed*
> *To free the kingdom, save the throne,*
> *So let this call be heeded.*
> *And as reward for such as can*
> *This monster overthrow,*
> *One-half this land Elysian*
> *Shall to the slayer go.'*

'What does "Elysian" mean?' asked the King, who had an aunt named Elizabeth Ann, and thought it might have something to do with her and didn't want to get aunts mixed up with state affairs.

'I don't like "such as can",' said the Queen, 'and anyway, who said a proclamation had to rhyme? Next, please.'

'Oyez, oyez,' began the Prime Minister, then feeling that he had done quite well so far, he went on in a louder voice, 'slay the dragon and win a handsome prize. Half the kingdom for a successful attempt. No entrance fee, no difficulties. Their Majesties' decision is final.'

'That sounds as if a dragon was a sort of crossword puzzle,' said the Queen, who didn't hold with crossword puzzles because the King could do them better than she could. 'Next, please.'

This was the Lord High Marshal of Heralds. He popped up very quickly and in a voice that could be heard all over the place read out:

'Oyez, oyez, oyez. Whereas the Kingdom of Urgburg-under-Ug is suffering under the onslaughts of a dragon, be it known that we by our royal privilege do hereby offer half the said kingdom, together with all the appurtenances thereof, as prize or reward to whomsoever shall slay the monster. Given under our hand this so and so day.'

22

Of course that was by far the best attempt of any, but the King said he thought the Lord High Marshal of Heralds knew too much about proclamations.

Then the rest of them had a go at reading out their attempts except two of the ministers who had not been able to get any further than chewing the end of a pencil, and one who had been looking over the Lord Chancellor's shoulder, but hadn't been able to read his writing.

'Well,' said the Queen, rather briskly. 'I did one myself.' She read out:

'Oyez, oyez. We have had the most terrible dragon ravishing the kingdom lately, and what do you think it's been doing? I mean to say, too devastating, you know. Why, my dears, positively stamping on places and all that. Something must be done about it, so the King and myself thought that if we could get someone to slay the dragon, because we feel sure that nobody really likes the nasty thing, we would give him half the kingdom for his trouble. So –'

23

'Here, here,' broke in the King.

'Don't applaud until I've finished,' said the Queen, thinking he meant an applauding sort of thing like 'Hear, hear!'

'But you can't have a proclamation like that,' said the King.

Then the King and Queen started arguing, partly about the proclamation but very much more so about the small prize, chiefly because the Queen's idea of a small prize was a very big one.

'I tell you what we'll do,' said the King at last, 'you shall have a nice diamond necklace for your prize for the proclamation, but we'll use the Lord High Marshal of Heralds' proclamation because it sounds better.'

'All right,' replied the Queen, who didn't mind so long as she got the prize, and as nobody else minded either because the King promised them all consolation prizes, the matter was settled.

But although the proclamation was settled, the dragon wasn't, and next day news came that he had kicked down two more castles.

The dragon sat at the mouth of his cave cleaning his claws with a tree-trunk.

'Huh! Huh!' he growled, 'so they want to get me killed, do they? I'll teach them to send out proclamations. I'll teach them a thing or two about killing dragons.'

He had heard the proclamation read out because he had rather good ears and four of them at that, two on each of his two heads.

'Disgraceful, I call it,' said one head.

'I've got an idea,' said the other.

'Well, out with it,' said the first.

'Psp, psp,' said the other, trying to whisper.

'What say?' said the first head.

'Get suit of armour, disguise self as champion, pretend kill own self, claim half kingdom as reward.'

'Good idea, but don't talk like telegram,' said the first head, talking like one itself.

The dragon shook one head and nodded the other, and went round to one of the castles he had kicked down and rummaged about to find some armour. He had a very severe portion of trouble getting himself into the armour, partly because his tail was rather

24

long and he had to wind it round himself which made him rather fat, and partly because he had to get both his heads into one helmet.

'They say two heads are better than one,' said the first head.

'I can't see it myself,' said the second.

'Move over a bit,' said the first.

At last the dragon got himself

all fastened up by using about four-and-a-half suits of armour to cover him, and set out for the King's palace.

'Majesty,' he said, bowing before the throne as he was ushered into the King's presence, 'I come as your champion. I will kill the dragon if you promise me the reward you have offered.' He said this with both his heads at once, so it sounded nice and loud even though the visor of his helmet was down so that no one could see he was really the dragon himself.

'Ask him to open his hat,' said the Queen, who was not used to people talking through their helmets at her, although she used to say that some of the ministers talked through their hats, but that, of course, was a different thing.

'Shush,' whispered the King, 'you may upset him, and look what a nice big champion he is. No dragon will stand a chance against such a whopper.' Then aloud he said, 'Certainly, go and slay the dragon, bring back proof that you have slain it and half the kingdom shall be yours.'

'Majesty,' boomed the dragon's two heads, 'it shall be done.'

And with a clatter and clang of all four-and-a-half suits of armour, he strode out of the palace with such a swish that all the blinds came down and three of the ministers thought it was night-time and went to bed.

Once again the dragon was sitting outside his cave, but this time he wasn't cleaning his claws. He was very carefully cutting a circular piece out of the side of a large tray. Then he put the tray on his shoulder with the cut-out piece round one of his necks, held it there with one paw, put his other head on one side, and looked at his reflection in the pond.

'Excellent,' said the first head.

'Looks just as if you are carrying the dragon's head on a tray,' said the second head.

'Entirely satisfactory,' said both heads together.

The dragon put his helmet on again, putting it on to one head only this time, and back he went to the palace. He strode up the throne-room, making the windows rattle as he went. He held the head on which he wore the helmet slightly on one side and he kept the eyes on his other head closed, and as he held the tray on his shoulder, it looked for all the world as if he was a mighty champion bearing the head of the slain dragon on the tray.

Cheers went up as he went by.

'Hoorah for the dragon-slayer! Hail champion of Urgburg-under-Ug! The dragon is slain!'

'Majesty,' said the dragon, being careful to talk only with the

head that was inside the helmet, 'I have slain the dragon. See, I bring his head as proof. I come to claim my reward of half the kingdom.'

'Lovely,' said the Queen, clapping her hands. 'What a horrid-looking dragon it was.'

'Terrible,' said the King.

And the dragon who didn't know whether he wanted to laugh because his plan was succeeding so well, or to be angry because they were saying such rude things about him, but who knew he mustn't do either until he got his reward, passed round the throne-room, pretending to show off the head on the tray.

Oh! dreadful situation, think of it! The dragon about to be given half the kingdom for slaying himself! Not that it would have mattered if he had slain himself, but of course he hadn't. He was tricking the King. He was tricking the entire kingdom. When he had got half the kingdom for himself he would still go on ravaging the other half. Instead of Urgburg-under-Ug being delivered from the dragon, it would be delivered to the dragon. Everything would be terrible. Oh! crafty monster! Oh! to think that nothing could be done to save the kingdom!

The King stood up.

'According to the terms of the proclamation,' he cried, 'I have much pleasure in presenting to our valiant champion one-half of the kingdom of Urgburg-under-Ug.' Then, turning to the disguised dragon, 'Won't you put the head down, sir, and take a cup of wine?'

'Oo-er,' thought the dragon, 'can't put my own head down. I'd better pretend to be a bit dashing.' Then aloud:

'Majesty, I prefer to keep the head of this monster as a trophy.'

The Queen was just going to ask what a trophy was, when from amongst the spectators a young man pushed his way forward, and ran towards the dragon.

'Go back,' cried the King, 'go away.'

But the young man didn't go back or away. He ran forward with a small bright object clasped firmly in his hand. It was a pepper-box. He shook its contents on to the tray in front of the dragon's head.

'Arrest him,' roared the King.

The guards had taken hardly a step when –

'ATISHOO!' A most frightfully monstrous noise rang out. The head of the supposed-to-be-slain dragon had sneezed!

Pandemonium raged. The cheers that had gone up before gave place to screams of fear and howls of alarm. The King jumped up so suddenly that he kicked the throne over backwards and the Queen with it, but happily she fell on some cushions.

'He is no champion,' said the young man, pointing to the dragon who had torn the helmet off his other head and was beginning to puff out sparks, 'he is the dragon himself.'

'Huh, huh,' roared the dragon in a voice that blew all the guards' hats off in a shower. 'Yes, I am the dragon and I will have not half the kingdom but all of it. It's just my dinner-time – what a meal I'll have!' He rolled his eyes round the throne-room and blew out a jet of blue flame.

Forty-seven duchesses fainted all at once. The Lord Chamberlain climbed up on the chandelier, the Prime Minister and the Lord Chief Justice tried to get up the chimney but got stuck half-way.

The dragon advanced, a terrifying form, upon the young man.

'Have at ye!' cried the young man, who had read in a book that champions always said that when attacking the foe. He drew his sword with a flourish. Horrors! the blade flew off the handle. Urgburg-under-Ug was undone! The last hope was gone. No, it wasn't! Marvels of all marvels! The shining sword blade flew like a streak of silver across the room and through both the dragon's heads at once, skewering them like an enormous pennyworth of cat's meat.

With a sensational crash that shook all the pictures down in the Queen's spare bedroom, the dragon fell lifeless to the floor. Serve him right for cheating. The pieces of armour from his four-and-a-half suits rolled and clanged all over the place like so many milk-churns or even more.

More cheers went up. Forty-six of the fainted duchesses came unfainted again and asked for cups of tea. The Queen climbed out of the cushions and helped the King stand the throne up again. The Lord Chamberlain dropped off the chandelier with a loud 'bong' into the middle of the floor, but didn't hurt himself much as he wore thick trousers. The Prime Minister and the Lord Chief Justice came out of the chimney followed by a large helping of soot.

The kingdom of Urgburg-under-Ug was saved!

'But tell me,' said the King to the young man, when they were sitting down to a nice banquet to celebrate the great occasion, 'who are you and how did you guess the dragon's trick?'

'I am Prince Diddinott Dottimwun,' said the young man. 'My kingdom which is near here was stamped out of existence by the dragon the Thursday before last. I followed him and saw him preparing to trick you into giving him half your kingdom.'

'Splendid,' said the King, 'now you can have half of my kingdom, and marry the Princess, and everything will be all lovely.'

'Shush,' said the Queen, 'we haven't got a princess. You said so yourself.'

'Neither we have!' exclaimed the King, it being his turn to look rather silly.

'Never mind,' said the young man, 'everything is quite all right. I never did care much for girls, anyway.'

So the Prince ruled over half the kingdom of Urgburg-under-Ug, but whether he cared much for girls anyway, or not, it wasn't very long before he fell in love with a rather special young duchess. So this rather unlikely sort of story comes to a nice usual sort of end because they were married and lived happily ever after.

NORMAN HUNTER

THE SNOWTIME EXPRESS

The snow came down all through the night.

Down, down, down – all through the quiet night.

In the morning, when Jonny woke up, he looked out of his window.

The whole world was white.

'Yipee!' cried Jonny. 'Where's my sled?'

Across the street, Carol looked out of her window.

What a surprise!

Carol had never seen so much snow.

'Hurray!' cried Carol. 'Where's my sled?'

Mothers and fathers were busy looking out of windows, too.

Up and down the street, they were looking out at the snow.

But the fathers didn't say, 'Yipee!'

No indeed.

They shook their heads and said, 'No cars today! It will be hard to get to work!'

The mothers did not say, 'Hooray!'

The mothers were thinking, 'Mr Vick will not be able to send us any food from his store.'

Mrs Nally lived next door to Jonny.

She had a little baby.

'Oh, dear,' said Mrs Nally. 'How will I get a box of baby food for little Tommy?'

Mrs Dorman lived next door to Mrs Nally.

She was taking care of two little grandchildren.

'Oh dear,' said Mrs Dorman. 'Not a bit of bread in the house today! How can I get some bread?'

Down the street lived old Mrs Green.

She was very old.

It was hard for her to walk.

She looked out at the snow and said, 'Oh, dear! I did so want some cheese for my lunch today.'

Jonny was the first one out with his sled.

Then Carol came out with hers.

She came slowly through the deep snow to play with Jonny.

First they pulled each other on the sleds.

Then they tried to run with their sleds and get a ride.

Then they tied the two sleds together and played they had a sled train.

Soon Jonny's mother came out.

'Jonny,' she said. 'Do you think you could get all the way down the street to the store? We need some lunch meat today, and Mr Vick can't send it.'

Jonny looked down the street. How deep the snow was!

'I don't know,' he said.

'Maybe you can go on your sled train,' said his mother.

Jonny looked at Carol.

Carol looked at Jonny.

'Yipee!' cried Jonny. 'Let's go! Here comes the Snowtime Express!'

And off they went.

'Let's make stops, like a train,' said Carol.

So they made a stop.

They rang Mrs Nally's bell.

'Snowtime Express going to Mr Vick's,' said Jonny. 'Do you want us to bring anything for you?'

'Oh, yes, yes!' said Mrs Nally. 'Please bring me some baby food for little Tommy.'

'Toot! Toot!' said Jonny, and the sled train went on its way.

'Let's make another stop,' said Carol.

So they made another stop.

They rang Mrs Dorman's bell.

'Snowtime Express going to Mr Vick's,' said Carol. 'Do you want us to bring anything?'

'Oh, yes,' said Mrs Dorman. 'Please bring me some bread.'

'Toot! Toot!' said Jonny. 'All aboard!'

And the sled train went on its way.

'Let's make one more stop,' said Carol.

So they made one more stop.

They rang old Mrs Green's bell.

'Snowtime Express going to Mr Vick's,' said Jonny. 'Do you want us to bring anything back for you?'

'Oh, yes, yes,' said Mrs Green. 'Please bring me some yellow cheese.'

Toot! Toot!

The Snowtime Express went on its way to the store.

It had to go slower and slower as it got down the street.

Carol and Jonny took turns pulling and pushing.

Sometimes the sled train got stuck in the snow.

One time Jonny had to pull and pull. He gave a hard pull, and Carol tumbled right into the snow.

The sled train stuck again near the store.

This time it was Carol who pulled. She pulled and pulled. Then she went on.

But where was Jonny?

Sitting in the snow!

'Wait for me!' cried Jonny.

At last they got to the store.

'Toot! Toot!' they cried. 'Here comes the Snowtime Express!'

What a surprise for Mr Vick!

'Well, well,' he said. 'A sled train is just what we need today.'

He got a box and tied it on the sled.

Into the box went the baby food, and the bread, the cheese and the meat.

'There,' said Mr Vick. 'You can take out one thing at a time. The box will stay on your train.'

'All aboard!' cried Jonny.

'All aboard!' cried Carol.

And the Snowtime Express started back.

Slowly, slowly, the sled train made its way back up the street.

First Carol pulled and Jonny pushed. 'Toot! Toot! Clear the track!' cried Carol.

Then Jonny pulled and Carol pushed. 'Out of the way for the Snowtime Express!' cried Jonny.

It was hard work, but lots of fun.

'Toot! Toot!' cried Carol. 'First stop at Mrs Green's.'

How happy Mrs Green was to get her yellow cheese!

'Thank you,' she said. 'That's the best train running today.'

Toot! Toot!

The next stop was at Mrs Dorman's.

How glad she was to get the bread!

Then the train stopped at the Nally house.

'Thank you, Snowtime Express,' said Mrs Nally. 'Now little Tommy will have a good lunch.'

The last stop was at Jonny's house. He ran in and gave his mother the lunch meat.

When he came out again Carol said, 'Look, Jonny!'

In the box on the sled train was a white paper bag.

'Say, what's this?' asked Jonny. 'We made all our stops, didn't we?'

'Yes,' said Carol; 'I guess Mr Vick made a mistake.'

But it was no mistake.

Carol and Jonny opened the bag.

There were two lollipops in it!

Two big lollipops!

The red one said, 'For Carol'.

The green one said, 'For Jonny'.

So Carol and Jonny sat down on the Snowtime Express, and they ate their lollipops right then and there!

LILIAN MOORE

JACK JACKDAW

I must tell you about Jack. Jack won't like it. He'll squawk and fluff out his black feathers in a huff, but he's our school bird and we're proud of him – even if he is rather bad-tempered.

I first met Jack on the day I started school. He was walking up and down on the wall at the end of the playground during morning break.

I was standing by the wall because I didn't like the big wide space in the middle of the playground. For a while I watched this strange black bird with a grey head and then I said.

'Hello, birdie. Pretty birdie.'

Jack looked at me with a beady eye and said 'Jack-Jackdaw,' very clearly.

A boy was standing beside me.

'He's not pretty,' the boy said. 'Do you like birds? I like birds. My Grannie's got a budgie that can talk.'

That boy was my first friend at school. He still is my friend too. He's called Robert and I'm called Sarah.

After that Robert and I always went to talk to Jack if he was perched on the wall. Sometimes he made a lot of noise.

'Jack-Jack-Jack-Jackdaw,' he would squawk. Then he would laugh and whistle and make a funny hubbub noise like a lot of children in a distant playground.

But at other times he would not talk at all, even though the whole class would try to make him. He would walk and hop along the wall opening his beak at us and wagging his head.

We asked our teacher, Mrs Stacey, about Jack.

'Now, let me think,' she said. 'He's a jackdaw, you know. And he's been around the school for a couple of months now. He seems so tame that the headmistress thought he might be someone's pet. We put a notice about him in the village post office. But nobody claimed him. I don't suppose anybody wanted him. He isn't a pretty sight, is he? All those scrawny grey feathers standing up on his head.'

Robert and Mrs Stacey were right. Jack was not a pretty bird.

His feathers standing up in spikes made him look as if he was always cross about something. And the way he squawked wasn't very appealing either. Some of the children said they were frightened of him. But I don't think they were really. Although he sounded fierce, he never pecked anybody.

He used to eat out of the pig bins which stood in a row near the school kitchens. All the scraps which didn't get eaten at dinner time used to go in those pig bins. Sometimes Robert and I picked up the lids to look inside because it was so horrible. We saw mashed potato and gravy and vegetables all mixed up with custard and lumps of pudding. It really looked disgusting. Jack loved it. He used to walk up and down nearby pretending to think of other things. Then, if a lid was left a bit askew, he would flap up on to the edge of a bin, grab a piece of pastry or half a fish finger, and make off to the top of the games shed to eat it.

While he ate it he would jump and flap and bash his food on the shed roof. He made rather a mess of the roof and Mr Hudson, the school caretaker, didn't like him at all.

But Robert and I liked Jack more and more. We looked for him every morning when we arrived at school, and we said good-bye to him if he was around when it was time to go home.

And Jack began to like us.

Robert and I spent a year in Mrs Stacey's class. After a while we got used to the big empty playground and played in the middle of it as well as by the wall. And after a while Jack got used to it too. He flapped around Robert saying 'Aark-aark', and tried to join in our games. He particularly liked skipping. As soon as he saw a rope he would bob up and down as if he were jumping over it. Robert tried to teach him some skipping rhymes.

'Come on, Jack,' Robert used to say. 'I like coffee. I like tea. I like Jackdaw in with me.'

But Jack used to turn and walk off, hunching his shoulders.

'Jack-Jack-Jackdaw,' he would say looking back at Robert.

'Perhaps he's too old to learn new words,' said Robert.

But Robert was wrong. Jack was taking things in all right. And he began to make himself unpopular.

Our headmistress was a kind lady and always said good morning to the children in the playground when she arrived at school each day. Usually she said 'Good morning, Robert,' or 'Good morning, Sarah,' because she knew all our names. But sometimes she said 'Good morning, dear,' if she wasn't thinking of names just then, and Jack picked it up.

One morning the headmistress walked in at the school gate and Jack was waiting for her on the wall.

'Good morning, dear,' said Jack loudly in exactly the head-mistress's voice.

The headmistress looked very surprised but she laughed.

'You saucy bird, Jack,' she said and walked on across the play-ground.

Jack flopped down on to the ground and hobbled after her.

'Good morning, dear. Good morning, dear. Good morning, dear,' he said.

'Yes, Jack. I heard you the first time,' said the headmistress as she went into the school.

But Jack didn't take the hint. He carried on saying 'Good morning, dear' to the headmistress every time he saw her. And I could see she got tired of it.

There were a lot of children in our school but Robert was the one Jack liked best. Robert used to bring him little tit-bits from home. Once he even brought him some of his seventh-birthday cake. Robert put it down on the ground for Jack to peck. Jack squawked and tossed bits of cake in the air, laughing in a cackling voice as he did so.

'You've got no manners, Jack,' said Robert.

'Aark-aark,' said Jack happily.

Not long after that Robert was made goal-keeper for the school football team. Jack liked that. He was able to perch on the crossbar of the football goal and keep Robert company. Whenever the ball came anywhere near the goal Jack used to flap and squawk and nearly fall off his bar with excitement. Robert said it was encour-aging to have such a noisy fan. But the sports master said Jack was a 'plaguey nuisance'.

One day a team from the school in the next village came to play our school at football. I was able to watch, although I hadn't been chosen for the team.

A boy from the other school team saw Jack flap across the football pitch and land on the goalpost.

'Look at that old crow,' he shouted.

'That's a jackdaw,' I shouted back at him. 'He's our mascot. He brings us luck.'

And Jack did bring us luck. The visiting team were very good footballers and the ball kept coming dangerously close to Robert's goal. But Jack flapped and yelled and kept distracting the players so that Robert was able to get the ball each time it was kicked towards the goal. But at half time the teams changed ends and Robert went off down the pitch to defend the other goal. Jack decided to stay put. He perched above the other goal-keeper's head and peered down at him. Then he opened his beak and gaped at him. And just as one of our players was about to kick the ball hard into the goal Jack said 'Good morning, dear' to the goal-keeper, and the ball slammed into the back of the net.

38

We all cheered and jumped and clapped. Jack squawked and flew off towards the school.

'It's that old crow,' shouted the goal-keeper. 'He distracted me. He did. He did it on purpose.'

The sports master from the visiting school looked very annoyed.

'I'm sorry about that jackdaw,' said our sports teacher. 'He's becoming a plaguey nuisance around the school. He won't leave us alone.'

Have you ever heard stories about magpies and jackdaws stealing things? Well, it's true. It isn't that they are dishonest or anything like that. They just like collecting things, especially shiny things.

Jack was always on the look-out for something new to add to his collection. The litter bin in the school playground was filled with bits of tin-foil wrappings from sweets and biscuits. Jack used to sort out the bin, hurling any litter he didn't want on the ground.

'That bird makes this school look like a slum,' Mr Hudson, the caretaker, used to say as he cleared up after Jack.

For a while we wondered what Jack did with all his bits of foil and rubbish. Then Mr Hudson found out. Jack stuffed them down the narrow gap between the games shed and the wall of the school. He must have been doing it for months, perhaps even for years. The gap was almost filled up with rubbish and Mr Hudson spent hours pulling it all out with a pair of tongs on a long stick.

'I'll wring that bird's neck if I get half the chance,' I heard him mutter.

Robert and I were beginning to worry about Jack being in so much trouble. Several of the teachers thought he was nothing but a nuisance. Then he made matters worse by trying to visit Robert in school.

We were in Mr Maynard's class when Jack dropped in on Robert one morning. We had been set some geography work to get on with when suddenly Jack flap-flapped in at an open window of the classroom and landed with a flump and a squawk on Robert's exercise book. He lay there for a moment with his beak open as if the drop had been further than he expected. Then he stood up,

shook himself a little, and said, 'Good morning, dear,' to Mr Maynard.

Mr Maynard was not pleased. He could see what a muddy mess Jack had made of Robert's geography book.

'Get that bird out of here Robert,' he said crossly.

'Sorry, Mr Maynard,' said Robert as if he had invited Jack to come and ruin his work. 'I'll take him out.'

But Jack had a different plan. He jumped down on to the floor and hopped around under the desks squawking and grumbling. Luckily he spotted a metal pencil sharpener which somebody had dropped on the floor and he began to pick this up in his beak and hurl it about. This gave Robert a chance to grab him and carry him out. Strangely enough, Jack seemed to like being held by Robert and he gave a chirpy sound. But then he caught sight of Mr Maynard and said 'Aark-aark' in a cross voice.

'Aark-aark yourself,' said Mr Maynard. 'And don't come back.'

Half an hour later Jack came back.

There was a scratching at the door leading out to the big school corridor. Mr Maynard opened the door to see what the noise was.

'Good morning, dear – Aark,' said Jack, standing up very straight with all his head feathers standing up straight as well.

All the class roared with laughter and Jack laughed too in a screaming, showing-off sort of voice which made Mr Maynard furious.

'Robert,' he said, 'get that fowl out of here and shut the school door. And tell him that if he comes in again I'll wring his neck.'

'The teachers don't like Jack,' said Robert as we went home that evening.

'Do you think Mr Maynard would really wring his neck?' I asked.

'No,' said Robert. 'But I know Mr Hudson wants to get rid of him.'

'How will they do it?' I asked.

'I don't know,' said Robert. 'But I think we ought to get Jack away from school for a while.'

Two evenings later we had a plan to save Jack. We didn't tell anyone else. But when we were going home we searched for Jack and found him perched on top of the games shed.

'Good morning, dear,' he said to Robert in a friendly way. So Robert clambered up on to my shoulders and tried to grab him. But he didn't have to. Jack walked on to his arm and made those chirpy noises he had done in the classroom.

Robert was delighted, although it was difficult to climb down again without letting go of Jack.

Then we had to run home because we were late and our mothers might have been worried. Jack was jolted rather a lot and looked more beady-eyed than usual by the time we reached my house. We just had time to push him under our garage door and shut it down before Robert had to run off home.

A little while later Robert came back with some biscuits and an apple for Jack.

'We must give Jack some food,' he said. 'Then he'll like it here and stay.'

So I took some of the chocolate cake I had had for my tea and we went to the garage.

41

Very carefully we pulled up the swing door and crept inside.

'Jack,' we whispered. 'Here's your tea.'

'Come on, Jack. Where are you?' said Robert.

Then we both saw the open window. We had forgotten about the window. Usually it was shut. But this evening it was open and Jack had gone.

We searched the garden. We searched the trees down the road. We went all the way back to the school. But Jack was nowhere. He had vanished. And it was all our fault.

'I expect he'll turn up at school tomorrow,' said Robert as he went back home that evening.

'I hope so,' I said.

But Jack didn't turn up. Every day Robert and I searched for him. We asked Mr Hudson if he had seen him, but he said, 'No. And good riddance. I reckon.'

We asked Mrs Stacey and all the teachers who hadn't minded Jack too much. But nobody had seen him.

We felt terrible. The football team wondered where their mascot was and Robert kept letting balls into the goal. We looked hopefully at every passing rook or crow that flew overhead, but it was never Jack.

I told my mother what I had done and how sorry I was. She was very kind and said she was sure Jack could look after himself. She also said the village school was better off without him. But I didn't really agree with that.

All that happened two years ago. Since then there has been no sign of Jack. No sign, that is, until yesterday morning.

You see, Robert and I started at our new school in town yesterday. We had to go in on a school bus with lots of other children from our village. The new school has green railings along the front on to the main road where the buses stop.

As we got off the bus Robert grabbed my arm and pointed. Way down the road at the very end of the railings was a small black hunched figure.

'Aark,' it said as we ran up the road. 'Good morning, dear.'

'JACK JACKDAW,' yelled Robert. 'It is. It really is JACK.'

I think I have never been so happy. And Jack was happy too.

He flapped and bowed and squawked before jumping clumsily on to Robert's shoulder and rubbing his beak against his ear.

Robert walked into school with Jack still perched on his shoulder. A teacher came out of the main door.

'Don't bring that bird into school,' said the teacher. 'He's a terrible nuisance. He's become the school mascot and lives in a heap of rubbish behind the bicycle sheds. We wouldn't be without him now. But *not* inside the school buildings, you understand.'

So Robert put Jack gently down on the grass in front of the school.

'It's nice to see a friendly face in a new school,' said Robert, blowing his nose because he was so pleased.

'Aark-aark,' said Jack, and waddled off around the corner.

'I expect he's going to the pig bins,' I said happily.

In the afternoon Robert told our new teacher about Jack's story. He was very interested and said he would tell the local newspaper about it. So a photographer came to the school this morning to take Jack's picture. Jack was on the railings preening himself when the photographer came up to him and held up his camera to take a picture.

'Aark,' said Jack and swooped down to take a close look at the camera. It was just the sort of thing Jack likes for his load-of-rubbish collection. But the photographer was alarmed and flapped his arm at Jack to keep him away.

'Good morning, dear,' said Jack and flew away over the school, as if he had more important things to do.

'Bother,' said our teacher, 'I was thinking of getting the regional television people to come and film him too.'

But Jack isn't the sort of bird to sit nicely for cameras. So I thought I had better write down his story and you could see what he's like from the drawings.

ANNE ROOKE

EGGS

'Oh, how I wish I had an alarm clock,' sighed Mrs Smith each morning. 'Every single day little Sam is late for school, and William is late for work.'

William, her husband, took no notice of this. He was spraying his roses. Nothing but roses grew in Mr Smith's garden, which lay right by the road. People walking along could lean over the low wooden fence and breathe in the scent, which was like warm Madeira cake mixed with raspberry trifle. And they could gaze at the gorgeous colours of flowers, red, white, pink, flame, yellow, and orange. People walked very slowly along that stretch of road. Bees hummed among the roses all day; they came from all over the country to make honey from Mr Smith's roses. And from March to November Mr Smith spent every free hour in his garden, watering, digging, raking the ground, picking off dead flowers, pruning, and spraying the roses and plants to get rid of greenfly, caterpillars, and nibbling insects.

There wasn't any room for little Sam in the garden. *He* had to play on the cement strip by the back door. And he would have liked a kitten, or maybe a puppy, but his father said animals would damage the flowers.

Every day little Sam was late for school because his father, who drove him there, had to be called in from the garden where he was caring for his roses; and every day Mr Smith was late for his job in the garden shop where he worked, selling roses and mowers and wheelbarrows.

Mr Smith liked working in the garden shop because he could get rose plants at half price.

'Hurry, William!' cried his wife. 'You'll be late! And Sam will be late for school. Here're your sandwiches, Sam, and your school bag. And, William, will you *please* buy me an alarm clock, so we can all get up earlier in the morning?'

'If I remember,' said Mr Smith. But she knew he would not remember. He would just buy another rose plant.

Father and son were leaving by the back door, to get to the shed where Mr Smith kept his old pick-up, when, guess what happened! With a crash louder than eighty tons of boulders falling on an ice rink, a lorry skidded off the road – across the pavement – through the wooden fence – and straight into Mr Smith's garden, ploughing over the roses, and ending up with its radiator jammed into the next-door fence. Then it fell on its side, because Mr Smith's garden was on quite a steep slope.

If Mr Smith had stayed in his garden *one minute* longer, *he* would have been run over too, along with his roses!

'Mercy!' cried Mrs Smith, running out of the back door. '*Mercy*, what's happened? Sam! William! Are you all right?'

'Oh, my lord! Oh, my roses!' wailed Mr Smith.

For the roses that had not been mashed by the truck were now completely buried under its load, which had tumbled out all over the garden.

What was that load?

Eggs! The truck had been taking forty thousand eggs to a cake factory. And every single one was now lying smashed all over Mr Smith's rose bed.

'What *happened*?' Mrs Smith asked the driver, who had clambered down, gulping and trembling, from his cab.

'A bee stung me, that's what! Made me swerve.'

'I'll want compensation for this,' moaned Mr Smith, looking at his ruined rose-bed. 'Compensation! My roses would have taken all the prizes at the County Show tomorrow.'

'My firm will pay you,' said the driver.

'Maybe we can buy an alarm clock with the money,' said Mrs Smith. But she didn't really believe so. She knew the money would go to buy more rose plants. 'Look at all those broken eggs! Not a whole one among them. What a shame! What a waste!'

The garden was bright yellow, and all gooey. Little Sam was up to his knees in egg yolk.

'Sam, come out of that! *Look* at you!'

But Sam called, 'Hey, Ma, look what I found! One egg isn't broken. Just one! Can I have it?' he asked the driver, who was limping indoors to phone for the breakdown service.

'Help yourself, son. No one's going to count those eggs...'

As Sam gently held the egg in his hand, he felt something alive, moving about inside it.

'Oh! It made a noise! There's a live chick in there! Ma, can I keep it? Can I hatch it?'

'Dad doesn't want chickens in the garden,' began Mrs Smith. But then she looked at the ruined roses and said, 'Oh, what's the difference? Put it in a basket by the stove where it'll keep warm. Now, clean yourself up for school. I never did *see* such a sight –'

'Egg yolks must be good for the ground,' sighed Mr Smith.

When little Sam came home at tea time, the egg in the basket was beginning to bump and joggle about. And then, crack! It opened. Out crawled a damp and yellow chick.

'Give it a spoonful of cereal,' said Sam's mother. 'And a drink of water.'

Soon the chick was dry, and yellow and fluffy.

'I'll call him Herbert,' said Sam.

'Perhaps it's a hen,' said his mother.

But Herbert was a cock. Long before Mr Smith had dug in the broken eggshells, and before the new roses were planted and blooming, Herbert had grown into a splendid rooster. He had a scarlet comb, black and green tail feathers, a gold-brown chest, and orange legs with black feather breeches. He followed Sam everywhere, sat beside him on the new patch of grass that had been planted, and ate all the slugs and snails in the garden.

And, every morning, sharp at half-past six, he shouted:

'Cock-a-doodle-doo! Time to get up! Cock-a-doodle-doo!'

Never again did Mrs Smith need to wish for an alarm clock. Or Sam for a kitten.

JOAN AIKEN

46

THE PAPER PALACE

Caroline had a bad leg and it kept her in bed for a long time. She was fearfully bored, because she had read all her books and used up all her paints.

Then her grandmother bought her a present. A nice present: a pair of scissors.

'For my nails?' asked Caroline.

'No,' said Grandmother. 'To cut things out of paper.'

'What kind of things?' asked Caroline.

'People,' said Grandmother. 'And animals and trees and houses and anything you can think of.'

It was not at all easy. First Caroline cut out a car, but it looked more like a jam jar on legs. Then she made a hare and a rabbit, but they looked more like funny hats.

She took a new sheet of paper and cut out another animal.

'Did *you* make that dog?' her father asked. 'With your grandmother's scissors? Jolly good!'

Caroline practised and practised and after a week she could cut out anything she liked with the scissors. Even little houses, which she would cut out and then stick together. Everyone had heard about it and everyone in the neighbourhood came to look. There was the farm which sick little Caroline had made, with barns and stables and chickens and cows and pigs. And ducks, in a silver-paper pond.

'Good gracious, Caroline, how clever!'

One night Caroline had a strange dream. A tiny man, smaller than her little finger, skipped on to the table. 'You must make a palace,' he said.

'A palace?' asked Caroline. 'What for?'

'For the Queen,' said the little man. 'In three days' time she is giving a party and it's got to be in a beautiful new palace.'

'Made of paper?' asked Caroline.

'Naturally,' said the little man. 'And you must cut it out. With a big ballroom and two kitchens with stoves and a broad staircase to the upper rooms and turrets with flags and battlements and parapets and a double front door with a flight of steps. And you must make footmen too, and cooks and dancing girls. Lots of dancing girls, because it's going to be a big party.'

Caroline had to laugh about it next morning, and yet she could not forget her dream. 'You know,' she thought, 'I'm really going to make it. A whole palace. For my own pleasure.'

She began to snip and stick and stick and snip. Walls with windows in them, turrets with battlements, the ballroom floor, the steps leading upwards.

'What are you making, Caroline?' her mother asked.

'Oh, a palace.'

By evening she had stuck two walls together and part of the stairs.

That night she dreamed of the little man again. He tripped across the ballroom and gave the walls a push which made the paper crackle. 'Is it really sturdy enough?' he asked.

'Yes, of course,' said Caroline.

'And where are the kitchens?'

'I've still got to do them,' said Caroline.

She made the kitchens the next day and the upper rooms with the broad staircase leading up to them and the turrets with flags on them.

'You'll have to hurry up,' said the little man on the third night of her dream. 'You've only got one day left. What about the flight of steps? Where are the cooks and footmen and dancing girls? And one of the towers must be higher.'

Caroline began immediately after breakfast. She cut out twelve dancing girls and stuck them on one leg in a circle round the ballroom. She cut out seven cooks and stuck them on two legs by the stoves in the kitchens. She stuck an extra bit on the tower and made the steps and two big trees for the outside.

'Marvellous, child. Marvellous,' said her mother. 'Shall I put it away now?'

'On the table,' whispered Caroline.

But that night Caroline did not dream. No, she woke up instead. A light was shining in the room, a strange white light. She turned her head and then she saw it. In the middle of the table her paper palace stood sparkling and glittering as if a thousand lamps were burning inside it. Music was pouring from the windows and shadows were moving against the transparent paper walls – the shadows of people dancing.

'The party!' thought Caroline. She was longing to sit up, but her bad leg wouldn't let her.

Then the people in the palace started to sing and clap their hands and laugh and shout hooray and 'Long live the Queen!' and Caroline saw the shadows of skipping, swaying, leaping and whirling people dancing across the white walls.

Then she looked at the tall tower. There at the top stood the little man of her dream, on guard.

'Hello!' Caroline called to him.

At that moment everything fell dark and silent.

How strange, thought Caroline, and next morning she thought again: how strange. Of course it was only a dream, but it seemed just as real as if I were awake.

'I say, how strange,' her mother was saying, as she set the castle beside Caroline's bed. 'I didn't remember that you had put a little man on the tower as well.'

Caroline's eyes opened wide. 'It wasn't a dream,' she whispered.

'What do you mean?'

But Caroline didn't answer. She peered with one eye through the window into the ballroom. And there, in the middle of the dance floor, inside the ring of twelve dancing girls on one leg, stood another figure, in a wide cloak and with a crown on her head: the Queen.

And when the neighbours said, 'You did cut out *that* one cleverly, she's so real it looks as if she were alive,' Caroline would say, 'I didn't make that one.'

But no one believed her.

PAUL BIEGEL

THE FARM
BROTHERS' BAND

There were once four brothers who lived with their sister, Betsy Ann, on a small farm just outside a little seaside village in Wales.

Now, nearly all the people who live in Wales are very fond of music. The four Jones brothers were real Welshmen. They were never happier than when they were making music. First, there was Davy-the-Drum with his *Rum-ti-tum-tum*! Then came Freddie-the-Flute with his *Tootle-too-toot*! The third brother was Triangle Tim with his *Ting-a-ling-ling*! The youngest brother was Trumpeter Tom with his *Too-too*! *Pom-pom*!

You can see they were almost like a band when they all played together. The only one who didn't join in was the brothers' sister, Betsy Ann. She said she was far too busy cooking and mending and cleaning – not to mention her hens and ducks – to make music with her brothers.

'The best I can do,' she would say, 'is to ring the dinner bell to fetch you all in before my good food gets spoiled.'

Of course, the brothers couldn't spend all their time playing their instruments. Davy-the-Drum was the porter at the small village station that only had a single-track line and four trains passing through it all day.

Freddie-the-Flute was the village postman, but, if there weren't too many letters to be delivered, he would pedal along the lanes gaily on his Post Office bicycle practising tunes on his flute.

Triangle Tim was the milkman and he took the milk from the farm cows all round the village each day.

Trumpeter Tom helped Betsy Ann with the farm work. He was a big strong cheery fellow and drove up and down the fields in his tractor or rounded up the sheep on the hillside with his old dog, as happy as could be.

One fine spring day when the blackthorn blossoms had sprinkled the hedges like snow and Triangle Tim found the first clump of pale primroses smiling up at him from a sheltered bank, Freddie-the-Flute came back to the farm full of excitement. But it wasn't until the brothers were all sitting round the big kitchen table enjoying Betsy Ann's steaming helpings of stew that he said anything to the rest of the family.

Then he put down his knife and fork, mopped up the last of the good rich gravy with a hunk of bread, and gave an important sort of cough.

'Well, brothers,' he said, as they looked at him in surprise, 'I've a bit of news for you all – good news, I fancy, and fun for our Betsy Ann, too.'

They all stopped eating and stared at Freddie-the-Flute who was generally a very quiet fellow.

'Mr Roberts-the-Bank was telling me this morning,' he went on, 'there's to be a Grand Carnival this summer and it's to be held in the field behind the station. People are coming from all the villages for miles around, and there's to be competitions and prizes and a fair and I don't know what. It'll be a real grand do, I can tell you.'

The brothers looked at Freddie-the-Flute in amazement and Betsy Ann gave a squeal of excitement. 'Well there's news, if you like!' she cried. 'Fancy Mr Roberts telling you all that, Freddie. We'll have to start saving up right away.'

Then they all began to chatter and laugh and ask questions till Freddie-the-Flute said, 'That is all I know yet, but there'll be posters and things so we can see what's on.'

'If there're musical competitions, I'm going in for a prize, that's for sure,' said big Trumpeter Tom.

'Me, too,' cried Davy-the-Drum.

'Why don't we make a band and do something all together?' suggested Triangle Tim.

Everyone thought that was a splendid idea.

How the brothers worked! They practised and practised till they knew their music so well they could have played it in their sleep!

At last the great day came. Betsy Ann had their Sunday suits and clean shirts all pressed and ready for them and she even found time to put a new ribbon in her straw hat. They *did* look smart as they set off for the village in their old car. It was quite a squash with their band things, too, but no one minded and they got to the field in plenty of time. And how everyone cheered and waved as the carnival procession marched along in the sunshine in all its finery. The four brothers walked together, playing away for all they were worth. Their faces grew as red as the rosebuds Betsy Ann had popped in their button-holes.

And then the judging began.

There were cheers for all the competitors, of course, but the biggest cheer of all seemed to be for Davy-the-Drum, with his *Rum-ti-tum-tum*, Freddie-the-Flute, with his *Tootle-too-toot*, Triangle Tim and his *Ting-a-ling-ling* and Trumpeter Tom and his *Too-too! Pom-pom!*

'It's the liveliest band I've heard for many a year,' said the judge. 'You have won first prize!' and he handed the brothers a shining silver cup and £2.50 in fifty-pence pieces!

'Well,' sighed Tom, who hadn't much spare breath left after all his blowing, 'that was a grand do, wasn't it?'

'Grand!' echoed his brothers and Betsy Ann.

'And this lovely silver cup!' cried Freddie.

'And all the money, too,' said Tim.

53

'I think we should have fifty pence each and give the other fifty pence to Betsy Ann who helped us so much,' said Trumpeter Tom.

'Good idea!' cried the other three as they went back through the farm gate to milk the cows, feed the chickens and ducks, and settle the farm for the night.

And can you guess how Betsy Ann spent her fifty pence? The very next time she went into market she spied a lovely little mouth organ in the toy shop window and she went right in and bought it! So, next time the brothers played their band, Betsy Ann had an instrument too. And, as she went round the house and farm doing her work, every now and then you could hear a faint little humming buzz. It was Betsy Ann practising on her mouth organ that she kept handily in the pocket of her apron!

URSULA HOURIHANE

GALLDORA AND THE MERMAID

One day Galldora was given a new dress and taken by Marybell to the seaside for a holiday.

'What a strange doll,' said the landlady, Mrs Cockle, when she saw Galldora.

'She's not really strange,' answered Marybell, 'she's just a rag doll.' Marybell spoke as stiffly as she could, because she was upset that the landlady was so rude about Galldora.

'Yes, my dear, I can see she is a rag doll,' said the landlady slowly, 'but she's strange all the same. She's very faded and flabby, poor thing, but perhaps the sea air will do her good. Let's hope so.'

'It's just her new dress that makes her look washed out,' explained Marybell, talking very fast to get in all she wanted to say; 'It is rather a bright colour. It's a piece of Mummy's worn-out dance dress. Mummy calls it flame colour. I'm not sure I like that colour myself. Blue's my favourite colour, that's why I bought a blue ribbon for Galldora's hair. I spent a whole four-pence on that ribbon. The colour's called king-fisher blue, and it doesn't look quite right with flame colour, but it is pretty all the same.'

'Very pretty,' Mrs Cockle said, adding, 'It's a pity about the safety-pin though, it's so large that it hides most of the ribbon.'

'Well, but, you see, Mrs Cockle, I had to pin it on Galldora's hair, because Galldora can't keep ribbons on her hair. It's wool hair, Mrs Cockle, and it's got a bit moth-eaten, and her head's such a funny shape too, sort of flattish, do you see what I mean?'

Galldora was held up for inspection. Mrs Cockle inspected Galldora's head. 'Yes, very flat, my dear, and a very odd shape.'

Now, Galldora was not at all pleased at this conversation. She loved being looked at, but she felt it was very rude indeed of people to make remarks about the shape of her head.

Human beings, she thought to herself, have no manners, no manners at all. Certainly none where dolls are concerned.

I think the discussion on Galldora's head would have spoilt the whole of Galldora's holiday if it hadn't been for an adventure that came her way on the first evening.

It was a wonderful adventure, and Galldora was able to tell all the other dolls and the teddy bears about it when she returned to the nursery. It happened like this. Marybell was so eager to rush down to the sands and the sea at once that her mother promised to take her down as soon as they had unpacked the spade, the bucket, and the swimsuits.

'We won't wait for lunch,' said Marybell's mother, 'we'll ask Mrs Cockle if she could make us some sandwiches and we'll eat them on the sands.'

Mrs Cockle understood all about little girls wanting to rush on to the sands and not waste a moment so she bustled about and produced a packed lunch.

'There you are, my dear,' she said to Marybell's mother, as she handed over the lunch, and turning to Marybell she added, 'That's right, love, you take that doll down and give her a good sea blow, that will do the poor thing a power of good.'

The sands and the sea were all that sands and sea should be.

The sands were silver white, stretching as far to the right and as far to the left as Marybell could see, and the great ocean was in a very gentle mood.

'Oh, Mummy,' said Marybell, 'I want to stay here always and always.'

'Well, we have till six o'clock,' answered Marybell's mother. 'Now, how about a paddle, Marybell, while I get the lunch set out? Then after lunch I'll help you build a sand castle, and later we will go and have a real swim.'

So after their lunch Marybell's mother helped Marybell to build the hugest and the most magnificent sand castle that Galldora had ever seen. It was so large that Marybell could stand in the middle courtyard without knocking any of the castle walls down. The castle had turrets and windows, and a moat, and a wall round the moat, with more turrets and more windows. When the castle was finished Galldora was sat on a sand-throne made especially for her. She sat there happily and proudly, staring out over the castle walls.

After a swim Marybell decided to look for shells. She and her mother were so happy collecting shells and shining wet pebbles

that Marybell's mother forgot all about the time. When she did look at her watch she was horrified.

'Quickly, Marybell,' she said, 'we mustn't be late the very first day. Mrs Cockle said she would have a high tea waiting for us at six, and it is six o'clock now.'

There was a lot of collecting up to be done. Wet towels and bathing-suits were crammed into one basket. Then into another basket went the paper wrappings of the lunch and the sun-hats and the sun-glasses, while in the bucket went the pebbles and shells. With all the pushing of this here and that there, both Marybell and Marybell's mother forgot Galldora. Marybell's mother did say, 'Have you got Galldora, Marybell?' and Marybell had answered, 'Yes, Mummy, I put her with my swim-suit.' And Marybell really thought she had. Galldora couldn't be seen, for the sand-throne she had been sitting on had collapsed, and she had sunk forward against the wall. She was still upright, and her head rested against a turret, but she was hidden and she couldn't see anything but sand. Galldora heard Marybell chattering as she and her mother hurried away from the beach, back to Mrs Cockle and high tea. Soon the beach grew very quiet except for the wild noises of sea-birds. Then the noise of the sea seemed to grow louder.

The half-hours went by, and the sky changed from blue to a flush of pink and yellow gold. If only Galldora could have seen how wonderful the sky was, for it looked as if some giant child of the sky-lands had tipped up a basket full of rose petals and set them floating down. Then the colour left the sky, and a silver bloom lingered on the sea and the sands. All the while the sound of the sea grew louder.

I know I'm not fancying it, said Galldora to herself. It's true, the sea is coming towards me inch by inch.

It was true. The tide was rolling in the white surf, and with the incoming tide a low wind had sprung up. The wind stirred the white sand and set the white horses riding far out at sea. It may have been the dragging of the sands, as the sea washed out before each incoming wave swept up, or it may have been the low wind shifting the sands, but whatever was the cause, the walls of the castle cracked and slowly, very slowly, crumbled.

'Gracious me,' gasped Galldora, 'I can see now – and how very different everything looks. Mrs Cockle wouldn't approve at all. Why, everything looks as pale and as washed-out as my face.'

The silver bloom about the scene turned clearer and harder. Shadows sprang like seaweed in a silver wash. All in the dark and the light of the waves were a million phosphorous sea life, that glowed so gaily it looked as if the fish were holding a great ball, far down below. The moon, like a full-sailed ship riding high, seemed to let drift a fishing-net of light to glitter and shimmer on the sea.

It's very beautiful, thought Galldora, but I rather wish I wasn't here. I think Mrs Cockle's boarding-house would be more cosy. Still, it's no good me wishing, as here I am and here I'll have to stay until Marybell finds me tomorrow.

All the time the sea crept closer, wave by wave. This began to worry Galldora.

I wish the sea would stop – just stop where it is, thought Galldora. If it doesn't my castle will soon be washed away and I with it. And then she sighed, 'Oh, dear, poor Marybell, she won't have a rag doll any more.'

Just then Galldora thought she heard sweet singing. I've got myself into such a state of nerves, I'm imagining all sorts of things, she told herself crossly. Why, that's only the noise of the sea or the wind or a bird. But try as Galldora would to make herself believe the singing noise was just natural noises, she couldn't. The singing grew louder and higher. I don't think I like that singing at all, thought Galldora, it makes me feel uncomfortable.

Then Galldora noticed a shape on one of the white horses far out in the sea. As the shape came nearer Galldora thought it was a girl. A girl with long, shining hair. And it was a girl. The girl was singing.

Nearer and nearer came the white horse and the girl with the long hair, until, with a sudden *splosh*, she was washed up on shore. Then Galldora saw she was not a proper girl, but a mermaid.

The mermaid was in a shocking temper. She clearly hated being on the shore. She stopped singing and lashed her tail, and was very thankful when the next wave lifted her up and washed her out into the sea again.

'Oh, do stop and talk to me, please!' called Galldora. 'I've never talked to a mermaid before. But perhaps you can't talk.'

'Of course I can, silly,' answered the mermaid. 'But where are you?'

'In here,' called Galldora. 'Here in the sand castle.' The mermaid swam closer to the shore to have a look.

'I can't see with all this hair,' said the mermaid at last, and she tossed her hair this way and that.

'I'm just near you,' explained Galldora, 'for the sea has come up to my castle walls, and I'm terribly afraid it will wash it and me away.'

The mermaid lifted up her silvery hair with her two hands. 'That's better,' she said. 'Ah, yes, I can see you now. My, aren't you small, and you haven't got much hair – how very strange.'

'Oh, yes, I know all about that,' said poor Galldora. 'And I've got a funny-shaped head, but I'm used to it, and it's *my* hair and *my* head, and, anyway, talking of hair, you've got far too much. You ought to have it cut off.'

'Cut it off – how do you do that?' asked the mermaid. Then Galldora realized at once she had made a very silly remark, because, of course, who would have scissors in the sea? 'Oh, I've changed my mind,' she said hurriedly, 'I shouldn't cut your hair off if I were you; it suits you.'

'If you had to choose between one eye and three eyes,' said the mermaid, 'which would you choose?'

'I've often had one eye,' said Galldora, 'and another one can always be sewn on, but three would look ugly, very ugly indeed. So I would choose one.'

'I'd choose three,' said the mermaid, 'a third one in the middle of my forehead, then when I opened my middle eye, the lashes would lift my hair a little, so I could see. It's a dreadful nuisance not being able to see properly. Look what happened just now. I got washed ashore, just because I couldn't see where I was going.'

'Yes, I do understand what you mean,' said Galldora thoughtfully.

'Can't you think of something to help me?' asked the mermaid.

'I'll try,' said Galldora. 'You can see now, though, can't you?'

'Yes, because I'm lifting my hair with my hands, but it gets trying.'

'Of course,' said Galldora. Then she asked, 'Do other mermaids have this trouble?'

'No,' answered the mermaid. 'It's because I'm a bad mermaid I have this trouble. The good mermaids sit on rocks and sing to the sailors, and it makes the sailors muddled and then they wreck their ships on the rocks. The ships sink, and the mermaids go swimming down and down into the wrecks and they find all sorts of treasures, like string and mirrors and combs. The mermaids make their hair behave by combing it, then they tie it up with the string, and then they look at themselves in the mirrors.'

'Just a moment,' said Galldora. 'I'm getting a bit muddled, or are you? Surely if mermaids wreck ships that's being very wicked and bad.'

'No, that's being good,' said the mermaid. 'Being bad is being like me, not wrecking ships, but just playing about in the sea. Oh, I love playing!'

'I think I'll have to think this out,' muttered Galldora, feeling very muddled.

Just then a crab who had been silently listening started to laugh and said, 'What a joke – thinking.'

'It's all very well for you to laugh,' said Galldora crossly, 'but you don't have to think this out like I do. You understand the sea and sea-creatures. I don't.'

'Don't try,' answered the crab. 'Some folks do things sideways, like me, some folks do things flat ways, like plaice, while other folks do things along, like eels do. But mermaids, they do things upside down.'

'Yes,' Galldora had a long think. 'That's very helpful,' she said. 'Thank you, Mr Crab, for telling me. I understand now. Being good is being bad to mermaids and being bad is being good, is that it?'

'It is and it isn't,' answered the crab, 'it just depends. Now, for wrecking their ships. You can't reason with mermaids, it's better to give them a "hello" in passing and let them be. Don't have no conversation with mermaids and above all don't listen to them singing. It will muddle you.'

'Thank you,' said Galldora, 'thank you very much, Mr Crab.'

'You're welcome,' mumbled the crab, as he walked away sideways.

'That was very kind of him,' said Galldora out loud.

'Oh, was it?' snapped the mermaid. 'I think it was most spiteful of that crab and he was just talking rubbish. Oh, do hurry up and think of something to keep the hair out of my eyes. My arms are aching, and I want to go and play!'

'I know,' said Galldora, 'I've got the very thing for you – my ribbon.'

'Give it to me,' said the mermaid, putting out a hand and letting half of her long hair fall down.

'Well, I can't exactly give it to you,' answered Galldora sadly, 'you will have to come and get it. I'm a doll, you see, and I can't walk.'

The mermaid swam about on the edge of the waves and peered at the rag doll, and got very cross. She pouted and flicked her tail and then said, 'I can't walk either, so we'll just have to wait for the sea to come up and wash you to me, that's all.'

'Oh, I do hope not, what will become of me then?' gasped Galldora.

'Don't you like the sea?' asked the mermaid in surprise.

'No.'

'That's funny, the sea is safe.'

'Yes, to you, because you are a mermaid, but I'm a rag doll, and rag dolls find the sea very unsafe, I can assure you.'

'What colour is your ribbon?' asked the mermaid, changing the subject.

'Blue,' said Galldora.

'I like blue,' said the mermaid.

'It's got a silver safety-pin holding the ribbon to my hair.'

'What's a safety-pin like? I can't see.'

'You've let your hair go all over your face again, that's why,' said Galldora.

'Well, my arms were aching so,' answered the mermaid. 'Oh, I do wish the sea would hurry up and wash you out!'

'Do you think it really will?' gasped Galldora in alarm.

'Oh, yes, of course,' answered the mermaid, 'I know it will. It's still coming in, and your castle wall is slowly crumbling.'

'If I am a good rag doll –' began Galldora, then she stopped. 'Of course,' she mumbled to herself, 'it's the other way round with mermaids.' So she started again. 'If I am a bad rag doll and let you have my ribbon for keeps and my safety-pin, will you be a bad mermaid in return and throw me out of the sea far behind the castle, where I will be safe?'

'Oh, yes, all right,' said the mermaid, 'let's be bad together,' which, of course, to the mermaid meant being good.

So when at last the sea broke through the castle walls and washed Galldora out the mermaid picked her up. The mermaid took her blue ribbon and the safety-pin, and then threw her over the crumbling castle on to the far dry sand.

'Thank you,' shouted Galldora, lying on her back in the sand-dunes. 'Does the ribbon work?' she called.

'Yes, rather,' shouted back the mermaid, 'I've tied some of my hair one side with the ribbon and pulled some of the other through the safety-pin. It's lovely. I can see now. I can go and play and play and play. I'll be able to play catch with the porpoises like I never did before, and grandmother's steps with the whales. What fun!'

Then, as the mermaid swam away singing, she turned just for a second and waved a last good-bye to the rag doll. Soon her song was lost in the song of the sea, and the silver flick of her silver tail was lost in the silver of the moon's light that spread upon the waters.

Galldora was found next day by Marybell, and Marybell knew at once that she must have had some strange adventure, for how else did the rag doll leave the sea-washed castle, and how did she lose her ribbon and the safety-pin?

'I hope it was a happy adventure,' said Marybell to Galldora. Galldora's shoe-button eyes shone back so brightly that Marybell knew it had indeed been a very happy adventure, and she was glad.

MODWENA SEDGWICK

THE PUDDING LIKE A NIGHT ON THE SEA

'I'm going to make something special for your mother,' my father said.

My mother was out shopping. My father was in the kitchen looking at the pots and the pans and the jars of this and that.

'What are you going to make?' I said.

'A pudding,' he said.

My father is a big man with wild black hair. When he laughs, the sun laughs in the window-panes. When he thinks, you can almost see his thoughts sitting on all the tables and chairs. When he is angry, me and my little brother Huey shiver to the bottom of our shoes.

'What kind of pudding will you make?' Huey said.

'A wonderful pudding,' my father said. 'It will taste like a whole raft of lemons. It will taste like a night on the sea.'

Then he took down a knife and sliced five lemons in half. He squeezed the first one. Juice squirted in my eye.

'Stand back!' he said, and squeezed again. The seeds flew out on the floor. 'Pick up those seeds, Huey!' he said.

Huey took the broom and swept them up.

63

My father cracked some eggs and put the yolks in a pan and the whites in a bowl. He rolled up his sleeves and pushed back his hair and beat up the yolks. 'Sugar, Julian!' he said, and I poured in the sugar.

He went on beating. Then he put in lemon juice and cream and set the pan on the stove. The pudding bubbled and he stirred it fast. Cream splashed on the stove.

'Wipe that up, Huey!' he said.

Huey did.

It was hot by the stove. My father loosened his collar and pushed at his sleeves. The stuff in the pan was getting thicker and thicker. He held the beater up high in the air. 'Just right!' he said, and sniffed in the smell of the pudding.

He whipped the egg whites and mixed them into the pudding. The pudding looked softer and lighter than air.

'Done!' he said. He washed all the pots, splashing water on the floor, and wiped the counter so fast his hair made circles around his head.

'Perfect!' he said. 'Now I'm going to take a nap. If something important happens, bother me. If nothing important happens, don't bother me. And – the pudding is for your mother. Leave the pudding alone!'

He went to the living room and was asleep in a minute, sitting straight up in his chair.

Huey and I guarded the pudding.

'Oh, it's a wonderful pudding,' Huey said.

'With waves on the top like the ocean,' I said.

'I wonder how it tastes,' Huey said.

'Leave the pudding alone,' I said.

'If I just put my finger in – there – I'll know how it tastes,' Huey said.

And he did it.

'You did it!' I said. 'How does it taste?'

'It tastes like a whole raft of lemons,' he said. 'It tastes like a night on the sea.'

'You've made a hole in the pudding!' I said. 'But since you did it, I'll have a taste.' And it tasted like a whole night of lemons. It tasted like floating at sea.

'It's such a big pudding,' Huey said. 'It can't hurt to have a little more.'

'Since you took more, I'll have more,' I said.

'That was a bigger lick than I took!' Huey said. 'I'm going to have more again.'

'Whoops!' I said.

'You put in your whole hand!' Huey said. 'Look at the pudding you spilled on the floor!'

'I am going to clean it up,' I said. And I took the rag from the sink.

'That's not really clean,' Huey said.

'It's the best I can do,' I said.

'Look at the pudding!' Huey said.

It looked like craters on the moon. 'We have to smooth this over,' I said. 'So it looks the way it did before! Let's get spoons.'

And we evened the top of the pudding with spoons, and while we evened it, we ate some more.

'There isn't much left,' I said.

'We were supposed to leave the pudding alone,' Huey said.

'We'd better get away from here,' I said. We ran into our bedroom and crawled under the bed. After a long time we heard my father's voice.

'Come into the kitchen, dear,' he said. 'I have something for you.'

'Why, what is it?' my mother said, out in the kitchen.

Under the bed, Huey and I pressed ourselves to the wall.

'Look,' said my father, out in the kitchen. 'A wonderful pudding.'

'Where is the pudding?' my mother said.

'WHERE ARE YOU BOYS?' my father said. His voice went through every crack and corner of the house.

We felt like two leaves in a storm.

'WHERE ARE YOU, I SAID!' My father's voice was booming.

Huey whispered to me, 'I'm scared.'

We heard my father walking slowly through the rooms.

'Huey!' he called. 'Julian!'

We could see his feet. He was coming into our room.

He lifted the bedspread. There was his face, and his eyes like black lightning. He grabbed us by the legs and pulled. 'STAND UP!' he said.

We stood.

'What do you have to tell me?' he said.

'We went outside,' Huey said, 'and when we came back, the pudding was gone!'

'Then why were you hiding under the bed?' my father said.

We didn't say anything. We looked at the floor.

'I can tell you one thing,' he said. 'There is going to be some beating here now! There is going to be some whipping!'

The curtains at the window were shaking. Huey was holding my hand.

'Go into the kitchen!' my father said. 'Right now!'

We went into the kitchen.

'Come here, Huey!' my father said.

Huey walked towards him, his hands behind his back.

'See these eggs?' my father said. He cracked them and put the yolks in a pan and set the pan on the counter. He stood a chair by the counter. 'Stand up here,' he said to Huey.

Huey stood on the chair by the counter.

'Now it's time for your beating!' my father said.

Huey started to cry. His tears fell in with the egg yolks.

'Take this!' my father said. My father handed him the egg beater. 'Now beat those eggs,' he said. 'I want this to be a good beating!'

'Oh!' Huey said. He stopped crying. And he beat the egg yolks.

'Now you, Julian, stand here!' my father said.

I stood on a chair by the table.

'I hope you're ready for your whipping!'

I didn't answer. I was afraid to say yes or no.

'Here!' he said, and he set the egg whites in front of me. 'I want these whipped and whipped well!'

'Yes, sir!' I said, and started whipping.

My father watched us. My mother came into the kitchen and watched us.

After a while Huey said, 'This is hard work.'

'That's too bad,' my father said. 'Your beating's not done!' And he added sugar and cream and lemon juice to Huey's pan and put the pan on the stove. And Huey went on beating.

'My arm hurts from whipping,' I said.

'That's too bad,' my father said. 'Your whipping's not done.'

So I whipped and whipped, and Huey beat and beat.

'Hold that beater in the air, Huey!' my father said.

Huey held it in the air.

'See!' my father said. 'A good pudding stays on the beater. It's thick enough now. Your beating's done.' Then he turned to me. 'Let's see those egg whites, Julian!' he said. They were puffed up and fluffy. 'Congratulations, Julian!' he said. 'Your whipping's done.'

He mixed the egg whites into the pudding himself. Then he passed the pudding to my mother.

'A wonderful pudding,' she said. 'Would you like some, boys?'

'No, thank you,' we said.

She picked up a spoon. 'Why, this tastes like a whole raft of lemons,' she said. 'This tastes like a night on the sea.'

ANN CAMERON

67

GREEN GROBBLOP

At first nobody knew what the green grobblop was or even where it came from. Ben found it on the doorstep one Monday morning. He came running in from the garden calling to his mother.

'Come and see! There's a funny green hairy thing out here. It's ever so small and ever so sad. Can I play with it?'

Ben's Mum, who was in the kitchen doing the washing, came to have a look.

'I don't know what it is,' she said, 'and it doesn't look very clean. I think I'd better give it a good wash before you play with it.'

She always washed everything on a Monday. So she washed it. She was going to peg it up to dry when she heard it say, 'Don't peg me up on the clothes line. A green grobblop like me should be put in a nice warm room.'

Ben's Mum was so surprised to hear the grobblop speak, she said, 'Oh, I'm sorry!' and asked, 'What did you say your name was?'

'I'm a green grobblop,' it said, and it did look so small and sad. Ben's Mum was a kind lady. She took it at once and put it on the curly cuddly rug in the sitting-room.

'That's much better,' said the grobblop, nodding its small green head. 'Now I should like tea and chocolate biscuits and some bananas.'

'There is only one banana,' said Ben, who was looking forward to eating it for his tea.

'Well, that will have to do for now then,' sighed the grobblop, looking smaller and sadder than ever. 'But in future, I would like three for my tea.'

After he had eaten the banana, the grobblop had four helpings of biscuits. He was just drinking his fifth cup of tea when Ben's Dad came home from work.

'What's that?' asked Ben's Dad. When Ben and his Mum told him, Ben's Dad had to agree that the grobblop did look small and sad.

'And it will need to be well looked after,' he said.

All the rest of the week the grobblop sat on the curly cuddly rug. Ben's Mum fed him and Ben played with him whenever he wanted. At the end of the week Ben's Mum said: 'I'm afraid I shall need some more money now that we have a grobblop to feed. It does eat rather a lot.'

'I can see that,' said Ben's Dad, and he looked worried. He wasn't at all sure that his boss would pay him more money just because he now had a green grobblop to feed.

'Perhaps,' he said, 'when the green grobblop gets bigger and stronger, he'll be able to do some useful jobs about the house.'

'I hope so,' agreed Ben's Mum. She had been doing everything for the grobblop, giving him the biggest helpings, letting him have the most comfortable place to sit in the sitting-room and the warmest blankets on his bed.

'I can think of lots of useful things he could do,' said Ben's Mum.

No sooner was this said than the grobblop said, 'I'll have to go to bed. I'm not at all well.'

The doctor was called and he came almost at once. He wasn't used to treating grobblops, but he said, 'He does look green and small and sad! He needs someone to look after him. He's to stay in bed a day or two and take this medicine to make him well and strong.'

The grobblop liked his medicine almost as much as he liked tea and biscuits and bananas. He liked staying in bed even better than he liked lying on the curly cuddly rug in the sitting-room. So he stayed in bed and had all his meals brought up. All the time he was growing bigger and stronger, Ben's Mum grew thinner and more tired, until one day, she said, 'I'm quite worn out.' Ben's Dad sent her to bed and called the doctor who said, 'You're to stay in bed a day or two and let someone look after you.'

The grobblop heard what the doctor said. He peeped in to see Ben's Mum. 'She does look so sad and small,' thought the grobblop who was now big and strong. He felt ashamed. He went downstairs at once.

He cleaned the kitchen, dusted the rooms, and made a delicious meal which he took up to her on a tray. He did this every day until Ben's Mum was well again. Then he said to her, 'I've come to say it's time I went away.'

'You don't have to go,' said Ben's Mum. 'You really can stay as long as you like.'

But the grobblop replied, 'No, I'm big enough and strong enough to look after myself now. I won't forget how well you looked after me and I'll write to you sometimes.'

Ben and his Mum and Dad were quite sorry to say goodbye to the grobblop. He went to live at the seaside and he did write to them. He sent them some lovely picture postcards and he's asked them all to come and stay with him for their next summer holiday.

EUGENIE SUMMERFIELD

MISS HICKORY

Miss Hickory heard heavy footsteps, clump, clumping along the stones of the pasture, then approaching her lilac bush. Out of the corner of one sharp little black eye she could see a pair of large yellow feet but she did not turn her head. As a matter of fact Miss Hickory had difficulty in turning her head. It was a hickory nut that had grown with an especially sharp and pointed nose. Her eyes and mouth were inked on. Her body was an apple-wood twig formed like a body with two arms and two legs, hands and feet, as twigs sometimes grow. To this body Miss Hickory's nut head was glued. She wore a blue-and-white checked gingham dress. A white cap with ruffles was tied in a smart bow beneath her chin. Many persons, looking first at Miss Hickory, would have said that she was a country doll, made by Miss Keturah who kept the notions store in Hillsborough, and given to Ann. But not you or I. The tilt of her sharp little nose, her pursed mouth and her keen eyes were not those of a doll. You and I would have known Miss Hickory as the real person that she was.

A black shadow passed the doorsill of Miss Hickory's house. A coarse *caw* seemed intended to catch her attention, but she continued sweeping with her broom that was made of pine needles. She had just finished her tea and her acorn cup and saucer, neatly washed, stood on a shelf above the stove. A bed of discarded pullets' feathers covered with a bright quilt of patched sumac leaves was ready for pleasant dreams. Miss Hickory's house was made of corncobs, notched, neatly fitted together and glued. It stood beneath the lilac bush that was so sweet and purple when in bloom, so thickly green and cheerful with birds all summer long. If one had to live in town, Miss Hickory had always said, take a house under a lilac bush.

Soon, through her front door, the sunset would toss a few coloured pieces from the orchard sky. Soon, too, the sun would drop like the biggest apple in the world, red and round, behind Temple Mountain that guarded the orchard spring, summer, autumn and winter, world without end. The sun set earlier now, for it was late September. Miss Hickory swept more briskly to warm herself. Thinking of cold weather made her shiver. But a large dark head with beady eyes and a long bill, thrust in through the window, stopped her.

'Are you at home, Miss Hickory?' Crow asked in his hoarse voice.

'Well, what do you think, if you ever do think?' she asked. 'I

71

heard your big yellow clodhoppers, and I saw you pass by. If you think there is one kernel of corn left in my house walls that you can peck out you are mistaken. You have eaten them all.'

'Dear lady!' said Crow, stopping, entering and making himself at home. 'Always so polite, so generous!'

A small smile seemed to move the wrinkles of Miss Hickory's face. 'Here.' She took from her pocket a few hard yellow kernels and held them out. Crow gobbled, choked, bowed low.

'Don't try to thank me,' she urged. 'You'll get the hiccups. What is the news? If there is any, you have heard it.'

'Precisely why I am here, as they put it over the radio,' he said. 'News indeed, and it concerns you.'

Miss Hickory sat down on her toadstool, spreading her skirts neatly to cover her ankles. Crow rested his wings comfortably, eased his toes and leaned against the wall. These two might spit and tiff, but they had fellow feelings. Crow made no pretensions; he was a country man. The earth owed him a living and so he helped himself to cherries and corn. Summer boarders, the bluebirds, thrushes, and larks, could fend for themselves, Crow felt, paying high prices for any berries and seeds that they got from his feeding ground. But he knew what was going on throughout the entire countryside. He was tough and weatherwise. He set the date for Old Crow Week in Hillsborough every spring, and so started the season with noisy promise. He could walk as well as fly, which meant that he got around more than most birds. He knew that Miss Hickory had once been part of a tree and he respected her for that ancestry. In certain ways they were alike. He waited for her to speak.

'Well,' she said at last.

Crow folded his wings over his stomach and pointed his beak at Miss Hickory.

'Great-granny Brown is closing this house for the winter. She plans to live in the Women's City Club on Beacon Hill, Boston, until spring.' The house was full of stillness for a while, thick with thoughts that could not break it. His words stunned Miss Hickory. She could not speak.

'I know,' Crow said at last, 'that you expected to live another winter, house and all, on Great-granny Brown's kitchen window-sill. You expected Ann to drop in almost every day and bring you something useful, a little iron stove, a pot or a tin tea-kettle. But the entire family is going to Boston. Ann is to be put into school there.' Crow rolled his eyes towards the ceiling, pretending to be shocked. Truly, however, he was enjoying himself. A love of gossip is hatched from every crow's egg.

Miss Hickory arose. She came close to him, her sharp little nose almost touching his face.

'They could not! They would not!'

'Ah, yes, Miss Hickory,' he assured her. 'Two-leggers who have been to Boston long for wings. Only we country people who can fly never feel the need of a city. Now, I once knew a starling who went to the Public Gardens in Boston for a visit, but –'

'Stop! Don't gabble.' Miss Hickory twisted her hands in distress. 'Come to the point.'

'The point is yours, dear lady.' Crow tapped her shoulder playfully with one wing-tip. 'You have seen through Great-granny Brown's kitchen window how deep the snowdrifts are in New Hampshire. I'll wager that there were days when you could not see through the windows. The winters are long and hard here, Miss Hickory.'

'What could one do?' she begged. She would not believe him yet.

'Don't feel too badly, as if they had forgotten you,' he said kindly, 'Ann has other matters than dolls to fill her mind now. Great-granny Brown was born and bred in New Hampshire. She expects you to be equal to any weather. You'll have to move, Miss Hickory.'

'Where?' She went over to the window and looked west. There each year the forest, wild and deep, marched closer to the Old Place. They had both forgotten to admire the sunset. The afterglow, like a blanket of woven rainbows, had folded about Temple Mountain.

'Aye, that's the rub!' Crow replied hoarsely.

Miss Hickory stamped her foot.'Don't talk like a Poll-Parrot. Whatever you hear, either the radio or William Shakespeare, you repeat. You know you can't read a word.'

Crow bowed his head humbly. 'Right you are, but what I meant was that we shall have to make a plan, and make it speedily. You can't live under a lilac bush all winter.'

'We? This isn't your home. It belongs to me. I like it here, I can't move. Where would I take my stove, my pot and my tea-kettle, my cup and saucer and my bed? If I lived in a crow's nest, with no nice house furnishings and no good housekeeping . . .' She could not say any more. She could only look with love and fear at her four corncob walls.

'You give me an idea, Miss Hickory.' Crow balanced himself on one foot and scratched his head with the other.

'I will have no idea of yours.'

'But a little change is good for us all,' Crow said, smirking. 'You must remember, dear lady, that you weren't born with a cup and saucer in your hand.'

It was more than Miss Hickory could stand. She lost her temper. 'I believe that this is all a piece of gossip on your part, Crow. I shall never believe that the Old Place is empty until I ask Mr T. Willard-Brown. He will tell me the truth. As for you, Crow –' She stood as tall and brave as she could beside her door. 'Get out of my house!' she ordered.

'As you wish.' Crow walked in a dignified manner towards the door. 'But don't worry. Something is bound to turn up!'

'I won't move!' she repeated as he stepped across the threshold. But he tapped her head lightly with his beak.

'Hardheaded, that's what you are!' And with that Crow walked off in the direction of the pine wood, he and the falling night one, in the colour of dusk.

Miss Hickory put her twig hands up to her nut head. Crow, she knew, was right. Her head was undoubtedly hard. She moved slowly about her house, lifting a stove lid to poke the red coals, turning down her bedspread. But as she comforted herself with these homely tasks, a feeling that she had never experienced before came to Miss Hickory. Perhaps it was caused by the sap that was still in her twig body. Perhaps it was the essence of the sweet nut inside the hard shell of her head. Whatever caused it, Miss Hickory began to cry. Tears came out of her eyes and rolled down her wrinkled cheeks. They fell so fast that she had to staunch them with her cap ties. It was dark then, so no one saw her break down. No one heard Miss Hickory sob, 'It isn't true! I won't move! Mr T. Willard-Brown will tell me tomorrow that I only had a bad dream.'

'A good day to finish my canning,' Miss Hickory said to herself as she built up a wood fire and started towards the forest for berries.

It was a beautiful day, crisp but with warm sunshine that made her forget Crow's warning visit. Crow was so ready with raucous chit-chatter that she did not take him seriously. 'He always has something to say and likes to hear himself say it,' she reminded herself as she put a small rush basket over her arm and stepped briskly off on her twig feet. Although the torches that the goldenrod had lighted along the October road towered above Miss Hickory's head, she found her way easily in and out among them. Their brightness made her feel gay. Farther on the purple asters made a royal canopy beneath which she walked proudly until she came to the edge of the woods. She left the road and was at once in the deep green of the pines.

Miss Hickory's nose was as keen as a fox's. The smell of pine trees never failed to go to her head. She could not explain why, but when she was alone in the woods, sniffing rich earth, wandering through the lacy lanes of ferns, and smelling the pines, she felt like another person. She wished that she had time to dig up one of the tiny new hemlock trees to set out at the front of her corncob house, an idea that she had treasured for some time. But the cold of the woods, now that she had left the sunny road, made her realize that there would not be many more berrying days. She knelt down, dug away the leaves that already were making a thick covering on the earth.

It always surprised her to feel how warm the earth kept under the leaves, even on a cold day. She dug them aside, here and there, uncovering the vines that she wanted. It was as delightful to thrust her twig arms up to the elbows in the warm tangle as to sniff the woods. She began to pick the bright red berries and fill her basket. There was no time to lose, she knew. Cock-Pheasant lived close by and was a famous berry-picker.

Checkerberries first! They stood up straight, in plain sight on their stems, and could be picked fast. But for preserving and storing away in her acorn jugs for the winter, Miss Hickory knew that checkerberry preserve needed a good deal of sweetening, more honey than she had been able to save that season. She picked up a few checkerberry leaves. They were tasty and crisp served with a cup of tea.

Next, the partridgeberries that ripened close to the ground, little crimson balls in twins, two growing side by side secretly on their low-lying running vine. Miss Hickory canned partridgeberries whole in their own sweet juice. As she finished gathering berries and started home with her filled basket she remembered something that Cock-Pheasant had once told her.

'When the partridgeberries are ripe,' Cock-Pheasant had said, 'it is only two full moons before the first snowfall.'

When she came home, Miss Hickory saw that the entire front of her house was covered by the fat brindled haunches of Mr T. Willard-Brown. He was enjoying the sunshine that trickled down through the bare lilac bushes and waving his long tail to and fro like a banner. He was a wandering barn cat, a hunter of renown, but Miss Hickory liked him. Mr T. Willard-Brown lived a secret life closer to the ground than did Crow. He was a newsy man and willing to share his stories.

'You are late this morning,' she told him.

'The milking was late,' he explained. 'I can't start the day without my regular breakfast of a dish of warm milk, right from the cow.'

Miss Hickory set down her basket of berries, came close, and looked sharply into Mr T. Willard-Brown's green eyes.

'That would have been a better story, my friend,' she said, 'if you had washed your face before you told it. There is a feather sticking out of your mouth.' She flipped it off.

'Oh, my ears and whiskers,' he explained in mock chagrin. 'However did I get into feathers so early in the morning? Now, if it had been teatime here at the Old Place and I had dropped in and someone had urged me to take a nap on one of those soft feather pillows –' He purred loudly to cover his embarrassment.

'Never mind,' she said. 'We all know your habits, Mr T., and I am glad to see you this morning. Crow called yesterday.

'Don't speak of him!' Mr T. Willard-Brown spat. 'I wouldn't eat crow on a wager. The last time I saw Crow he walked right towards me and said a bad word. I spat at him.'

'If you ate crow occasionally you might be a better man,' she told him. 'What I was about to say when you interrupted me was that Crow spoke of the family as planning to leave Hillsborough for the winter. He said that Great-granny Brown was thinking of living at the Women's City Club on Beacon Hill, Boston, and Ann was going to school there. Nothing but hearsay on his part, of course.'

Mr T. Willard-Brown arose, stretched and yawned. 'Not a plan, not hearsay, my love,' he told Miss Hickory, 'but the truth. They have gone!'

She listened without words, her eyes full of terror. He continued:

'You ought to get about more, Miss Hickory. All summer you have stayed here under the lilacs, only going to the woods for berries, or on Sunday when Jack-in-the-Pulpit preached. If you had gone around to the front of the house lately you would have seen trunks coming down from the attic.'

'Gone!' she breathed at last. Now she knew that it was true. She would not let him see her cry. Instead she stamped her twig feet.

'It's all your fault, Mr T. They had to leave to get away from *you*, scratching on doors and purring in the kitchen for milk. You are only a cat with a cat's ways. I shall tell all Hillsborough what your given name is. *Tippy*, because you have a white tip to your tail. Willard is for the barn where you were born. Brown is pretence. The hyphen is putting on airs. You are sly, Tippy. I always suspected it.'

He purred loudly, curling his claws and smiling. 'I am so famous a mouser that my given name and my humble birth are always overlooked. If you doubt Crow and me, why not go around to the front of the house and look in? See for yourself.' He walked, with flowing tail, towards the barn.

Miss Hickory was unable to move for a space. She watched Mr T. Willard-Brown, swinging his sides and disappearing at last through the wide red doors of the barn. Then she walked slowly away from the lilac bush, the corncob house, her basket of berries. She skirted the garden, crossed the lawn and came to the pink rambler-rose trellis beside the front porch. Up the trellis she climbed, braving the sharp thorns, up, up, until she could peer underneath the crack of the window where the shade was not completely pulled down.

Blue Rocking Chair stood empty and still. The fireplace was boarded. The family bible on the centre table was folded carefully in a white towel. The shining brass pendulum of the grandfather cluck hung motionless and the hands pointed to eight o'clock. It must, by the shadow on the lawn sundial, be noon now. The Old Farmer's Almanac that had hung by a loop of string on the wall was gone. She had been alone, without knowing it, for some time.

She knew now that everything that Crow and Mr T. Willard-Brown had told her was true. Her head would have whirled if it could. She felt too weak to hold on to the rose trellis, but she backed slowly down. Mr T. Willard-Brown was waiting for her, having come softly around the corner of the house.

'Well, there you are, Miss Hickory,' he purred. 'Two of us in the same fix. Why not come over to the barn with me? It is to be kept open all winter and I have been offered a permanent position as head ratter.'

'I wasn't born to live in a barn,' she told him desperately.

'Where then?' he asked.

'I am going home,' she said. 'Today I shall finish my canning.'

'Home?' He smiled. 'Amusing, that! I just passed your house and it was occupied. You know Chipmunk of course, who lives in the stone wall and has been so spoiled with gifts of peanuts that he expects to be supported? He has moved into your house, Miss Hickory. I should say that he is there for the winter. He was finishing his dinner when I saw him, your basket of berries.'

Miss Hickory never remembered how long she sat on the ground under the rambler-rose trellis. If she had been living in her own home at the back of the house she might have cried, but that small corncob home, so cosy and familiar, was now occupied by Chipmunk. Here, with the open road in front, she was too proud to show her sorrow. More than sorrow, she felt despair. She became damp with the heavy dew and then stiff with the first frost. The wind whistling down from Temple Mountain whipped her wet skirts around her shivering legs. None of the few passers-by noticed her. Mr T. Willard-Brown, warm and busy in the barn, gave her no thought. A light flurry of snow powdered her cap.

But one day, when Miss Hickory was sure that her end was near, down the road from the orchard, walking briskly, came Crow. Would he, too, pass her by? No, Crow turned into the front path and approached. He came close to the spot where Miss Hickory huddled under the poor shelter of the rambler-rose trellis. He raised one foot in salute.

'Dear lady!' Crow croaked, ignoring her bedraggled state. He understood that she had suffered a great loss. He was a busybody and had heard about Chipmunk.

'Don't try to explain, Miss Hickory,' he said hoarsely. 'We all have our troubles. I told you that something would turn up. It has.'

'What?' She stood up and leaned against the trellis.

'First of all,' he told her, 'you must realize that a change, travel, a new scene, are good for all of us. You especially, Miss Hickory, need a change. You have been living for two years with those who feel that they need a grocery store, a Ford car, a stove, and storm windows. You have grown soft.'

She held out her arms, no longer proud.

'Don't preach to me, Crow! What has turned up?'

'A new home for you.' He gave a hop-jig step and a swing for show. 'Don't ask any questions, but come along with me. There isn't any time to lose. I shall very likely be off for good tomorrow and I want to see you well settled-in before I leave. Come with me, dear lady.'

Miss Hickory stumbled weakly towards Crow, but he caught her underneath one wide black wing. His wing was like a tent, warm and strong. His big yellow feet guided her small twig ones and the two left the Old Place behind and took to the road. He shortened his steps to suit hers, talking earnestly in his rough voice as he led her towards the orchard.

'You spoke of the untidiness of my nest. How right you are, Miss Hickory. Sticks, chaff and bark are all I ever use. But please realize that I am a man of affairs. I spend my days here and there, in the cornfield, the orchard, the vegetable garden. All I need in the way of a home is a place to hang my hat. But my nest is built high at the top of a tall pine tree as a lookout. From it I saw your new home.'

They reached the orchard.

'Turn this way,' he told her. 'We are going to follow McIntosh Lane along the hillside. You can't imagine how sheltered it is there, under the lee of the mountain with the pine woods up above for a windbreak. Lean on me, Miss Hickory. We are almost there.'

As they found and took the stubble-grown path where the older apple trees had twisted in odd bent shapes, the better to climb the hillside of the orchard and reach the sun, Miss Hickory felt herself floating, rather than trudging along. She was lifted off her feet every now and then as she clung to Crow's wing. She felt again the energy that the woods always gave her. The exercise of trying to keep up with Crow warmed her. Her heart pounded with excitement, for she believed that Crow was helping her to begin a great adventure. Perhaps a small log cabin with a fireplace and a chimney was waiting on beyond. When she had signed the lease she would return, evict Chipmunk and move her things up there to the hillside on McIntosh Lane.

'Is it much farther?' she gasped.

Crow was muttering and did not answer at once. He had never been able to count above one. One cherry, gulp it down. One plump green pea. One mouthful of corn. His father had taught him the corn-planting Rule.

> One for the cut-worm
> One for the crow,
> One for the farmer . . .

'Never mind the rest of it,' Crow's father had said. 'It signifies nothing for us until later: "Two to grow".'

So Crow was not counting the trees on the hillside, but naming them.

'Cherry. Northern Spy. Clapp's Favourite Pear. McIntosh. McIntosh. Mc – Mc – Tosh – Tosh.' His tongue was becoming twisted. 'Here we are!' he told her at last as they were halfway or so along the hillside and deep among the leafless gnarled shapes of the apple trees. He stopped beneath one that had not seemed worth pruning that spring. The branches touched the ground and it leaned comfortably towards the slope of the hill, away from the wind. He loosed his hold on Miss Hickory and hopped towards a low-lying bough. 'Climb up!' he ordered.

'But – I don't understand.' She hesitated.

Crow spread his wings and disappeared among the branches of the apple tree but his voice croaked down to her:

'He who hesitates is lost. Do you or do you not want to live until spring? Climb, I told you!'

She grasped the low bough. How homelike it felt in her strong little twig fingers!

'Swing a bit and then jump!' Crow's call came to her from higher up. This, she decided, was a game that he wanted her to learn. She pulled on the bough, swayed pleasantly a moment and then jumped to another branch farther on.

'Keep on!' Crow croaked. 'Climb along up.'

So she continued to swing, jump and climb, feeling more adventurous and bold with each step. Up, up, Miss Hickory climbed into the apple tree until the ground was dizzying to look down upon and she could see Temple Mountain, keeping vigil to the west.

'How much farther?' she called.

'Here you are,' he answered from a perch right beside her. 'Carefully now. Easy does it. How's this, dear lady, for your new home?'

She looked in astonishment at what he pointed out to her: a large and deep nest resting securely in a crotch of the apple tree. Crow knew that it might not suit her at first sight so he began to argue and boast, like a real estate agent.

'Light and heat free, whenever the sun shines. A long lease. Although Robin built it for his own use and planned to stay north this winter, Mr T. Willard-Brown drove him away. Hooks for hanging your clothes; Robin builds carelessly and leaves twigs sticking out. Insulated against the cold with good country mud.' Crow's sales talk went on and on, but Miss Hickory had not listened after he had mentioned Mr T. Willard-Brown. No cat, she decided, would drive *her* out of her home. She balanced on a bough and inspected the empty nest. It was indeed well placed, sheltered and strong. As she peered inside she saw that the wind had cushioned the empty nest deeply with milkweed down and lined it with rose-brown oak leaves. She stepped inside and sank down deliciously into its warm comfort.

'Not bad at all, Crow,' she admitted.

'It struck me favourably,' he croaked.

The nest was so well suited to her size that when she stood up, she had to stretch a bit to pull herself out. When she lay down, as she now did, for she was very tired, she was snug and unseen. She was alone in a world that had no need of the things she had left behind.

'I don't know what I shall do here all winter,' she said, 'without a broom in my hands.'

'You'll find plenty to do,' he told her. 'New things to collect, new friends, new places to explore. Well, it's time I was off.'

'I am greatly obliged to you, Crow.' She leaned over the edge of the nest as Crow opened his wings.

'Don't give it a thought,' he said.

'How long until spring?' she ventured to ask. 'They took the Old Farmer's Almanac to Boston.'

'It doesn't matter,' he assured her. 'Spring always comes. Remember this, though, dear lady. This is important. Get it through your head. *Keep your sap running!*'

Crow spread his wings, cawed loudly and started. Miss Hickory watched Crow cross the Old Place, the barn, the woods, then disappear as he flew towards the south.

CAROLYN SHERWIN BAILEY

FATHER CHRISTMAS

One day Polly was in the kitchen, washing currants and sultanas to put in a birthday cake, when the front-door bell rang.

'Oh dear,' said Polly's mother, 'my hands are all floury. Be

a kind girl, Polly, and go and open the door for me, will you?'

Polly was a kind girl, and she dried her hands and went to the front door. As she left the kitchen, her mother called after her.

'But don't open the door if it's a wolf!'

This reminded Polly of some of her earlier adventures, and before she opened the door, she said cautiously, through the letter box, 'Who are you?'

'A friend,' said a familiar voice.

'Which one?' Polly asked. 'Mary?'

'No, not Mary.'

'Jennifer?'

'No, not Jennifer.'

'Penelope?'

'No. At least I don't think so. No,' said the wolf decidedly, 'not Penelope.'

'Well, I don't know who you are then,' Polly said. 'I can't guess. You tell me.'

'Father Christmas.'

'Father Christmas?' said Polly. She was so much surprised that she nearly opened the front door by mistake.

'Father Christmas,' said the person on the doorstep. 'With a sack full of toys. Now be a good little girl, Polly, and open the door and I'll give you a present out of my sack.'

Polly didn't answer at once.

'Did you say Father Christmas?' she asked at last.

'Yes, of course I did,' said the wolf loudly. 'Surely you've heard of Father Christmas before, haven't you? Comes to good children and gives them presents and all that. But not, of course, to naughty little girls who don't open doors when they're told to.'

'Yes,' Polly said.

'Well, then, what's wrong with that? You know all about Father Christmas and I'm pretending to be – I mean, here he is. I don't see what's bothering you and making you so slow.'

'I've heard of Father Christmas, of course,' Polly agreed. 'But not in the middle of the summer.'

'Middle of the what?' the wolf shouted through the door.

'Middle of the summer.'

There was a short silence.

'How do you know it's the summer?' the wolf asked argumentatively.

'We're making Mother's birthday cake.'

'Well? I don't see what that has to do with it.'

'Mother's birthday is in July.'

'Perhaps she's rather late in making her cake?' the wolf suggested.

'No, she isn't. She's a few days early, as a matter of fact.'

'You mean it's going to be her birthday in a day or two?'

'You've got it, Wolf,' Polly agreed.

'So we're in July now?'

'Yes.'

'It's not Christmas?'

'No.'

'Not even if we happened to be in Australia? They have Christmas in the summer there, you know,' the wolf said persuasively.

'But not here. It's nearly half a year till Christmas,' Polly said firmly.

'A pity,' the wolf said, 'I really thought I'd got you that time. I must have muddled up my calendar again - it's so confusing, all the weeks starting with Mondays.'

Polly heard the would-be Father Christmas clumping down the path from the front door; she went back to the currants.

The weeks went by; Mother's birthday was over and forgotten, holidays by the sea marked the end of summer and the beginning of autumn, and it was not until the end of September, when the leaves were turning yellow and brown, and the days were getting shorter and colder, that Polly heard from the wolf again. She was in the sitting-room when the telephone bell rang; Polly lifted the receiver.

'I ont oo thpeak oo Folly,' a very muffled voice said.

'I'm sorry,' Polly said, politely, 'I really can't hear.'

'Thpeak oo Folly.'

'I still can't quite hear,' Polly said.

'I ont oo – oh BOTHER these beastly whiskers,' said quite a different voice. 'There, now can you hear? I've taken bits of them off.'

'Yes, I can hear all right,' Polly said puzzled. 'But how can you take off your whiskers?'

'They weren't really mine. I mean they're mine, of course, but not in the usual way. I didn't grow them, I bought them.'

'Well,' Polly asked, 'how did you keep them on before you took them off?'

'Stuck them on with gum,' the voice replied cheerfully. 'But I haven't taken that bit off yet. The bit I took off was the bit that goes all round your mouth. You know, a moustache. It got awfully in the way of talking, though. The hair kept on getting into my mouth.'

'It sounded rather funny,' Polly agreed. 'But why did you have to put it on?'

'So as to look like the real one.'

'The real what?'

'Father Christmas, of course, silly. How would I be able to make you think I was Father Christmas if I didn't wear a white beard and all that cotton woolly sort of stuff round my face, and a red coat and hood and all that?'

'Wolf,' said Polly solemnly – for of course it couldn't be anyone else – 'do you mean to say you were pretending to be Father Christmas?'

'Yes.'

'And then what?'

'I was going to say if you'd meet me at some lonely spot – say the crossroads at midnight – I'd give you a present out of my sack.'

'And you thought I'd come?'

'Well,' said the wolf persuasively, 'after all I look exactly like Santa Claus now.'

'Yes, but I can't see you.'

'Can't See Me?' said the wolf, in surprise.

'We can't either of us see each other. You try, Wolf.'

There was a long silence. Polly rattled the receiver.

'Wolf!' she called. 'Wolf, are you there?'

'Yes,' said the wolf's voice, at last.

'What are you doing?'

'Well, I was having a look. I tried with a small telescope I happened to have by me, but I must admit I can't see much. The trouble is that it's so terribly dark in there. Hold on for a minute. Polly, I'm just going to fetch a candle.'

Polly held on. Presently, she heard a fizz and a splutter as the match was struck to light the candle. There was a long pause, broken by the wolf's heavy breathing. Polly heard him muttering: 'Not down there . . . Try the other end then . . . Perhaps if I unscrew this bit . . . Let's see this bit of wire properly . . .'

There was a deafening explosion, which made poor Polly jump. Her ear felt as if it would never hear properly again. Obviously the wolf had held his candle too near to the wires and something had exploded.

'I do hope he wasn't hurt himself,' Polly thought, as she hung up her own receiver. 'It sounded like an awfully loud explosion.'

She saw the wolf a day or two later in the street. His face and head were covered with bandages, from amongst which one eye looked sadly out.

'Oh Wolf, I am so sorry,' said kind Polly, stopping as he was just going to pass her. 'Does it hurt very much? It must have been an awfully big explosion.'

'Explosion? Where?' said the wolf, looking eagerly up and down the street.

'Not here. At your home. When you rang me up the other day.'

'Oh that!' said the wolf airily. 'That wasn't really an explosion. Just a spark or two and a sort of bang, that's all. I just got the candle in the way of the wires and they melted together, or something. Nothing to get alarmed about, thank you, Polly.'

'But your face,' Polly said, 'the bandages. Didn't you get hurt in that explosion?'

'No. But that gum! Whee-e-e-w! I'll tell you what, Polly,' the wolf said impressively. 'Don't ever try and stick a beard or whiskers on top of where your fur grows, with spirit gum. It goes on all right, but getting it off is – well! If it had been my own hair it wouldn't have been more painful getting it off. Next time I'm going to have one of those beards on sort of spectacle things you just hook over your ears. Don't you think that would be better?'

'Much better.'

'Not so painful to take off?'

'I should think not,' Polly agreed.

'Well you just wait till I've got these bandages off,' the wolf said gaily, 'and then you'll see! My own mother wouldn't know me.'

Perhaps it took longer than Polly expected to grow wolf fur again: at any rate it was a month or two before Polly heard from the wolf again, and she had nearly forgotten his promise, or threat, of coming to find her. It was just before Christmas, and Polly was out with her mother doing Christmas shopping. The streets were crowded and the shop windows were gay with silver balls and frosted snow. Everything sparkled and shone and glowed, and Polly held on to Mother's hand and danced along the pavements.

'Polly,' said her mother. 'Would you like to go to the toy department of Jarold's? I've got to get one or two small things there, and you could look round. I think they've got some displays of model railways and puppets, and they generally have a sort of Christmas fair with Father Christmas to talk to.'

Polly said yes, she would very much, and they turned in at the doors of the enormous shop and took a luxuriant gilded lift up to the third floor, to the toy department. It really was fascinating. While her mother was buying coloured glass balls for the Christmas tree, and a snowstorm for Lucy, Polly wandered about and looked at everything. She saw trains and dolls and bears; she saw bicycles, tricycles, swings and slides, boats and boomerangs and cars and carriages. At last she saw an archway, above which was written 'Christmas Tree Land'. Polly walked in.

There was a sort of scene arranged in the shop itself, and it was very pretty. There were lots of Christmas trees, all covered with sparkling white snow, and the rest of the place was rather dark so that all the light seemed to come from the trees. In the distance you could see reindeer grazing, or running, and high snowy mountains and forests of more Christmas trees. At the end of the part where Polly was, sat Father Christmas on a sort of throne. There was a crowd of children round him and a man in ordinary clothes, a shop manager, was encouraging their mothers to bring them up to Father Christmas so that they could tell him what they hoped to find in their stockings or under the tree on Christmas Day.

Polly drew near. She thought she would tell Father Christmas that what she wanted more than anything else in the world was a clown's suit. She joined a line of children waiting to get up to the throne.

The child in front of Polly was frightened. She kept on running out of line back to her mother, and her mother kept on putting her back in her place again.

'I don't want to go and talk to that Father Christmas,' the little girl said, 'he isn't a proper Father Christmas.'

'Nonsense,' her mother said sharply. 'Don't be so silly. Stand in that line and go up and tell him what you want in your stocking like a nice little girl.'

The little girl began to cry. Polly, looking sharply at Father Christmas, couldn't help rather agreeing with her. Father Christmas had the usual red coat and hood and a lot of bushy white hair all over his face. But somehow his manner wasn't quite right.

He certainly asked the children questions, but not in the pleasantest tone of voice, and his reply to some of their answers was more of a snarl than a promise.

The little girl in front of Polly was finally persuaded to go up and say something in a breathy, awestruck whisper. Polly, just behind her, was near enough to hear the answer.

'Box of sweets,' said Father Christmas in a distinctly unpleasant tone. 'What do you want a box of sweets for? You're quite fat enough already to satisfy any ordinary person, I should think.'

The child clutched her mother's hand tightly, and the manager who was standing near, looked displeased. 'Come, come,' Polly heard him say sharply in Father Christmas's ear, 'you can do better that that, surely.'

Father Christmas jumped, threw a sharp glance over his shoulder at the manager and leant forward to the little girl. 'Yes, of course you shall have a box of sweets,' he said. 'Only wouldn't you like something more interesting? For instance a big juicy steak, with plenty of fried potatoes? Or what about pork chops? I always think myself there's nothing like ...'

'Next please,' the manager called out loudly. 'And a happy Christmas to you, dear,' he added to the surprised little girl who was being led away by her mother, unable to make head or tail of this extraordinary Father Christmas.

Polly moved up. The Father Christmas inclined his ear towards her to hear what she wanted in her stocking, but Polly had something else to say.

'Wolf, how could you!' she hissed in a horrified whisper. 'Pretending to be Father Christmas to all these poor little children – and you're not doing it at all well, either.'

'It wasn't my fault,' the wolf said, gloomily. 'I never meant to let myself in for this terrible affair. I just put on my costume – and I did the beard rather well this time, don't you think? – and I went out to see if I could find you, and this wretched man' – and he threw a glance of black hate at the shop manager – 'nobbled me in the street, and pulled me in here, and set me to asking the same stupid question of all these beastly children. And they all want the same things,' he added venomously. 'If it's boys they want space guns, and if it's girls they want party frocks and television sets. Not one of them's asked for anything sensible to eat. One of them did ask for a baby sister,' he said thoughtfully, 'but did she really want her to eat, I ask myself?'

'I should hope not,' Polly said firmly.

'And I'm much too hot and my whiskers tickle my ears horribly,' the wolf complained. 'And there's not a chance of snatching a bite with this man standing over me all the time.'

'Wolf, you wouldn't eat the children!' Polly said in protest.

'Not all of them,' the wolf answered. 'Some of them aren't very –'

'Next please,' said the manager loudly. A deliciously plump juicy little boy was pushed to stand just behind Polly. He was reciting to himself and his mother, 'I want a gun, an' I want soldiers, an' I want a rocking 'orse, an' I want a steam engine, an' I want . . .'

'I think you're going to be busy today,' Polly said, 'I probably shan't be seeing you for a time. Happy Christmas,' she added politely, as she made way for the juicy little boy. 'I hope you enjoy yourself with all these friendly little girls and boys.'

'Grrrrrr,' replied Father Christmas. 'I'll enjoy myself still more when I've unhooked my beard and got my teeth into one unfriendly little girl. Just you wait, Polly: Christmas or no Christmas, I'll get you yet.'

CATHERINE STORR

A FISHY TALE
OR HOW I JOINED THE MIXED
MAGGOTS AND BOTTOM FEEDERS,
TOLD TO GENE KEMP BY JOHN
SWEET

My Dad says the best thing to do is to forget all about it. Especially as I lost my wellingtons. I suppose he's right, really, but since you asked about it, here goes, Mzz Kemp.

I was getting tired, I reckon, and my concentration slipped and so did I, into the canal, at the edge where all the tall plants and reeds line the bank, deep and green and mysterious, full of insects and weird crawlies. And there in the middle of the canal is the deep channel where all the fish swim along. Yes, I love fishing. I like going fishing with my Dad better than anything else. Better even than football, I think ... All them fish, browny red dace, roach with orange fins, spotted perch, all spiky, you need a rag to protect your hands when you get him off the hook, and down at the bottom of the centre channel there's the spotted brown gudgeon, a bottom feeder, and the stone loach with stick-out lips, like this, whuwh, see? Of course you do get the nobs putting in a grand appearance sometimes, the salmon and the silver brown trout, but not for me with my licence at £1.50. If you do nabble one, you put it back quick.

Oh, it's a fantastic sport.

And the sport isn't just to catch the fish, but to land it, easy, easy. If you wind in too quickly the line will break, because of the friction, so you must do it slowly to let it move around in angles which tires the fish, and it's easier to pull out smoothly. Don't let the line go loose or the fish jumps, the hook slides and the fish escapes.

You need the feel, like.

92

This Sunday I'm telling you about, my Dad took me out about four. It was a smashing day, hot for October, with brown and yellow leaves lying in heaps to shuffle your feet through, scrunch, scrunch. I was glad to go, not only because, as I've told you, I like going fishing with my Dad better than anything, but because it had been that sort of a Sunday. My elder brother was out of the house somewhere, but the rest were hanging about all over the place, shouting and bossing me about, that's the worst of having four sisters, and you know what our Sandra is like, Mzz Kemp. Our house isn't very big neither, and my Mum made me do jobs, but it didn't really matter, not inside, because I knew I was going fishing with my Dad.

We set off, and it was still warm and sunny, though the mist was beginning to stir in little smoky spirals as we walked down the long hill that goes to the river and beyond to the canal. It's called Fore Street, and our teacher, you, Mzz Kemp, told us the Romans marched down there, long ago, and people before that, and it's a pretty steep hill, though that didn't bother me, *then*.

At last we reached the canal, and there's a road on one side for cars, and a path on the other for people and dogs, but half-way to Double Locks is a bridge, a really narrow bridge, and there the road crosses over, becoming a path, and the path becomes the road on the other side, bit daft really, not that it bothered me and Dad, because we were walking anyway, but it is tricky to drive across. Two posts stop cars trying to drive on to the path. Just beyond the bridge, where it's fine for fishing with the banks all green and quiet and beautiful, I sat down with my tackle and Dad wandered on a bit. I put down my bag for the fish and my rag to handle them with, then I made sure the eyes were level, pulled the lines up through them, fixed the little round band, the float and the hook, judged the weights, put them on, stood up straight and cast without maggots. Then I got the maggots on to the hook, pushing them with my thumb, and cast. My landing net was ready and the float was okay. The red bit goes under when you've got a bite.

Only I hadn't. And I didn't. I waited and I waited and I waited.

The sun painted the sky, pink and purple and orange and red, while I sat there on my little folding stool, waiting. No bite at all.

93

Not a sausage. Not a dicky bird. Not a dicky bird of a sausage. Not a nibble.

I could feel a nibble inside, though.

I was hungry. I was very hungry. I was starving.

Roast pork with apple sauce and crackling when we got home, Mum had said. I thought about roast pork and apple sauce and crackling. I pictured it on my plate. I pictured me eating it. I felt even hungrier.

The sun pushed off to the other side of the world or wherever it goes, taking all the colour with it. Grey mist trailed everywhere. My fingers grew cold and stiff. Dad came along and asked how I was doing, no good I said, him neither, we'd pack it in soon and go home.

'Another minute, Dad,' I asked, as he turned away. I didn't want to return with no catch and Sandra laughing like a drain, and I don't know why, but at the very thought of Sandra, my chair slipped, so did I, and there I was, slip, sliding away on my back into the reeds, and down, down, down into the water, coming up over my wellies, colder than cold, shock, horror. Somehow I turned, grabbed a rough and unkind sort of plant and yelled for Dad, who had gone some way away.

And a car came over the bridge, a man's head stuck out of the window, yelling. 'Look at that little kid. He's gonna drown! Stop!'

It didn't stop. It came roaring on. Towards me. My cold hands were slipping. Any minute now, I'd be among the fish I'd been after, earlier, and I didn't fancy the idea much. I didn't want to meet the bottom feeders on their own level. I didn't think we'd have much to say to each other down there amongst all that cold mud. 'Dad!' I yelled even louder. I couldn't see him, and I was slipping further all the time.

But if I couldn't see Dad, I could see the car. It was heading straight towards me and it didn't look as if it knew how to stop. It seemed as if I had a choice. Either be run over or drowned. I thought fast, very fast. And there was only one way to go so I went. Backwards into the canal. Right up to my neck in cold slimy canal right down into what seemed enough mud to submerge a submarine. I thought I could hear the fishes laughing all the way to Double Locks.

The car swerved, hitting the posts, one went into the water, just missing me, the other stayed put and the car rose up on it. The back door flew open and out jumped a man.

'Don't worry, son. I'm here.'

He certainly was. Water splashed everywhere, as if some huge whale was spouting off. He grabbed me by the neck and headed for the bank.

'I'm all right. I can swim,' I shouted, but he wasn't listening. Holding me like he was a dog with his favourite bone, he stumbled on, then fell forward, me with him.

'I can't swim,' he shouted, dropping me, and waving his arms about.

'I'm coming,' shouted another man, leaping towards us. I managed to move just in time. This splash was more like a freak tidal wave. Nowhere was left untouched. But I'd seen Dad on the bank and I was getting to him fast.

'It's all right,' shouted my Dad. 'Don't all go in!'

Too late. Another flying body hit the water, now full of bodies and one post. The canal was having a busy evening. Together we arrived at the bank where Dad pulled us out one by one. A lot of panting and spitting and coughing went on. That canal water doesn't taste nice at all.

'We saved your boy,' said one.

'Yeah,' said my Dad.

'Aren't you gonna thank us?'

'Well, thank you, yes, and I hope you enjoyed your bit of fun in there, but I feel I must say that first of all, he's the school swimming champion, and next, you couldn't drown a rabbit in there, let alone three big blokes like you. John, where's your wellingtons?'

'In the mud, Dad. They came off.'

'Well, we'd better get walking then, before you catch cold. It's a fair step.'

The driver had righted the car by now. The others climbed in dripping wet.

'We can't offer you a lift,' one said.

'Funny you not being able to swim, Reg. I never knew that,' I heard one of them say. Reg made a sort of angry roaring noise as the car drove off.

It was a long way home. Especially in wet-socked feet. And I thought I'd got a fish down my back, but it turned out to be a slimy weed. I kept thinking of them Roman soldiers as we walked back up that hill, Mzz Kemp, and how they had to keep going when they didn't feel like it. Once a dog came out and barked at us, but he soon stopped when my Dad said a few words to him. But it was a long way home.

Roast pork and apple sauce and crackling's scrumptious when you eat it in front of a hot fire after a bath. Even Sandra was nice to me. She didn't laugh. Much.

Guess what I'm doing next Sunday?
Going fishing, of course.

GENE KEMP

THE BORING BEAR

One day Julie came to John's house. She hung her coat on the low peg in the hall, then she saw something unusual.

'Why's this bear hiding under the coats?' she said.

'Because he's boring,' said John.

'He looks all right,' said Julie.

'That's all he does,' said John. 'He always looks like that.'

Julie looked at the bear. His face wasn't sad or happy. It was printed on, like his clothes: black trousers and red jacket, printed buttons, printed pockets.

'My gran made him,' said John. 'He's got washable stuffing.'

Then he put the bear back under the coats and they played monsters. They often played monsters. They liked being a little bit frightened.

When Julie put her coat on to go home, she looked at the bear. He was quite smart.

'Can I have him?' she said.

John thought.

'I'll swop him for your bell,' he said.

Julie's tricycle was old, but the bell was new. She'd rung it a lot for the first week, but she did like the look of the bear.

'All right,' she said.

So bear and bell changed hands.

When John went to Julie's house, he hung his anorak on the low peg in the hall. He saw a paw he'd seen before. 'Why's my bear hiding under the coats?' he said.

'He's Bear now,' said Julie. 'He likes it there. He thinks it's a warm, dark cave. He jumps out and frightens people.'

97

John brought Bear into the light. He was the same underneath, black trousers and all, but he looked different on top. He was wearing a blue sweater with the sleeves rolled back, he had a patch over one eye and a bandaged leg.

'What did he do?' said John.

'He fell off a mountain,' said Julie. 'I pushed him.'

John looked more closely.

'It's a good bandage,' he said. 'What can he do today?'

'Well, if his leg's better, the bandage can come off,' said Julie.

'And the leg?' said John.

'No,' said Julie. 'He'll need both legs for exploring. He's Action Bear. We can make him an exploring kit.'

John made Bear a paper hat for hot weather and wound string round his shoulder for a climbing rope. Julie drew a map in case he got lost.

98

Then her mother gave them some iron rations. Iron rations are not nails and things, you know; more dates and cheese and chocolate, if you're lucky.

At last they set off. They hauled themselves upstairs, then they pulled Bear up by his climbing rope. Then suddenly they heard noises.

'Monsters,' said Julie and they rushed downstairs while Bear slid down the bannister.

'He's hurt his arm,' said John. 'I'll make a sling.'

Then they sat on the bottom stair and ate their iron rations.

'Can I have him back now?' said John.

'No,' said Julie.

That week John rode his tricycle a lot. He rang the bell until his thumb was tired and so was everyone else.

'It's time that fire engine went home,' said his mother.

The next time Julie came to John's house, she was carrying a big shopping bag, and looking out was Bear. He still had a patch over one eye, but this time he was wearing a wooden sword in his string belt.

'He's very fierce,' said Julie, 'but he knows me.'

'And me,' said John. 'My gran's coming this week.'

Julie thought. Her tricycle was a bit quiet without the bell.

'All right,' she said. 'You can have him back. Do you want the sword?'

'No,' said John. 'I'll make one.'

He liked making things for Bear.

The next day John's gran really did come. Bear was lying near the fire after a hard day. His leg was bandaged, his arm in a sling.

'Goodness,' she said. 'Is that the bear I made?'

'Yes,' said John. 'With washable stuffing.'

'I thought he might be too dressed up,' said his gran. 'A bit boring.'

'His clothes don't take off,' said John, 'they put on. You never know what he'll do next.'

'I can see he isn't boring now,' said his gran.
Perhaps, thought John, he never was.

JOAN WYATT

THE SEVENTH
PRINCESS

Did you ever hear the tale of the Six Princesses who lived for the
sake of their hair alone? This is it.

There was once a King who married a gypsy, and was as careful
of her as if she had been made of glass. In case she ran away he
put her in a palace in a park with a railing all round it, and never
let her go outside. The Queen was too loving to tell him how much
she longed to go beyond the railing, but she sat for hours on the
palace roof, looking towards the meadows to the east, the river to
the south, the hills to the west, and the markets to the north.

In time the Queen bore the King twin daughters as bright as the
sunrise, and on the day they were christened the King, in his joy,
asked what she would have for a gift. The Queen looked from her
roof to the east, saw May on the meadows, and said:

'Give me the Spring!'

The King called fifty thousand gardeners, and bade each one
bring in a root of wild-flowers or a tender birch-tree from outside,
and plant it within the railing. When it was done he walked with
the Queen in the flowery park, and showed her everything, saying:

'Dear wife, the Spring is yours.'

But the Queen only sighed.

The following year two more Princesses, as fair as the morning,
were born, and once again, on their christening day, the King told

the Queen to choose a gift. This time she looked from the roof to the south, and, seeing the water shining in the valley, said:

'Give me the river!'

The King summoned fifty thousand workmen and told them to conduct the river into the park that it should supply a most beautiful fountain in the Queen's pleasure grounds.

Then he led his wife to the spot where the fountain rose and fell in a marble basin, and said:

'You now have the river.'

But the Queen only gazed at the captive water rising and falling in its basin, and hung her head.

Next year two more Princesses, as golden as the day, were born, and the Queen, given her choice of a gift, looked north from the roof at the busy town, and said:

'Give me the people!'

So the King sent fifty thousand trumpeters down to the market-

place, and before long they returned, bringing six honest market-women with them.

'Here, dear Queen, are the people,' said the King.

The Queen secretly wiped her eyes, and then gave her six beautiful babies into the charge of the six buxom women, so that the Princesses had a nurse apiece.

Now in the fourth year the Queen bore only one daughter, a little one, and dark like herself, whereas the King was big and fair.

'What gift will you choose?' said the King, as they stood on the roof on the day of the christening.

The Queen turned her eyes to the west, and saw a wood-pigeon and six swans flying over the hills.

'Oh!' cried she, 'give me the birds!'

The King instantly sent fifty thousand fowlers forth to snare the birds. While they were absent the Queen said:

'Dear King, my children are in their cots and I am on my throne, but presently the cots will be empty and I shall sit on my throne no more. When that day comes, which of our seven daughters will be Queen in my stead?'

Before the King could answer the fowlers returned with the birds. The King looked from the humble pigeon, with its little round head sunk in soft breast-feathers, to the royal swans with their long white necks, and said:

'The Princess with the longest hair shall be Queen.'

Then the Queen sent for the six nurses and told them what the King had said. 'So remember,' she added, 'to wash and brush and comb my daughters' hair without neglect, for on you will depend the future Queen.'

'And who will wash and brush and comb the hair of the Seventh Princess?' they asked.

'I will do that myself,' said the Queen.

Each nurse was exceedingly anxious that her own Princess should be Queen, and every fine day they took the children out into the flowery meadow and washed their hair in the water of the fountain, and spread it in the sun to dry. Then they brushed it and combed it till it shone like yellow silk, and plaited it with ribbons, and decked it with flowers. You never saw such lovely hair as the Princesses had, or so much trouble as the nurses took with it. And wherever the six fair girls went, the six swans went with them.

But the Seventh Princess, the little dark one, never had her hair washed in the fountain. It was kept covered with a red

handkerchief, and tended in secret by the Queen as they sat together on the roof and played with the pigeon.

At last the Queen knew that her time had come. So she sent for her daughters, blessed them one by one, and bade the King carry her up to the roof. There she looked from the meadows to the river, from the markets to the hills, and closed her eyes.

Now, hardly had the King done drying his own, when a trumpet sounded at his gate, and a page came running in to say that the Prince of the World had come. So the King threw open his doors, and the Prince of the World came in, followed by his servant. The Prince was all in a cloth of gold, and his mantle was so long that when he stood before the King it spread the whole length of the room, and the plume in his cap was so tall that the tip touched the ceiling. In front of the Prince walked his servant, a young man all in rags.

The King said:

'Welcome, Prince of the World!' and held out his hand.

The Prince of the World did not answer; he stood there with his mouth shut and his eyes cast down. But his Ragged Servant said, 'Thank you, King of the Country!' And he took the King's hand and shook it heartily.

This surprised the King greatly.

'Cannot the Prince speak for himself?' he asked.

'If he can,' said the Ragged Servant, 'nobody has ever heard him do so. As you know, it takes all sorts to make the world: those who speak and those who are silent, those who are rich and those who are poor, those who think and those who do, those who look up and those who look down. Now, my master has chosen me for his servant, because between us we make up the world of which he is Prince. For he is rich and I am poor, and he thinks things and I do them, and he looks down and I look up, and he is silent, so I do the talking.'

'Why has he come?' asked the King.

'To marry your daughter,' said the Ragged Servant, 'for it takes all sorts to make a world, and there must be a woman as well as a man.'

'No doubt,' said the King. 'But I have seven daughters. He cannot marry them all.'

'He will marry the one that is to be Queen,' said the Ragged Servant.

'Let my daughters be sent for,' said the King, 'for the time is now come to measure the length of their hair.'

So the Seven Princesses were summoned before the King. The six fair ones came in with their nurses, and the little dark one came in by herself. The Ragged Servant looked quickly from one to another, but the Prince of the World kept his eyes down and did not look at any of them.

Then the King sent for the court tailor, with his tape-measure; and when he came the six fair Princesses shook down their hair till it trailed on the ground behind them.

One by one they had it measured, while the six nurses looked on with pride – for had they not taken just as much care as they could of their darlings' hair? But, alas! as neither more care nor less had been spent upon any of them, it was now discovered that each of the six Princesses had hair exactly as long as the others.

The Court held up its hands in amazement, the nurses wrung theirs in despair, the King rubbed his crown, the Prince of the World kept his eyes on the ground, and the Ragged Servant looked at the Seventh Princess.

'What shall we do,' said the King, 'if my youngest daughter's hair is the same length as the rest?'

'I don't think it is, sir,' said the Seventh Princess, and her sisters looked anxious as she untied the red handkerchief from her head. And indeed her hair was not the same length as theirs, for it was cropped close to her head, like a boy's.

'Who cut your hair, child?' asked the King.

'My mother, if you please, sir,' said the Seventh Princess. 'Every day as we sat on the roof she snipped it with her scissors.'

'Well, well!' cried the King, 'whichever is meant to be Queen, it isn't you!'

That is the story of the Six Princesses who lived for the sake of their hair alone. They spent the rest of their lives having it washed, brushed, and combed by the nurses, till their locks were as white as their six pet swans.

And the Prince of the World spent the rest of *his* life waiting with his eyes cast down until one of the Princesses should grow the longest hair, and become his Queen. As this never happened, for all I know he is waiting still.

But the Seventh Princess tied on her red handkerchief again, and ran out of the palace to the hills and the river and the meadows and the markets; and the pigeon and the Ragged Servant went with her.

'But,' she said, 'what will the Prince of the World do without you in the palace?'

'He will have to do as best he can,' said the Ragged Servant, 'for it takes all sorts to make the world, those that are in and those that are out.'

ELEANOR FARJEON

MR ANTONIO

Mr Antonio was small and dark with a nice wiggly moustache, and he didn't just sell ice cream – he *made* it. It was soft and creamy and he had learned how to make it from his mother.

Mr Antonio and his mother came from a country called Italy, where they make a lot of ice cream. It's the place where the very first ice cream was made.

Mr Antonio made strawberry ice cream, vanilla ice cream, chocolate ice cream and pistachio – that's the one with the nuts inside.

Mr Antonio put his ice cream into little plastic boxes, and then he put the plastic boxes inside a big plastic box.

After that he put the big plastic box inside a big wooden box on the front of his tricycle. Then, he would ride along the road, ringing his bell ...

Every day Mr Antonio would cycle along a straight road with tall trees on each side, up a hill, down the other side, and over a little bridge to the village where the children lived.

When he arrived Mr Antonio rang his bell and all the children came running out of their houses to buy an ice cream.

'You tell me what you want,' said Mr Antonio, 'I gotta strawberry ice cream, vanilla ice cream, chocolate ice cream and pistachio – that's the one with the nuts inside.'

One morning, it was raining, but Mr Antonio made his ice cream, put it into little plastic boxes and those little plastic boxes were put inside a big plastic box. After that the big plastic box was put inside the big wooden box on the front of Mr Antonio's tricycle.

Mr Antonio cycled along the straight road with tall trees on each side, up the hill and then ... oh dear, the road was wet and going down the hill he went faster, and faster. The tricycle started to slide and slide, and then fell over, and it rolled over and over until it stopped at the bottom of the hill.

Poor Mr Antonio got up, brushed the mud off his trousers and put his tricycle back on its wheels. He rang his bell ... and it still worked, but when he looked inside the ice cream box, the lids had fallen off the little plastic boxes and all the ice cream was mixed up.

Poor Mr Antonio felt very unhappy, and pushed his tricycle along the road, over the bridge and into the village. He didn't ring his bell, but the children still came running out to buy their ice cream.

'Hello,' said Mr Antonio, 'I'm sorry but my tricycle fell over and all the ice cream is mixed up together,' and he lifted the lid of the ice-cream box to show them.

'That's all right,' said one little boy, 'I like things all mixed up. It's like the trifle my mum makes, I'll call it *trifle* ice cream.'

Now, when Mr Antonio rings his bell and the children come running out, he says: 'I gotta strawberry ice-a-creama, vanilla ice-a-creama, chocolate ice-a-creama, pistachio – that's the one with the nuts, and I got *trifle* ice-a-creama.'

He makes it specially, all the flavours mixed up together, because the children like it so much.

DAVID WILLMOTT

THE DUTCH DOLL

Once upon a time there was a little girl called Jenny.

One day her uncle gave her a shining fivepenny piece and she carried it about with her, tied in the corner of her handkerchief.

'Will you buy some sweets?' asked her father.

'Will you buy a book?' asked her mother.

'No,' said Jenny and shook her head. She knew what she was going to buy. She was going to buy a Dutch doll.

In the town where Jenny lived there was a market every Saturday. The market people came and set up tables and stalls right in the middle of the main street and on these they put all kinds of things to sell – fish and flowers and eggs and cabbages and clothes and books and toys.

Jenny loved going to the market, and there was one stall she liked better than all the others. It belonged to an old lady. Every Saturday she sat there and sold Dutch dolls, all costing exactly five pence each.

When Saturday came, Jenny asked her mother to take her to the market, so that she could choose her Dutch doll. Mother held her hand and they made their way through the crowds till they came to the old lady with her Dutch dolls.

The Dutch dolls had wooden heads and wooden bodies and wooden arms and wooden legs. Their arms were jointed at the elbow so that they could move up and down. The legs were jointed at the knee, so that they could move too.

Each doll had black shining hair painted on her flat wooden head, and black eyes and red lips, and a dab of red on each cheek as well. And a sharp little wooden nose sticking out in the middle of her face.

Jenny looked at them all and wondered which she should choose. 'Hurry up and choose, Jenny,' said Mother. 'They are all just the same.'

Oh dear, Jenny did not know which doll she liked best! One had specially red cheeks. Another had specially black hair. Then she noticed one that had a sad look on her face. Jenny stared at her for a long time. She looked as if she were lonely. 'I'll have *this* one please,' said Jenny, and she picked up the sad-faced doll. She untied the knot in the corner of her handkerchief and took out the money and gave it to the old lady.

'I shall call my Dutch doll Greta,' said Jenny as they hurried away. Now on the way home they had to cross a bridge over the river. Jenny stopped, because she liked to look down at the boats and the swans in the water below. 'Look, Greta,' she said, and held the little Dutch doll up so that she could see too. 'Look at the boats and the two big swans. Aren't they nice?'

But Greta still looked sad.

Suddenly, someone who was walking by bumped into Jenny and Greta fell out of her hand, over the railing of the bridge, down, down, down till she hit the water – splash!

'Oh!' cried Jenny. 'Oh! She's gone! Greta's fallen in the water!'

Then Jenny heard another splash. A big black dog jumped into the water from the side of the river and swam towards Greta. He thought Jenny had thrown a stick in for him, and he liked getting sticks out of the water. Because Greta was made of wood, she floated on the top of the water. Soon the dog reached her and took her in his mouth and swam back to the side of the river where his master was waiting for him.

He jumped out and shook himself, 'Brr brr,' and then he laid Greta at his master's feet. He wagged his tail proudly and his master patted his wet head and said, 'Good dog! Good dog!'

'Wuff, wuff,' said the big black dog, for he wanted his master to throw Greta in again.

But his master said, 'No – good dog – lie down,' then they waited for Jenny and her mother to come.

Jenny hurried over the bridge and ran fast along the side of the river. When she got to the man she bent down and patted the big dog's wet head and said: 'Thank you for saving Greta; she's only new today.'

'I'm afraid my dog's teeth have made some marks on your new doll and scratched off some of her paint, but if you'll let me keep her till tomorrow I'll make her as good as new. Where do you live?'

'Ivy Cottage, just along the road there,' said Jenny, and she pointed so that he'd know the way.

'Leave her with me today,' said the man, 'and I'll bring her back on my way past your house tomorrow.'

'Thank you,' said Jenny, though she knew she'd miss Greta badly, and would rather have taken her home even if she was scratched a bit.

That afternoon Jenny made a nice bed all ready for Greta out of a shoe-box, and she made some toy food for her – red apples and white eggs and yellow buns.

And next morning, sure enough, the front-door bell rang, and there was the man with the big black dog. He handed Jenny a brown paper parcel and said, 'There she is, young lady, as good as new.'

'Thank you,' said Jenny. 'Would your dog like a bone for his dinner? We kept one for him.'

'Yes,' said the man. 'He would.'

So Jenny gave him a big, juicy bone, wrapped up in paper, and he went away.

And then Jenny undid her parcel and took out Greta and had a good look at her.

'Oh, Greta,' she said. 'Your hair is blacker than it was, and your cheeks are redder, *and you've got a smile*. You don't look sad any more. Did you like falling in the river then? Did it cheer you up?'

But Greta just went on smiling and looking happy, so Jenny put her to sleep in the nice new bed she had made for her.

RUTH AINSWORTH

JAMIE'S DISAPPEARING LUNCH

One day Jamie's mother packed his lunch in a box. She put in a cold sausage, two honey sandwiches, a red apple and some milk in a drink bottle. Jamie put his lunch into a bag with a long strap, and slung it over his shoulder like the postman. He climbed over his back fence and went into the paddock. Then Jamie sat down under a shady tree.

He opened his lunch box and took out the cold sausage. Just as

111

he was going to take a bite, he saw a little white dog coming towards him. The dog's nose was sniffing along the ground and his tail was stuck up in the air. It was Scamp. He belonged to Jamie's friend, Mr Potter.

When Scamp saw the cold sausage in Jamie's hand he sat down. He put up his front paws to beg, as if to say, 'Mmmm, I'm hungry, Jamie!'

Jamie broke off a piece of his cold sausage. He threw it to Scamp who quickly gobbled it up. Jamie kept on throwing pieces of cold sausage to Scamp until it was all gone, and there was none left for Jamie.

Next, Jamie took out his sandwiches. Just as he was about to eat one, he saw lots of brown sparrows hopping around his feet. They cocked their little heads as if to say, 'We're hungry, Jamie!'

Jamie broke off little pieces of his sandwich and threw them to the sparrows. He kept on throwing pieces of his honey sandwiches until they were all gone, and there was none left for Jamie.

Then Jamie decided to have a drink of milk. He pulled the cork from his milk bottle. He was just going to drink some when he heard, '*Miaow, miaow!*' Jamie looked up. There was his own black cat, Fluff, running towards him. She must have followed Jamie from his house.

'*Miaow! miaow!*' wailed Fluff as if to say, 'I'm thirsty, Jamie!'

Jamie poured some of the milk into his lunch box and watched Fluff lap it up. Then he poured some more, and then some more, until it was all gone, and there was none left for Jamie.

He only had his red apple left. Just as he was about to bite into it, he heard 'Maaa! Maaa!' Without looking round Jamie knew who was calling. It was Gerda, the little white goat who lived in the paddock where Jamie was having his picnic lunch.

Gerda was tied behind the tree where Jamie was sitting. He knew that she liked apples. He gave her his red apple and watched her munch it to the very last bit.

Now there was nothing left for Jamie to eat. He packed his lunch things into the bag and slung it over his shoulder like the postman, and he went home.

He said to his mother, 'I'm hungry, Mother!' And his mother packed him another lunch.

This time Jamie sat in his garden, and ate it all by himself.

RUTH JONES

THE QUEEN IS COMING TO TEA

Pixie Parks and her mum and dad were an ordinary family, who lived in an ordinary house in an ordinary street, next door to ordinary Mr and Mrs Jones.

One day the Queen said: 'I should like to visit an ordinary house to see how my ordinary subjects live.' So her secretary sent a letter to Mr and Mrs Parks, saying that the Queen would come to tea with them on Friday, the twenty-fifth of June.

The letter was long and gold, with a royal seal on it. Mrs Parks was all of a flutter when she read it.

She took out the best tablecloth and held it up. 'That's not good enough for the Queen!' she said. 'We must buy a new one.' And she went out shopping.

113

But the new tablecloth had a fancy fringe that tickled Pixie's knees.

'I liked the old tablecloth best,' said Pixie. 'Besides, this new one is too fancy for our plain white cups and saucers.'

'You are right!' Mrs Parks declared. 'We must buy a new tea-set!' And she went out shopping.

But the new cups had curly little handles. Mr Parks could not hold them properly in his big fingers. 'I liked the old cups best,' he said. 'Besides, this new tea-set is too fancy for our plain old table.'

'You are right!' Mrs Parks declared. 'We must buy a new table.' And she went out shopping.

But the new table was so well polished that Pixie's plate went sliding all over the place. 'I liked the old table best,' said Pixie. 'Besides, this new one is too shiny for our dull old chairs.'

'You are right!' Mrs Parks declared. 'We must buy new chairs!' And she went out shopping.

But the new chairs had hard seats, and no little spindles to rest your feet on.

'We liked the old chairs best,' said Pixie and her dad. 'Besides, these new chairs are too fancy for our faded old carpet.'

'You are right!' Mrs Parks declared. 'We must buy a new carpet!' And she went out shopping.

But when the new carpet was laid, Mr Parks had to take off his boots every time he came into the room. 'I liked the old carpet best,' said Mr Parks. 'Besides, this new one is too fancy for our old dresser.'

'You are right!' Mrs Parks declared. 'We must buy a new dresser!' And she went out shopping.

But the new dresser had no room for books, or the pictures Pixie painted, or Mr Parks's pipes. 'We liked the old dresser best,' said Pixie and her dad. 'Besides, all this fine furniture is too grand for our little dining-room.'

'You are right!' Mrs Parks declared. 'We must move house at once!'

So Mr and Mrs Parks moved to a splendid new house. It had a fine, big garden with a fountain, a goldfish pond and statues made

of marble. It had sixteen windows, and a glass part at the side where plants were growing. But that house was far too big for the three of them. Pixie got lost upstairs, and Mr Parks got lost in the garden. 'We liked the old house best,' said Pixie and her dad.

Besides, the new house was not an ordinary house, so the

Queen did not want to see it. She went to tea with Mr and Mrs Jones instead.

HAZEL TOWNSON

WHAT WE NEED IS A NEW BUS

Not so long ago an old red bus ran down to the station and back again. It was a rumbling-grumbling bus. It was a rusty-dusty bus. It was a jumping-bumping bus. And because it was all of these things some people walked to the station rather than ride in the old bus. It shook them about too much.

'The trouble with this old bus,' the driver said, 'is that it's worn out. It needs a new engine to drive it. It needs new tyres to run on. It needs new seats, new windows, new paint, new everything. In fact what we need is a *new* bus!'

Now the bus wasn't surprised to hear this. It did feel worn out. It was worn out. Climbing the hills made its engine work so hard it went slower and slower and slower. Changing gears all the time made it feel exhausted. All it wanted to do was sleep in the sun for ever.

'*Ur, ur, ur!*' it grumbled. It didn't want to go another wheel turn.

Inside the bus the conductor was calling out, 'Fares, pliz! Fares! Fares, pliz!' He sold pink tickets from his book to the passengers, and their money dropped into his big black bag with a tinkling plink, plink, plink.

And inside the bus the driver was in his seat in front of the big steering wheel. He pushed the gear lever into place. He pulled off the brake and before it knew what was happening the old red bus was rolling down the road again.

'*Urr-uuuuur-urrrr-urrrrr!*' It grumbled. It mumbled. It groaned. '*Grrrr!*' It was as if it couldn't go another wheel turn. And to its surprise the old red bus didn't.

Ssssss!

The front tyre was shrinking smaller and smaller. *Sssssssss!* What was happening to the plump round sides? *Sssssssss!* Air hissed out. The tyre was as flat as a piece of paper.

The driver stopped the bus. Out he jumped. Out jumped the bus conductor. People poked their heads from their windows.

'The front tyre is as flat as a pancake,' the driver told them. 'We can't fix it here. You'd better walk to the station.'

'We'd better get the mechanic from the garage,' said the conductor. 'We could be here for hours,' he told the people. 'Yes, you'd be better off walking to the station.'

Now the people grumbled and mumbled and groaned and moaned and walked to the station. 'What we need is a new bus,' they muttered and some of them stopped to look at the flat tyre that had run over a big nail. It had stabbed a hole in the tyre's tube. *Sssssss!* Out hissed the air until the tyre, no longer fat and round, looked saggy-baggy, as flat as flat. A sad limp tyre.

When, at last, the mechanic came roaring up in his truck he tapped the old red bus with a spanner and said, 'This old crate needs more than a new tyre.'

'I know, I know,' agreed the bus driver. 'What we need is a new bus. When can you sell us one?'

'Not today.' The mechanic shook his head. He banged and tapped and looked at the insides of the bus and said nothing for a long time, then he said, 'In a couple of weeks we could make this old bus almost as good as new, up at the garage.'

Now that was a good idea. A wonderful idea, especially for the old bus. It helped as much as it could when the tow-truck came. There was a crane on the back of the tow-truck and it lifted the front wheels of the bus away, away off the ground. With just its two back wheels the old red bus ran along behind the tow-truck to the garage.

And when some people saw the old red bus being towed away they decided that it must be going to the scrap-heap. Where else could it go? 'Looks as if we'll get a new bus after all,' they told each other.

At the garage, mechanics took out the worn parts of the engine and put in new ones. They oiled and greased. They fitted new tyres and new seats. They repainted and repainted the old bus a sparkling red, a shiny red, a geranium red. It didn't look like an old bus. It didn't feel like an old bus. It felt like running a thousand miles or two – up hills, down hills and along lumpy, bumpy roads.

When the time came for the old red bus to drive along the road to the station everyone wanted a ride. They crowded in. Some people sat and some people had to stand. The bus was loaded but up the hill it went without a grumble or rumble, just a little *gr-grr-grrr* which was like a happy humming song. 'This isn't bad for our old red bus!' said the conductor with a grin.

'Not our old rumbling, grumbling bus!' shrieked someone. 'This can't be our old, dusty, rusty bus! Don't tell me that this is the bumpy, jumpy, worn-out old bus!'

It was, and we know that it was, don't we?

JEAN CHAPMAN

THE SECRET OF
THE STAIRS

Jo fell down the cellar stairs. As she rolled, she landed on each step.

Thunk

Thunk

Thunk

Thock

Thunk

'That was odd,' she thought.

Falling downstairs was not odd.

Jo was nearly two years old and was always falling downstairs.

It was one of the steps which was odd.

It had made a strange noise when she landed on it.

Jo went back upstairs for her ball and gently pushed it over the edge of the first step. She listened to the sound of the ball as it slowly bounced down the stairs.

Boing

Boing

Boing

119

Bonk

Boing

Boing
There it was again. What could it mean?

Jo bumped down the steps on her bottom. She picked up her ball from the cellar floor and clambered back upstairs.

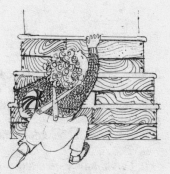

She heard her mother shout at her again to stop playing on the stairs. She had been shouting at them ever since they had arrived at their new house.

Their father said she worried too much.

Jo pushed the ball down the steps for the last time.
Boing

Boing

Boing

Bonk

Boing

Boing
This time her sister, Catherine, noticed it too.

Catherine left the dusty trunk of old plates she had discovered in a corner, and came to see.

She stamped noisily up the stairs to Jo.

They both listened to the sound of her feet.

Dunt

Dunt

Dunt

Donk

Dunt

Dunt

It was the third step from the bottom which was odd.

They both sat on the fourth step and stared down between their feet.

The steps were wooden. The third one from the bottom had two cracks in it.

Jo drummed her feet, just for fun.

The cracks moved a little. There was a loose plank.

Catherine found her last lolly stick in her pocket. She pushed it into one of the cracks and prised up the plank. They turned it over. Underneath, it was covered in soft, grey, woolly cobwebs thick with dust.

Jo stroked it.

Catherine rolled some into little balls to put on the plates she had found.

Later, peering into the dark hole they had made under the stairs, they saw a piece of cloth. Catherine lifted it out. It was a little bag. She pulled it open, breaking the faded ribbon around it.

Jo put the ribbon on her head. They both laughed.

Catherine emptied the bag on to Jo's lap.

There, on her knee, gleamed a heap of gold coins.

They looked like chocolate Christmas-tree money but they were hard and heavy. They clinked when Jo dropped them through her fingers.

'I know,' whispered Catherine, 'let's keep them in the bag, under the stairs, and we won't tell anyone and we can pretend it's our real treasure.'

And that is just what they did.

LYNNE RUSSELL

WHAT HAPPENED TO MUSTARD

This is a story about Mustard, the little yellow cat, and about something that happened to him not very long ago.

One morning he was sitting on the grass in the front garden. He had been very busy washing himself, licking his paw and wiping it round and round his face. Now he was quite clean. He didn't know what to do next, so he just sat and watched the road beyond the front garden, waiting for something to happen.

Very soon something did happen. A great big van, the biggest van Mustard had ever seen, stopped outside the garden gate. It was a green van, with yellow letters painted on it, and it was even bigger than the coalman's lorry, and *that* was the biggest thing Mustard knew. Presently two men, wearing white aprons, got down from the driving seat at the front and walked round to the back of the van. Mustard couldn't quite see what they were doing but ... clank ... clank ... clank ... clank ... what a noise! The men pulled down the back of the van, for it was really a sort of door.

123

Mustard ran across the grass and climbed quickly up one of the trees by the gate so that he could see right into the van. It was almost empty. Only a few sacks and boxes were inside. The two men in white aprons opened the garden gate and walked up to the front door of the house.

'I wonder what they want?' thought Mustard. 'I've never seen them before.'

He sat on the branch of the tree and his green eyes watched and watched. They watched the men go back to the van and bring the sacks and boxes indoors. Mustard could hear the men's heavy boots clumping about the house. 'Clump ... clump ... clump ... clump!' they went. It sounded as if they were walking on floors which had no carpets on them.

'Goodness me!' said Mustard to himself. 'Look what they are doing now! They are taking away the blue carpet from the hall and putting it into the big van. What *can* be happening?'

He watched the men bring out some more rolls of carpet. Then they brought out some chairs, then a table, then a sideboard, then a cupboard, and then ... and *then* ... they brought out Mustard's basket, Mustard's very own round basket with the brown cushion in it. And they put the basket into the van, with the carpets and the chairs and the table and the sideboard and the cupboard.

'Well!' said Mustard. 'My basket! Well!'

As soon as the men had gone inside the house again, Mustard jumped down from the tree and ran out of the front gate. He saw a wooden board which stretched like a hill from the ground to the floor of the big van. Up the hill he ran and into the van he pranced. This was fun.

'Miaow, miaow!' he laughed, showing his little pink tongue. 'Miaouw, miaouw.'

He ran round and round the inside of the big van, jumping on the chairs and on the table. And then, behind the cupboard, he found ... his very own basket. He jumped into the basket and curled himself round on the soft brown cushion.

'A ... a ... a ... ah! Mia-a-o-w!' he sighed. 'I *am* so tired.'

It was quite dark in that corner of the van behind the cupboard, and in a few minutes Mustard was fast asleep. He stayed asleep for a long time, and then suddenly, 'Clank ... clank ... clank ... clank!' What a noise! Mustard opened his eyes. Where *was* he?

What was this strange, dark place full of tables and chairs and cupboards and rolls of carpet? Oh, yes! Of course! He was inside the big van. And the clank ... clank ... clank ... clank must have been the noise the men made when they shut the van doors.

'Oh dear!' cried Mustard, sitting up in his basket. 'Oh miaow, miaow! I'm shut in.'

Now he could hear the children calling him from the front garden.

'Mustard!' they called. 'Mustard, where are you?'

'Miaow, miaow!' cried the little yellow cat.

'Mustard! Come along! We're going in the car to the new house and we want to take you with us.'

'Miaow! Here I am! Miaow!' called Mustard, from the inside of the van.

But the children couldn't hear him. They were terribly worried, for they couldn't think where he could be.

'Honk! Honk!' went the horn on the van. 'Honk! Honk!' And the big, green van began to move slowly away, with the yellow cat shut up inside it.

Mustard lay down again in his basket behind the cupboard. He didn't know where they were going, nor what was happening. But it was very comfortable on his nice brown cushion, and he was having a lovely ride.

After a little while, the van began to slow down. Then it stopped altogether.

'Clank ... clank ... clank ... clank!' What a noise! The men were opening the door at the back of the van. Mustard jumped out of his basket and ran towards them.

'Why, here's a little cat!' said one man.

'Oh, Mustard! Darling Mustard! He must have been in the moving van all the time. And we thought he was lost.'

'Miaow!' cried Mustard happily.

'Come and see the new house, Mustard. Come along! This is where we're all going to live now.'

They picked him up and carried him into the house.

'We'll bring the little cat's basket indoors in a minute,' promised one of the white-aproned men.

126

The children said, 'Thank you very much,' and then they hugged Mustard more tightly than ever.

'What a clever little cat!' they said. 'He found the new house all by himself.'

'Miaow!' said Mustard. And because he loved being hugged and stroked he purred as loudly as he could. Brr ... brr ... brr ... brr ...

DORIS RUST

THE MICE AND THE CHRISTMAS TREE

Now you shall hear the story about a family of mice who lived behind the larder wall.

Every Christmas Eve, Mother Mouse and the children swept and dusted their whole house with their tails, and for a Christmas tree Father Mouse decorated an old boot with spider's web instead of tinsel. For Christmas presents, the children were each given a little nut, and Mother Mouse held up a piece of bacon fat for them all to sniff.

After that, they danced round and round the boot, and sang and played games till they were tired out. Then Father Mouse would say, 'That's all for tonight! Time to go to bed!'

That is how it had been every Christmas and that is how it was to be this year. The little mice held each other by the tail and danced round the boot, while Granny Mouse enjoyed the fun from her rocking-chair, which wasn't a rocking-chair at all, but a small turnip.

But when Father Mouse said, 'That's all for tonight! Time to go to bed!' all the children dropped each other's tails and shouted: 'No! No!'

'What's that?' said Father Mouse. 'When I say it's time for bed, it's time for bed!'

127

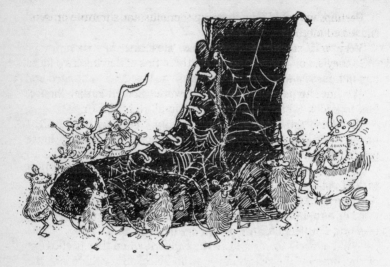

'We don't want to go!' cried the children, and hid behind Granny's turnip rocking-chair.

'What's all this nonsense?' said Mother Mouse. 'Christmas is over now, so off you go, the lot of you!'

'No, no!' wailed the children, and climbed on to Granny's knee. She hugged them all lovingly.

'Why don't you want to go to bed, my little sugar lumps?'

'Because we want to go upstairs to the big drawing-room and dance round a proper Christmas tree,' said the eldest Mouse child. 'You see, I've been peeping through a crack in the wall and I saw a huge Christmas tree with lots and lots of lights on it.'

'We want to see the Christmas tree and all the lights too!' shouted the other children.

'Oh, but the drawing-room can be a very dangerous place for mice,' said Granny.

'Not when all the people have gone to bed,' objected the eldest Mouse child.

'Oh, do let's go!' they all pleaded.

Mother and Father Mouse didn't know what to say, but they couldn't very well disappoint the children on Christmas Eve.

'Perhaps we could take them up there just for a minute or two,' suggested Mother Mouse.

'Very well,' said Father, 'but follow me closely.'

So they set off. They tiptoed past three tins of herring, two large jars of honey, and a barrel of cider.

'We have to go very carefully here,' whispered Father Mouse, 'not to knock over any bottles. Are you all right, Granny?'

'Of course I'm all right,' said Granny. 'You just carry on. I haven't been up in the drawing-room since I was a little Mouse girl; it'll be fun to see it all again.'

'Mind the trap!' said the eldest Mouse child. 'It's behind that sack of potatoes.'

'I know that,' said Granny. 'It's been there since I was a child. I'm not afraid of that!' And she took a flying leap right over the trap and scuttled after the others up the wall.

'What a lovely tree!' cried all the children when they peeped out of the hole by the drawing-room fireplace. 'But where are the lights? You said there'd be lots and lots of lights, didn't you? Didn't you?' the children shouted, crowding round the eldest one, who was quite sure there had been lights the day before.

They stood looking for a little while. Then suddenly a whole lot of coloured lights lit up the tree! Do you know what had happened? By accident, Granny had touched the electric switch by the fireplace.

'Oh, how lovely!' they all exclaimed, and Father and Mother and Granny thought it was very nice too. They walked right round the tree, looking at the decorations, the little paper baskets, the glass balls, and the glittering tinsel garlands. But the children found something even more exciting: a mechanical lorry!

Of course, they couldn't wind it up themselves, but its young master had wound it up before he went to bed, to be ready for him to play with in the morning. So when the Mouse children clambered into it, it started off right away.

'Children, children! You mustn't make such a noise!' warned Mother Mouse.

But the children didn't listen; they were having a wonderful time going round and round and round in the lorry.

'As long as the cat doesn't come!' said Father Mouse anxiously.

He had hardly spoken before the cat walked silently through the open door.

Father, Mother and Granny Mouse all made a dash for the hole in the skirting but the children were trapped in the lorry, which just went on going round and round and round. They had never been so scared in all their Mouse lives.

The cat crouched under the tree, and every time the lorry passed she tried to tap it with her front paw. But it was going too fast and she missed.

Then the lorry started slowing down. 'I think we'd better make a jump for it and try to get up the tree,' said the eldest Mouse. So when the lorry stopped they all gave a big jump and landed on the branches of the tree.

One hid in a paper basket, another behind a bulb (which nearly burned him), a third swung on a glass ball, and the fourth rolled himself up in some cotton wool. But where was the eldest Mouse? Oh yes, he had climbed right to the top and was balancing next to the star and shouting at the cat:

> *Silly, silly cat*
> *You can't catch us!*
> *You're much too fat,*
> *Silly, silly cat!*

But the cat pretended not to hear or see the little mice. She sharpened her claws on the lorry.

'I'm not interested in catching mice tonight,' she said as if to herself. 'I've been waiting for a chance to play with this lorry all day.'

'Pooh! That's just a story!' said the eldest who was also the bravest. 'You'd catch us quick enough if we came down.'

'No, I wouldn't. Not on Christmas Eve!' said the cat. And she kept to her word. When they did all come timidly down, she never moved, but just said: 'Hurry back to your hole, children. Christmas Eve is the one night when I'm kind to little mice. But woe betide you if I catch you tomorrow morning!'

The little mice pelted through that hole and never stopped running till they got to their home behind the larder wall. There

were Father and Mother and Granny Mouse waiting in fear and trembling to know what had happened to them.

When Mother Mouse had heard their story she said, 'You must promise me, children, never to go up to the drawing-room again.'

'We promise! We promise!' they all shouted together. Then she made them say after her The Mouse Law, which they'd all been taught when they were tiny:

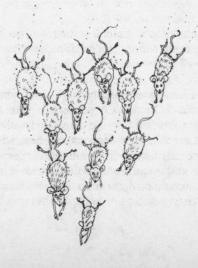

We promise always to obey
Our parents dear in every way,
To wipe our feet upon the mat
And, never, never cheek the cat.

Remember too the awful danger
Of taking money from a stranger;
We will not go off on our own
Or give our mother cause to moan.

Odd bits of cheese and bacon-scraps
Are almost certain to be traps,
So we must look for bigger things
Like loaves and cakes and doughnut-rings;

And if these rules we still obey
We'll live to run another day.

ALF PRØYSEN

THE CASTLE ON BUMBLY HILL

The big grey castle which stood at the top of Bumbly Hill was old – very old. No one had lived there for more than a hundred years. No one seemed to want to live in a big lonely old castle at the top of a hill.

The people who lived in Bumbly Town at the foot of the hill were very poor. They grew vegetables in their gardens and corn in the fields on the hillside but times were hard and often they looked up at the old castle and shook their heads.

'Soon the castle will fall down in ruins,' they said, 'for there is no one to keep the walls and roof repaired. If only a rich Prince and Princess would come to live in Bumbly Castle – how different it would be!'

'They would need kitchen maids and cooks, nursery maids and washerwomen,' sighed the young women and girls. 'It would be wonderful to work for a Prince and Princess.'

'Yes. We could be footmen and butlers, coachmen and grooms,' said the young men, picturing themselves dressed in smart uniforms, riding fine white horses and serving at banquets.

But no Prince came. The castle still stood empty and the people

of Bumbly Town grew poorer than ever. The town was very shabby and neglected for no one could afford to buy paint for their houses or wood to mend the fences and gates. Even the weathercock had fallen from the church steeple and there was a big hole in the Town Hall roof.

'People have no money to buy meat these days,' grumbled the butcher. 'If the castle were occupied I could sell big joints of meat and I should soon be rich.'

'I would make such lovely pastries for them to buy,' said the baker wistfully, for he was a very good pastry cook, and nowadays there was no sale for such luxuries in Bumbly Town.

Time went by and still the castle stood empty. Then one day, just as everyone in Bumbly Town was sitting down to their midday meal, a strange noise sent them all hurrying out of their houses. Such a rumbling and a banging came from the hill-top that it seemed as if a thunderstorm were about to break overhead. But the sky was blue, the sun shone and not a cloud was to be seen. Everyone gazed up the hillside.

'It's coming from the castle,' someone cried. 'Perhaps the walls are falling down.'

'Nonsense,' said the Mayor, 'the castle is strong enough to stand for a thousand years.'

Rumble ... bang. Rumble ... bang. The noise continued all through the afternoon and everyone was too frightened to go back to work. They huddled together in the town square looking fearfully up the hill. But there was nothing unusual to be seen and the strange noises went on until evening came and darkness fell.

'Look! Look!' called one old lady, pointing up to the castle.

'There's a light in one of the windows. Someone must be there.'

There was a long pause while the people of Bumbly Town gazed up at the lighted window. It was all very mysterious.

Then the Mayor cleared his throat, fingered his chain of office and looked very important.

'Er ... er ... We must find out who it is,' he said. 'Someone must go up to the castle this very evening and see what is going on.'

There was silence. No one volunteered to go. They were all too frightened.

Suddenly a small voice said, 'I'll go, Your Worship.' And Tim, the butcher's errand boy, stepped forward before the Mayor.

'I know the path up to the castle very well,' he said. 'I often go up there to play. I can find my way even in the dark. I'll climb quietly over the wall and peep in the window to see what is going on.'

'What a brave boy,' murmured the people, and the Mayor patted Tim on the head and said he was a great credit to the town.

'Go and find out what is happening in the castle,' he said. 'But take care and come back very quickly to tell us.'

The baker gave Tim two jam doughnuts to eat on the way and away he went to climb to the top of Bumbly Hill.

'Good luck,' called the people.

No one went to bed that night. They all gathered in the council chamber of the Town Hall and waited to see what news Tim would bring back. All was silent from the castle now but a light still shone from one of the windows.

As dawn broke the Mayor and all the people came out into the square and there, hurrying down the hill path, they could see Tim the errand boy. He was puffing and panting when he arrived in front of the Mayor.

'Oh ... Your Worship ...' he gasped. 'It's ... a ... it's ... a ...'

'Yes, my boy,' barked the Mayor, who was feeling very agitated. 'Yes, what is it? What did you see?'

'Tell us quickly, Tim,' implored the butcher.

Tim swallowed hard. 'There's a GIANT in the castle,' he said, 'a huge giant with red hair. He's sleeping in a chair by the fire and his boots are as big as WHEELBARROWS.'

'A GIANT,' gasped the astonished people, 'and in our castle. So that's what all the noise was about.'

'A giant has moved into Bumbly Castle,' moaned the Mayor. 'What is to become of us all?'

Everyone began to talk at once.

'He will stamp all over our fields with his big boots.'

'He will bump into our houses and knock off the chimney pots.'

'He will make so much noise that we shall all have bad headaches.'

'We're frightened of giants,' said the children, beginning to cry.

Then one by one they went off home to think over what had happened.

'He must GO. We must get rid of him ... AT ONCE,' muttered the Mayor. 'No one wants a giant for a neighbour.'

Hardly had they finished their breakfast, however, when out from the castle gateway with a bellow and roar came the giant, thundering down the hillside in his enormous boots and singing at the top of his voice,

> The Giant of Bumbly Hill I'll be,
> I hope you'll all be friends with me.

He laughed a big booming laugh as he walked into the Town Square and sat down on the Town Hall steps. Everyone closed their doors and peeped fearfully from behind their curtains.

They had often heard about giants but they had never seen one before. His hair was red and curly and hung down on to his shoulders. He wore a green velvet jacket trimmed with gold buttons as big as saucers and his brown baggy trousers were as wide as curtains. As for his boots ... as Tim had said they were as big as wheelbarrows. Everything about him was SO BIG. His hands looked as if he could pick up a cart quite easily and his hat must be as wide as a cartwheel. But the people had to admit that he looked very jolly and really rather nice.

No one dared to go outside, however. No shops opened. Mothers did not allow their children to go to school. The town was deserted. There was not a sound in Bumbly Town that morning.

The giant looked all round the square at the empty shops and the closed doors and the quiet street. He was not smiling any more. He began to look very unhappy and before long huge tears began to roll down his cheeks. He cried and cried and cried.

The people in Bumbly Town were so surprised to see a giant crying that they forgot to be afraid and came out of their houses and gathered round him in amazement.

'Whatever's the matter?' they asked kindly. 'Why are you crying Mr Giant?'

'It is always the same,' sobbed the giant. 'I have travelled north and south, east and west, all over the land searching for somewhere to live. But wherever I go people are afraid of me because I'm so big and noisy.'

He mopped his eyes on a handkerchief as big as a bath towel. 'No one believes that I am really a gentle giant,' he went on sadly. 'You see I'm so clumsy. I knock things over and stamp around and ... I can't help it.'

The people glanced at his big boots and nodded. They could understand how difficult it was for him.

'And now you are all afraid of me too,' said the giant sadly, 'and I do so want to live in Bumbly Castle and be friends with you all. It's just the place for a giant, you see. Plenty of room to move around ... it is very difficult too for a giant to make friends when he has to move from place to place so often.'

'And so you shall!' cried all the people, laughing and crowding round the giant.

'We have been wanting someone to come and live in our castle for a long time,' said the Mayor. 'We shall be very pleased if you will live there and be friends with us all.'

137

The giant dried his eyes and in no time at all was laughing and joking and they felt as if they had known him for years.

'I'll try to be as quiet as I can,' he promised. 'It's my boots, you know. They are so noisy.'

What a morning that was in Bumbly Town. The giant did his shopping and bought ten loaves of bread from the baker and a bag of gingerbread. From the butcher he collected fifty sausages and a big joint of beef. Then he met a farmer who sold him a sack of potatoes and a sack of carrots.

Then he sat down on the Town Hall steps again and the lady from the Café brought him a basin of coffee for his 'elevenses'.

Finally Tim helped the giant to load all the things he had bought on to a cart and the giant pushed it up the hill to Bumbly Castle with Tim riding on his shoulder and waving to all the people.

Never had there been so much to talk about in Bumbly Town before.

Now as the days went by the people of the town grew very fond of their giant. He helped them in so many ways. He put the weathercock back on the church steeple without even needing a ladder. He chopped down trees from a nearby forest and sawed wood to mend the fences and gates. He reached up and painted their upstairs windows and mended the hole in the Town Hall roof. Bumbly Town began to look really smart again. The children loved the giant and thought he was the best playmate they had ever had, for he was always ready to give them rides on his enormous shoulders.

The butcher, the baker and the farmer sold the giant so many things to eat that they became quite rich. The ladies sewed smart new shirts for the giant and knitted him enormous stripy socks to wear inside his huge boots. Even Tim had a new cart and great fun helping the giant take all his things up to the castle.

However, there was one big problem. The giant was terribly noisy and there were times when everyone in Bumbly Town wished he would not stamp around so much.

Nobody minded him being so noisy during the daytime when they were all busy working and the giant was helping them to do their jobs. They didn't even mind his big booming laugh when he played with the children or the sounds like explosions when he sneezed.

But during the evenings it was really very trying to hear him stamping around in the castle doing his housework or preparing his evening meal in the kitchen.

'We can't get the children off to sleep,' complained the mothers.

'All that rumbling and banging coming from the castle,' grumbled one old man who liked to have a snooze in the evening, 'it's as bad as a perpetual thunderstorm.'

'It certainly is very disturbing,' they agreed. But no one could think what to do about it. They didn't like to mention it to the giant in case they hurt his feelings.

'It's those boots of his,' muttered the Mayor. 'But I suppose he can't help having such big feet. I don't know W H A T we are going to do about him.'

Now one day when the giant had been particularly noisy, Tim went to call on the Mayor.

'It's the giant's birthday next week, Your Worship,' he said. 'Let's give him a party.'

'Well I don't see how that will cure him of stamping around so much,' said the Mayor crossly. But Tim just smiled and looked very thoughtful.

'Maybe it will,' he said. 'Wait and see,' and looking very mysterious he ran off to visit his Granny.

During the next few days there was great activity in Bumbly Town. The baker decided he must make the giant a birthday cake. But his tins were all too small so he made twelve cakes and stuck them together with icing and iced all over the top so the joins would not show. The cake was so big that it covered the whole of the top of his wife's kitchen table, and when they had put candles all around the edge it was so splendid that everyone had to come and look at it.

Meanwhile the butcher was busy making pork pies and sausage rolls and the most delicious-smelling meat pasties. The ladies made trifles and baked apple pies and the Mayor's wife whipped up big bowls of cream.

Tim just went backwards and forwards to his Granny's house looking very excited but not telling anyone why he had suggested a party for the giant's birthday. It was all very mysterious.

The day of the giant's birthday came at last and fortunately it was a lovely sunny day. Everyone wore their best clothes and came into the Town Square where the tea was all set out on tables. The giant had been invited for four o'clock and down the hill he came, wearing his best hat, his new shirt and his red and green striped socks. He was singing as he came,

I'm the Birthday Giant as smart as can be,
All ready to have my birthday tea.

He laughed and joked so much as he stamped round the square greeting everyone that the tea cups rattled and people were rather worried he might knock over the tables. But all was well and the food was delicious. There was enough for even the giant who was obviously enjoying himself immensely.

He ate three pork pies, ten sausage rolls, a whole trifle and three helpings of apple pie. When he blew out the candles on his cake a terrible gale passed through the square but no one grumbled as it was such a special occasion. After all, even giants have to have birthday candles.

Just as they were all finishing their cake, Tim came into the square pushing his cart with a simply enormous box on top, all wrapped up in birthday paper.

'It's a birthday present for you, Mr Giant,' he said. 'My Granny made it,' and he stood proudly by while the giant opened his present. The people were crowding round and standing on tiptoe to see what was in the box.

'Well, upon my word,' exclaimed the giant and he took out of the box a beautiful pair of red slippers, lined with soft warm fluffy material.

There was a gasp of surprise from everyone. 'What a good idea,' they whispered to each other.

'Just what I've always wanted,' chuckled the giant. 'A soft pair of slippers to wear in the evenings. It can be very tiring wearing these big boots all the time.'

Taking off his boots he put on the slippers which fitted him perfectly and which everyone agreed looked quite splendid with his stripy socks. Then the giant walked proudly round and round the square admiring his present.

No one said a word. They just listened. They could hardly believe

it. There was not a sound to be heard. That is ... until the giant started to sing in his jolly, booming voice:

> *The Giant of Bumbly Hill, that's me,*
> *The quietest Giant you ever did see.*

And from that day ... HE WAS.

PHYLLIS PEARCE

141

THE LOST KEYS

Barry was really a very good little boy – he was cheerful and kind, and almost always polite – but he had naughty fidgety hands. Barry's hands were always getting into trouble. They turned the salt cellar upside down at breakfast and made white trails of salt all over the red and yellow tablecloth. They played with lumps of coal and left marks on the sitting-room wall. They unrolled toilet rolls, touched Grandma's best and precious china dogs, knotted Mother's knitting wool, and once they even unscrewed the valves on his brother's bicycle so that the tyres went flat.

'What have you done now?' his mother would ask sorrowfully, and Barry would look at the little bits of china that had once been a cup, or the horrid worms of toothpaste all over the bath, or the rice spilt all over the kitchen floor, in astonishment.

'But I didn't mean to, Mummy,' he would answer.

And Mother said – and she said it several times each day – 'Really, Barry, I sometimes think that you don't even know when your hands are being naughty. They must be taught a lesson. I shall have to give them a hard smack.'

Poor Barry. Smacks never seemed to do any good.

But one sunny August day Barry's bad hands did something very tiresome – so tiresome that it taught Barry a lesson he will never forget.

Barry's big brother Geoffrey was on holiday from school, and all morning he and Barry played in the sandpit in the garden. They made themselves very sandy, but they had a lovely game making castles and tunnels, and even rivers and marshy places with water that Mother handed to them out of the kitchen window.

'I know,' said Geoffrey, 'let's get our toy soldiers and pretend the sandpit is a battlefield.'

'Yes, let's,' said Barry eagerly. He enjoyed playing with his big brother because he always had such good ideas. He didn't even mind when Geoffrey said, 'Will you go and fetch the soldiers then? They're in a big cardboard box in my bedroom cupboard.'

'All right,' said Barry, and off he went. Mother was washing woollen jumpers in the sink when Barry burst into the kitchen.

'I'm just going to get the soldiers from Geoffrey's room,' said Barry. 'We are having the most goodest game.'

'Are you?' laughed Mother. 'You're covered in sand if that's anything to go by! You stay in the kitchen, Barry, and I'll fetch the soldiers down. I don't want sandy footprints all up the stairs. It would look as if Man Friday had come to stay!'

Mother bustled upstairs, and Barry stood by the kitchen table, waiting. At first he stood as still as still, but then his naughty fidgety hands began to get up to their tricks. Mother's purse lay on the table, and Barry's hands undid the zip and spilt the money

out. They picked up a fifty penny piece – they liked its nearly round shape – and then put it back carefully. They picked up Mother's car keys, and then they found the biscuit tin. They opened the lid and felt inside ... but at that very moment, Mother came into the kitchen with the soldiers.

'Oh, Barry!' she cried, and Barry looked at the spilt money and the open biscuit tin.

'I'm sorry, Mummy,' he said in a little quiet voice. 'I didn't mean to.' He picked up all the money and put it carefully back into the purse, and he put the lid firmly back on to the biscuit tin so that the biscuits wouldn't go soft.

'Off you go,' said Mother in a tired, cross voice. 'You really are a terrible fiddler. Your hands will get you into trouble one day, my son.'

Barry carried the soldiers out to the sandpit, and from then until dinner-time the game became more and more exciting. It was the very best game Barry and Geoffrey had ever had together.

But somehow after they had eaten their dinner and watched Barry's programme on the television, the game just didn't seem very interesting any more. Geoffrey and Barry had a silly quarrel over whose turn it was to work the matchstick gun, and then the walls of the fort fell in.

'Let's not play any more,' said Geoffrey.

'All right,' agreed Barry, so they put the soldiers away and carried the box indoors.

'What can we do now, Mummy?' asked Geoffrey. 'We're tired of soldiers.'

'What about a swim?' suggested Mother. 'I saw you were clearing away, so I've made some sandwiches. I thought we could take a picnic to the swimming pool. You've been such good children all day that I've been able to finish all my jobs in record time.'

Geoffrey and Barry gave a loud cheer. 'You had better have a good wash first,' said Mother. 'They won't let you into the pool if you are covered in sand. Be quick. I'll collect all the swimming things and towels together and we can be at the pool before it becomes too crowded.'

The boys washed themselves very well, scrubbing at their knees and elbows, and helping each other dry the difficult parts. Mother was loading the picnic basket and the bag of swimming things into the car when they hurried downstairs.

'Jump in,' Mother called. 'I'll just fetch my purse with the car keys in it.'

The boys scrambled into the back seat of the car and waited for Mother. They waited and waited. After a few moments she came out of the house with her purse in her hand and a very worried frown on her face.

'I can't find the car keys,' she said. 'I'm sure I saw them in my purse when I paid the baker this morning. What can have happened to them?' Then Mother remembered.

'Barry!' she said, 'you've had them. You emptied my purse out while I was fetching the soldiers for you. What have you done with them?'

Barry felt very worried. 'I don't know,' he said in a small voice.

'Did you touch them?' Mother was very impatient.

Barry nodded miserably.

'Where are they then?'

'I don't know.'

Mother felt in all Barry's pockets, but the keys weren't there. They all looked on the kitchen floor, and under the mat, but they weren't there either.

'Perhaps Barry took them to the sandpit with the soldiers,' suggested Geoffrey.

'Well,' said Mother, 'we can't go swimming until the keys are found, because without the keys the car won't start. Barry, you go down to the sandpit, and don't come back until you have found the keys.'

Geoffrey went with Barry, who was very upset.

'Stop crying and look, you little nuisance!' said Geoffrey angrily. 'Your horrid hands spoil everything.'

All afternoon those two boys searched the sandpit. At first they scraped away gently, but after a while, when there was no sign of the keys on the surface, they dug holes and tried to remember where the tunnels had been. But it was no use. The keys had disappeared completely.

When she felt less angry, Mother came to help them look, but even she could find no trace of the keys.

The sun was very hot and the sky was very blue. Geoffrey kept saying that it was just the day for a swim. Barry grew more and more miserable.

'This is hopeless,' said Mother at last, standing up and rubbing away the sand that had stuck to her knees. 'I'll go and make some lemonade.'

In a few moments she was standing by the sandpit with three glasses of lemonade and the biscuit tin on a tray.

'Come on, boys,' she said. 'I think the keys are lost and gone for ever. Daddy has a spare set in his desk at work. I've just phoned him and asked him to bring them home with him this evening.

It's too late to go swimming today anyway. The pool would be much too crowded so late in the afternoon.'

'It's all Barry's fault,' said Geoffrey sulkily. And Barry began to cry again.

'Oh, that's enough!' said Mother. 'Barry has had his punishment. Here's your lemonade, love, and help yourself to a biscuit.'

Barry wiped the sand off his hands by rubbing them on the grass, and then he put his hand into the long tall biscuit tin. But it wasn't a biscuit his fingers pulled out. It was the bunch of car keys!

'How on earth did they get in the biscuit tin?' asked Mother when the excitement of the discovery had calmed down a little. 'I was sure Barry must have brought them out to the sandpit.'

'I remember now, my hands were fiddling with the biscuits, too,' said Barry. 'I must have dropped the keys in with the biscuits when I heard you coming. Oh Mummy, I am sorry!'

Poor Barry! But that unfortunate afternoon did teach his naughty hands a lesson. I don't think they will be so eager to fiddle with keys in future.

ANN STANDEN

THE FIEND NEXT DOOR

It was the last day of the holidays and I didn't want to play with Angela Mitchell from next door. All I wanted was to spend a nice peaceful morning, reading a book in my very own private play-shed in the garden. My dad built the play-shed for me when I was little, and it's got a couple of old chairs and a table and a furry rug and some shelves and a great big cupboard where I can keep all my junk. And it's a lovely place to be on a sunny September morning because you can open the window and listen to the birds singing and smell the woodsmoke from my dad's bonfire.

I was just making myself comfortable with a Mars bar and my favourite Paddington Bear story when the shed door suddenly flew open and Angela fell in. And she was in such a state that I couldn't help getting involved, even though I should have known better.

'Charlie!' she burst out. 'I've done something terrible!' She flung herself into the old armchair and put her hands over her face.

My name is Charlotte really, but everybody calls me Charlie. Except Miss Bennett at school. And my mum sometimes, when she's especially cross with me because I can't seem to stay out of mischief for five minutes.

Of course I know perfectly well why it is that I keep on getting into so much trouble. My dad is always telling me that it's time I found myself a new best friend and told that Angela Mitchell to get lost. And to be honest I think he's right, because most of the time it's all her fault. Like the time when I was climbing a tree on Cookburn Common and she went off and phoned the fire brigade and they came tearing along in a great big fire engine and I had to pretend I needed rescuing. And the fireman who rescued me was the same one who put out the fire when we burned down Angela's dad's garage last summer. He wasn't pleased to see me again, I can tell you.

I don't think Angela always means to be bad. It just sort of happens. And it seems to happen most often when she's with me. I once wrote in a composition at school, 'Angela Mitchell is my very best FIEND'. It was a stupid spelling mistake, and everybody laughed like mad. But my dad says there's many a true word spoken in jest and if anybody deserves to be called a fiend it's Angela. I don't know why I bother with her, sometimes. And then at other times she can be really nice. You never know where you are. But you're never bored, that's for sure.

Angela is very good at having hysterics. Like the time I cut all her lovely long hair off with her mum's new dressmaking scissors and made her look like a scarecrow. But sometimes it's very hard to tell whether or not Angela's hysterics are real. So I just sat there for a while, staring at her and trying to decide if it was all a fake. Finally I got up and put my arm round her shoulders.

'There, there,' I said. And it seemed a pretty useless sort of thing to say, but it's what everybody says when you get upset, even when it doesn't do the slightest bit of good.

'I've done it this time,' she wailed. 'They'll put me in prison and it serves me right. Please, Charlie. You'll have to help me.'

'What've you done now?' I said, and she sobbed and moaned a bit more. I patted her shoulder helplessly.

'Come on, Angela,' I said. 'It can't be all that bad. Whatever it is.' She looked up at me and her eyes were all dark and tragic and filled with tears.

'It is,' she gulped, 'It's the most awfullest, terriblest, dreadfullest thing I've ever done in my whole life!'

Well, that made my blood curdle a bit, I can tell you, because she's done some pretty bad things in her time.

'Worse than putting dead spiders in Miss Menzies' cucumber sandwiches?' I said.

'Much worse than that,' she groaned.

'Worse than setting fire to your dad's garage?' I said fearfully, and Angela gave a great sob.

'TEN times worse than that!' she said. I swallowed hard.

'What then?' I said weakly, not really wanting to hear. Angela took a deep breath.

'I'll get twenty years for sure,' she said hopelessly. 'I've kid-napped a baby. A little baby girl. From outside the supermarket.' And she started to howl all over again.

I stood there with my mouth hanging open and I couldn't think of anything to say. And then I remembered all the times she'd told fibs and played tricks on me and got me to believe all kinds of rubbish.

'I don't believe you,' I said at last. 'I bet you're having me on. Even you wouldn't do a thing like that.'

She didn't answer. Instead she jumped up from her chair, flung open the shed door and pointed outside with a dramatic gesture of her arm. I poked my head out and my heart gave a sort of lurch in my chest.

On the path beside the shed wall was one of those folding baby-buggy pushchairs. And in it was a baby. A pretty little baby girl, in a pink woolly suit and a pink knitted bonnet with a frill around it.

'Oh, no!' I breathed. 'Oh, lord!'

The baby waved her arms and kicked her feet about and made cooing noises when she saw me, and I think she was the nicest baby I have ever seen. She had blue eyes and pink cheeks and little blonde curls peeping out from under her bonnet. Angela must have looked just like that when she was little.

We stood together in the doorway and gazed at the baby without saying anything for a while. Then Angela went out and started dragging the pushchair into the shed.

'You'll have to help me to hide her, Charlie,' she said. 'They'll be searching the whole village.'

And so before I knew what I was doing I had pulled the buggy inside and shut and bolted the door. Angela unfastened the safety harness and lifted the baby out on to the floor. And the baby started to crawl about, pulling things down off the shelves and tipping all the papers out of the rubbish bin. Angela and I sat side by side on an orange crate and watched her, and bit by bit the story came out.

'She was sitting outside the supermarket,' sniffed Angela, blowing her nose. 'And she looked so cute I stopped to say hello. And when she gave me this huge smile I don't know what came over me. I just sort of wanted to keep her for myself. I grabbed the pushchair and ran all the way here. Oh, Charlie,' she cried, clutching my arm. 'Will they send me to Borstal? Will they put me in a horrible grey uniform?'

'They'll put you in a straitjacket if you ask me,' I said sourly. 'You must be off your head.' I suddenly got to my feet and started to put the baby back in the buggy.

'Come on, Angela,' I said firmly. 'This has gone on long enough. You've got to take her back. And the sooner the better. If you're lucky they may not have called the police yet.'

But when I mentioned the police Angela got all in a panic and started sobbing and moaning all over again.

'You do it,' she begged. 'Please, Charlie! You take her back. I just daren't.'

'NOT BLOOMING LIKELY!' I shouted. And I wasn't half mad,

I can tell you. 'I'm not getting the blame! I'm not that stupid, Angela Mitchell!' We both sat down again and glared at each other.

By now the baby was getting bored with playing by herself and was starting to whimper a bit. I picked her up to give her a cuddle, but she wriggled fretfully in my arms and sucked noisily at her fist.

'She's hungry,' I said crossly to Angela. 'Now what are we going to do?'

'Get some milk and biscuits from your mum,' she said, as cool as anything. 'It's about time for elevenses, anyway.'

I scowled at her. 'Why me?' I said. 'Why can't you ask your mum? It's all your fault in the first place.'

'I can't,' said Angela. 'My mum's got a visitor. And you know how she hates me to pester her when she's having one of her coffee mornings. Go on, Charlie. Your mum won't mind.'

I grumbled a bit more, but I had to go in the end. Not to please Angela, but because the baby was really crying hard and I thought somebody might hear her.

'Get your mum to warm the milk, Charlie,' Angela shouted after me as I hurried up the garden towards the house.

My mum was in the kitchen mixing a cake. The electric mixer was on and Leo Sayer was singing at full volume on the record player and I had trouble making her understand what I wanted.

'What?' she said. 'Milk and biscuits? For you and Angela? Yes, all right. But you'll have to help yourself, sweetheart. I'm a bit busy at the moment.'

So I put a few biscuits on a tray and poured some milk into a small saucepan on the stove. My mum switched off the noisy mixer and raised her eyebrows at me.

'You don't like hot milk, Charlie,' she reminded me. 'What are you doing that for?'

'I'm just er ... warming it a bit,' I said, feeling my face go pink. 'It's a bit chilly this morning.'

My mum looked out of the window at the blue sky and the sunshine and shook her head in a baffled way.

'Please yourself,' she shrugged. 'But don't leave dirty saucepans for me to clear up, will you. I've got enough to do as it is.'

So after I had poured the warm milk into two plastic beakers I had to wash the saucepan and dry it and put it away. I put the milk on the tray and opened the back door and just at that moment the record came to an end and everything went quiet and you could hear the baby crying in the distance.

'What's that?' said my mum, holding the door for me so that I could use both hands for the tray. 'Surely you haven't got a baby down in the shed?'

I gave a funny sort of giggle.

'A what?' I said. 'A baby? Good heavens, no. It's only Angela. We're playing, er ... a sort of game.' And I fled down the path with the cups wobbling like mad and a nasty shaky feeling in my stomach because I hate telling fibs to anybody. Especially my mum.

Angela pulled me into the shed and slammed the door.

'You've been ages,' she complained. 'The baby's frantic. What took you so long?'

I didn't bother to explain. I sat the baby on my lap and held a beaker of milk to her mouth. She stopped howling at once and began to gulp it down, clutching at the beaker with both hands. We hardly spilt any at all, and before long the beaker was empty. Angela sat and watched us, grinning and munching my mum's homemade shortbread biscuits.

'We're taking this baby back,' I said. 'I'll just have to come with you, I suppose, since you won't go yourself. Have you thought about what sort of state the baby's mother must be in by now? I don't know how you can sit there grinning like that.'

Angela jumped up at once.

'You'll really go with me?' she said, all smiles. 'Charlie, you're the best friend I ever had.'

I strapped the baby back in her buggy and gave her a biscuit to chew.

'We'll put her back outside the supermarket,' I said. 'Maybe nobody'll see us. But mind, I'm not taking any of the blame if we're caught.'

The baby seemed a lot happier now, cooing and gurgling and kicking her feet about, and she didn't seem to mind a bit when I put a stripy hat on her head and covered her from neck to feet in an old woolly blanket that almost reached the ground.

'What's that for?' said Angela. 'Oh, I see. It's a disguise. Charlie Ellis, you are clever!'

'You and me next,' I told her. 'We don't want to be recognized either.'

So we rummaged about in my dressing-up box and found some old clothes to cover our own. I wore a pair of dark sunglasses and a cowboy hat and a long velvet coat down to my feet. And Angela wore my Auntie Vida's old fur coat and the black wig my dad made when he went to the tennis club Hallowe'en party as a witch. In the end we all looked so funny I just had to giggle, even though I was scared to death and sure we were going to get arrested any minute.

Angela kindly offered to let me push the buggy, would you believe, but I wasn't having any of that. So off we went down the path and into the street, with Angela pushing the buggy and me looking nervously around for panda cars.

Well, we didn't get very far, I can tell you. In fact we only got as far as Angela's front gate. And suddenly there was Angela's mum coming out of the house with her visitor.

And in spite of being so worried I couldn't help staring, because even though I'd never seen that lady in my life before I could tell straight away who she was. I've never seen two people more alike. They were as alike as a pair of socks. It could only be Auntie Sally's sister from Canada.

Anyway, they both looked astonished when they saw us in our weird clothes. They raised their eyebrows at one another and then they burst out laughing.

'Whatever are you up to?' said Angela's mum. 'We were just

on our way to find you. What are you all dressed up like this for?'

My knees were shaking a bit and I thought I'd leave it to Angela to make up some sort of story. But I couldn't believe my eyes when I looked at her, because she was grinning all over her face and didn't look bothered in the least.

The other lady knelt down and took the rug off the baby's shoulders.

'Hello, my little poppet,' she said, in that soppy cooing voice that grown-ups always use when they speak to babies, as if babies were all halfwitted. 'Did Sarah Jane have a lovely time with her cousin Angela, then? Did you miss your mummy, darling?' Then she turned to Angela with a smile.

'Thanks for looking after her, Angela,' she said. 'Your mum and I had time for a nice long chat, and it was lovely to catch up on all the news. I expect we'll see quite a lot of you now we've moved to Barlow. Has Sarah Jane been any trouble?'

Angela shook her head.

'She's been as good as gold,' she said, her eyes all sparkly with mischief. 'We've been playing a fantastic game, pretending we were kidnappers wanted by the police and hiding in Charlie's old shed and getting dressed up in disguises and stuff. Haven't we, Charlie?'

I nodded dumbly. There didn't seem a lot I could say. I felt a proper fool, and I went on standing there with my mouth hanging open like an idiot while Angela's mum introduced her twin sister Beth, who had been living in Canada for ten years and that was why I had never seen the baby before.

And then off they all went, laughing and chattering together, to have lunch at the Wimpy bar, leaving me in the street all by myself with my arms full of disguises. I trudged off home swearing to myself that I'd get my own back one of these days, and I gave Angela's gatepost a good kick on the way past which didn't do any good at all.

I was in a rotten temper when I got home, but suddenly I felt much better, because I found that my dad had come home unexpectedly for lunch and had brought fish and chips in with him from that nice new fish and chip shop down the road.

So while we were eating fish and chips and tomato ketchup and bread and butter I started to tell my mum and dad all about what had happened. And somehow the more I told it the funnier it sounded until we were all falling about laughing and wiping our eyes and shaking our heads and saying what a villain Angela was, and all of a sudden I wasn't a bit mad with her any longer.

SHEILA LAVELLE

FORGETFUL FRED

The richest man in the land, even richer than the King, was Bumberdumble Pott. He lived in an enormous house with forty-four rooms, and he had nine cooks, twelve housemaids, four butlers, sixteen helpers, and a young man named Fred who did everything that was left over.

Fred was good-looking and bright, but he was very absent-minded. This was because his head was full of music. When he should have been thinking about his job, he was thinking of songs instead, and when he should have been working, he was playing on his flute. If Bumberdumble Pott said to him, 'Fred, throw out the rubbish and hang up my coat,' Fred was just as likely to throw away the coat and hang up the rubbish.

In spite of this, Bumberdumble liked him and so did everyone else, because he was merry, kind, friendly, and always polite.

One day, Bumberdumble called together all the servants in the great hall of his house. Standing on the staircase where everyone could see and hear him, he said, 'As you all know, I am the richest man in the land.'

Everyone nodded. They knew.

'You might think I'd be very happy,' Bumberdumble continued, 'but I'm not. There is one thing I've wanted all my life, and that is the Bitter Fruit of Satisfaction. When I was young, I could have

154

gone to find it but I was too busy making money. Now I am too old to make the journey. But if one of you will go and get it for me, I will give him half my wealth so that he will be as rich as I am.'

Everyone thought that over. At last, the youngest of the butlers said, 'Where is the Bitter Fruit of Satisfaction?'

Bumberdumble looked worried. 'I am afraid it is a long way off,' he admitted. 'It is beyond six mountains and six sandy deserts, beyond the Boiling River and the Grimly Wood. And it is guarded by a Fire Drake.'

'A Fire Drake? What's that? Something like a dragon?'

'Worse than a dragon,' said Bumberdumble gloomily. 'Much worse.'

'Well,' said the youngest of the butlers, 'I can't go. I have to finish my job polishing the silver.'

'I can't go,' said the chief cook. 'I have a wife and four children.'

'I certainly can't go,' said the oldest housemaid. 'I have a sore knee.'

And the more the others thought about the distance and the difficulties and the Fire Drake at the end of it, the more they thought of reasons why they couldn't go.

But finally, Fred said, 'I'll go.'

'You?' everyone cried.

'Why not?' said Fred, cheerfully. 'I haven't a wife or any children, I'm healthy, and you can always hire someone else to take over my jobs.'

'But you'll forget where you're going before you've gone a kilometre,' said the chief butler, with a chuckle.

'I will give him a map,' said Bumberdumble. He came down the stairs and clapped Fred on the shoulder. 'Bring me back the Bitter Fruit, my boy, and you will be richer than a king.'

The next morning Fred set out. He had a knapsack full of food on his back, his flute in his pocket, a staff to lean on, and twenty gold pieces in his purse. He also had a map showing where the Bitter Fruit was, and Bumberdumble had hung this round his neck so he wouldn't forget to look at it.

Fred travelled for a whole, long year. He climbed six high rocky mountains, almost freezing at the tops of them. He tramped across six sandy deserts, almost dying of thirst. He crossed the Boiling River by going to its narrowest place and jumping from one slippery stone to another.

One evening, he came to an old dark house that stood on the edge of a vast dark wood. He was very weary, hungry, and tattered. His money had long ago been spent. He felt as if he could go no farther.

He knocked at the door, and it was opened by a pretty girl with blue eyes, black hair, and a smudge of dirt on her nose.

'Good evening,' said Fred, politely, and then he dropped his staff and would have fallen, but the girl caught his arm and helped him into the house.

There was a bright fire burning and a good smell of cooking in the air.

The girl sat Fred down at the long table and put a bowl of soup in front of him. While he ate, she sat down opposite and watched him.

'You've come a long way,' she said.

Fred told her who he was and where he was going. 'And I have no idea how to take the Bitter Fruit when I find it,' he said sadly, 'or how I shall escape the Fire Drake. But if you will let me stay here until I'm rested, maybe I will think of something.'

'This isn't my house,' said the girl. 'It belongs to the Witch of Grimly Wood. She's at a witchery meeting now, and while she's away you may certainly rest here and get your strength back. But when she returns, I don't know whether she'll let you stay, for she is the stingiest person in the world. Perhaps you can pay her in some way?'

'All I have is some music,' said Fred. 'What's your name?'

'Melissa,' said the girl.

'Then I'll play you some special Melissa music, by way of thanks,' said Fred.

He put the flute to his lips. His music was like the clear calling of summer birds at evening. Melissa listened and sighed. That night, Fred slept on the floor in front of the fire. The next day he rested and played his flute and told stories about his travels and made Melissa laugh. Working for a witch, she didn't get the chance to laugh very often. She was a good cook and fed him well, and she thought she had never liked anyone half so much.

The following morning, she said, 'I am going to help you. I have three gifts my father gave me before he died, and I'll lend them to you. Maybe they will help you get the Bitter Fruit.'

She brought out a pair of red slippers, a hat with a feather in it, and a sword.

'These,' she said, 'are the Shoes of Swiftness, the Cap of Darkness, and the Sword of Sharpness. The shoes will make you run swifter than an arrow, the cap will make you invisible, and the sword will cut through anything.'

'Fine!' said Fred. 'If I'm invisible, maybe I can steal the Bitter Fruit. If not, maybe I can kill the Fire Drake with the sword. And if that fails, I can run like anything.'

At that moment they heard a noise outside.

'It's the witch,' said Melissa. 'Don't say a word to her about where you're going or how much Bumberdumble is going to pay you. She loves gold more than anything.'

The door swung open. In came a puff of cold grey air, and with it the witch.

'Aha!' she croaked. 'A stranger! Who are you, and what do you mean by sitting in my kitchen and eating my food?'

'My name is Fred,' said Fred. And then, being absent-minded, he promptly forgot about Melissa's warning. 'I'm on my way to get the Bitter Fruit of Satisfaction,' he said. 'When I take it back to Bumberdumble Pott, he will give me half his gold and I'll be richer than a king.'

'Is that so?' said the witch. 'I know where the Bitter Fruit is – it's just the other side of the Grimly Wood. I'll get it and give it to Bumberdumble Pott and collect the gold myself!' She spun round on her toe, jumped on her broomstick, and shot out of the room, slamming the door behind her.

'Quick!' cried Melissa. 'The shoes!'

Fred pulled on the red slippers. He leaped up and off he ran. But not very far.

He had forgotten to open the door. *Thump!* He ran headfirst into it and knocked himself flat.

He struggled up, rubbing his head. 'I told you I was absent-minded, didn't I?' he said.

'Never mind,' said Melissa. 'I'll show you a short cut. With the magic shoes, you can still get there first.'

She led him outside and showed him a secret path among the trees. 'This will take you straight through Grimly Wood,' said she, 'to a high hedge of thorns. On the other side of the hedge is the Bitter Fruit.'

The Shoes of Swiftness carried Fred along the path like a flash of light from the eye of a lighthouse. At the high thorny hedge he drew the Sword of Sharpness. One-two, he slashed, and made a hole large enough to get through.

On the other side, there was a glass table.

On the table stood a silver tree with one small, dry, brown fruit hanging from it. And behind the table was the Fire Drake. It was scaly and slithery, bigger than a dragon and twice as fierce.

Fred snatched out the Cap of Darkness and put it on his head. But he was so busy looking at the Fire Drake that he wasn't thinking about what he was doing, and he put it on backwards. At once, everything disappeared. Everything but Fred. He couldn't see the Fire Drake or the glass table or the tree. He couldn't even see the ground. It looked as if he were standing on nothing in the middle of nothing.

But he could still feel the earth under his feet. In a panic, he dropped to his hands and knees.

It was the best thing he could have done, for at the same instant the Fire Drake blew out a sheet of flame. It would have crisped Fred up like a piece of burnt toast if it had touched him, but it went right over him.

'Oh,' he groaned. 'If only I weren't so absent-minded.'

He reached up and turned the Cap of Darkness round on his head. Now he could see everything again, but *he* was invisible. He got shakily to his feet. He could see the Fire Drake looking this way and that in puzzlement. He tiptoed over to the silver tree.

The fruit was gone.

He understood what had happened. While the Fire Drake had been shooting its flames at him, the witch had sneaked up and stolen the fruit.

Fred ran back through the Grimly Wood to the witch's house. There was the witch, just packing her suitcase for the long broomstick flight to Bumberdumble's house.

'Stop!' yelled Fred.

With one chop of the Sword of Sharpness he cut her broomstick in two.

The witch snatched a handful of ashes from the fire and threw

159

them into the air. They settled over Fred and then she could see him, like a faint grey shadow.

'So it's you, miserable wretch!' she screamed. 'I'll turn you into a piece of waste paper and throw you away.'

She began to mumble a wicked spell.

'Stop her!' cried Melissa. 'Use your sword!'

Fred lifted the sword. Then he lowered it again. 'I can't,' he said. 'It wouldn't be polite.'

The witch raised her hands. The spell was ready.

'Then cut the ground out from under her,' snapped Melissa.

Fred whirled the sword. He sliced away the floor under the witch's feet. Down she fell.

Under the floor there was a bottomless well. The witch fell into it and that was the end of her.

Fred removed the Cap of Darkness and dusted himself off. He handed the cap, the shoes, and the sword to Melissa.

'Thank you,' he said. 'But do you know, I forgot something.'

'What?'

'The Bitter Fruit of Satisfaction. I forgot that the witch was holding it. She is still holding it, wherever she is.'

'What a shame,' said Melissa.

Fred scratched his head.

'Oh, I don't know,' he said. 'If you will marry me, I would really rather have you than be richer than a king.'

So they settled down in the witch's house – after fixing the hole in the floor – and they were happy together. And since Fred could play as much music as he liked whenever he liked, he was never absent-minded again except once in a while.

As for Bumberdumble Pott, if he never got the Bitter Fruit, at any rate he remained the richest man in the land, and that was better than nothing.

JAY WILLIAMS

QUAKA RAJA

There was once a poor widow who lived in a hut at the edge of the forest with her four children.

She favoured her three daughters – Minnie Minnie, Minnie Bitana, and Philambo – but she did not care a whit for her son, Quaka Raja. Yet Quaka Raja was obedient and worked hard in the vegetable garden in front of the hut while his three sisters quarrelled and fought among themselves all day. They made fun of Quaka because he was kind to the birds and animals of the forest, and always saved some of his food for them.

Every Friday the widow set out for the village market where she sold the vegetables and fruit from her garden. Everyone flocked to buy her dasheen, yams, sweet potatoes, mangoes, sapodillas, peas and beans, and soon her basket was empty. With the money she received she bought food to take home and filled her basket with all manner of goodies. There was *arape*, a cornmeal pancake with spicy meat filling, molasses balls, sugar cakes, black pudding, and many other things besides.

When she returned to the little hut she stood outside and sang:

> *Minnie Minnie, come here,*
> *Minnie Bitana, come here,*
> *Philambo, come here,*
> *Leave Quaka Raja one dey.*

As soon as the three daughters heard the song they ran to unlock the door, pushing Quaka Raja aside as the mother did not want him. Then the food was shared. But Quaka Raja's portion was always the least of all.

Now in the forest lived a man called Zobolak who was feared by all the villagers. He was a hideous-looking creature, with a deeply scarred face, fiery red eyes, and arms and legs that were huge and round, with clawlike hands and feet. Mothers warned their children to keep away from the forest, for whenever a child disappeared it was whispered that Zobolak had stolen it, though no one could prove this was true.

One Friday, when the widow returned from market, Zobolak, who had been hunting agouti, happened to be nearby. Peeping through the bushes he heard the widow's song and saw the three daughters run out to greet their mother. Zobolak could hardly restrain himself from rushing forward and seizing the three girls then and there, but he was as cunning as the wild animals which he hunted in the forest. He settled down to wait.

The next Friday the widow again set out for market. After some time had passed, Zobolak crept up to the hut and sang in a high voice:

> *Minnie Minnie, come here,*
> *Minnie Minnie, come here,*
> *Minnie Minnie, come here,*
> *Leave Quaka Raja one dey.*

The three daughters ran to open the door, but Quaka Raja said, 'Sisters, sisters, do not go out. That is not Mamma's song.' And he stood in front of the door and would not let them out even though they tugged and pulled until they were exhausted.

When the children did not open the door, Zobolak hid in the forest until the mother returned. But he stayed close by to listen carefully to the song.

The following Friday the mother set off once more for the village, and after a little while Zobolak crept up to the hut and sang in a high voice:

> Minnie Minnie, come here,
> Minnie Minnie, come here,
> Philambo, come here,
> Leave Quaka Raja one dey.

The three daughters ran to unlock the door, but Quaka Raja said, 'Sisters, sisters, do not go out. That is not Mamma's song.'

They tugged and pulled and scratched him but he stood fast in front of the door, and at last they fell down exhausted.

Once more Zobolak crept away into the forest when they did not open the door, but he waited close by until the mother returned.

At last Friday came. Zobolak's eyes gleamed with excitement as he waited. No sooner had the widow left than he crept up to the hut and sang in a high voice:

> Minnie Minnie, come here,
> Minnie Bitana, come here,
> Philambo, come here,
> Leave Quaka Raja one dey.

Quaka Raja stood in front of the door and begged his sisters not to go out. Their mother had just left. How could she be back so soon? But they tugged and pulled and scratched and kicked him so hard that he fell to the ground, senseless.

They ran out to greet their mother, but – 'Ayayayayay!' – there was Zobolak waiting for them. He threw them into his sack, slung it over his shoulder and off he went into the forest where he lived.

By the time Quaka Raja came to his senses Zobolak was far, far away. Quaka Raja ran hither and yon calling his sisters, but only the birds cheeped back at him. When his mother returned from the village and he told her what had happened, she was wild with grief. But Quaka Raja said, 'Do not cry, Mamma, I will go and look for my sisters and bring them back to you.'

At first his mother begged him not to go. 'Son, you are all that I have now,' she said; 'I cannot lose you too.'

But Quaka Raja pleaded with her until she agreed. So she packed him some of the food she had brought back and sent him off with tears in her eyes.

Quaka walked long and he walked far. He walked all day, and as night fell he saw a light in the distance. As he approached it he came to a hut half hidden by trees and creepers. Inside he could hear his sisters crying.

What to do? He could not rescue them without help. As he stood under a tree thinking, an owl overhead hooted and nearly frightened him out of his wits. At that moment he thought of a plan. He could ask his friends, the birds and animals of the

forest, to help him.

Much later that night, as the moon climbed down behind the mountain, the stillness of the forest was shattered by a horrible noise. Zobolak was startled out of his sleep as the sound grew louder and louder and came nearer and nearer, like the shrieks of a hundred demons coming after him. He rushed out of his hut like a hunted animal and ran deep into the forest, over the mountains, anywhere away from that terrible noise.

What was that noise? It was the sound of owls hooting, frogs croaking, wild cats yowling, wild pigs snorting and grunting, parrots screaming and birds chirping and whistling. They had all come to help Quaka Raja.

So Quaka Raja returned home with his sisters and his mother was so proud of him that if he weren't such a sensible child he would have been thoroughly spoiled.

And for all we know Zobolak is still running!

GRACE HALLWORTH

MANY MOONS

Once upon a time, in a kingdom by the sea, there lived a little Princess named Lenore. She was ten years old, going on eleven. One day Lenore fell ill of a surfeit of raspberry tarts and took to her bed.

The Royal Physician came to see her and took her temperature and felt her pulse and made her stick out her tongue. The Royal Physician was worried. He sent for the King, Lenore's father, and the King came to see her.

'I will get you anything your heart desires,' the King said. 'Is there anything your heart desires?'

'Yes,' said the Princess. 'I want the moon. If I can have the moon, I will be well again.'

Now the King had a great many wise men who always got for him anything he wanted, so he told his daughter that she could have the moon. Then he went to the throne room and pulled a bell cord, three long pulls and a short pull, and presently the Lord High Chamberlain came into the room.

The Lord High Chamberlain was a large, fat man who wore thick glasses which made his eyes seem twice as big as they really were. This made the Lord High Chamberlain seem twice as wise as he really was.

'I want to get the moon,' said the King. 'The Princess Lenore wants the moon. If she can have the moon, she will get well again.'

'The moon?' exclaimed the Lord High Chamberlain, his eyes widening. This made him look four times as wise as he really was.

'Yes, the moon,' said the King. 'M-o-o-n, moon. Get it tonight, tomorrow at the latest.'

The Lord High Chamberlain wiped his forehead with a handkerchief and then blew his nose loudly. 'I have got a great many things for you in my time, Your Majesty,' he said. 'It just happens that I have with me a list of the things I have got for you in my time.' He pulled a long scroll of parchment out of his pocket. 'Let me see, now.' He glanced at the list, frowning. 'I have got ivory, apes and peacocks, rubies, opals and emeralds, black orchids, pink elephants and blue poodles, gold bugs, scarabs and flies in amber, hummingbirds' tongues, angels' feathers and unicorns' horns, giants, midgets and mermaids, frankincense, ambergris and myrrh, troubadours, minstrels and dancing women, a pound of butter, two dozen eggs and a sack of sugar – sorry, my wife wrote that in there.'

'I don't remember any blue poodles,' said the King.

'It says blue poodles right here on the list, and they are checked off with a little check mark,' said the Lord High Chamberlain. 'So there must have been blue poodles. You just forget.'

'Never mind the blue poodles,' said the King. 'What I want now is the moon.'

'I have sent as far as Samarkand and Araby and Zanzibar to get things for you, Your Majesty,' said the Lord High Chamberlain, 'but the moon is out of the question. It is thirty-five thousand miles away and it is bigger than the room the Princess lies in. Furthermore, it is made of molten copper. I cannot get the moon for you. Blue poodles, yes; the moon, no.'

The King flew into a rage and told the Lord High Chamberlain to leave the room and to send the Royal Wizard to the throne room.

The Royal Wizard was a little, thin man with a long face. He wore a high red peaked hat covered with silver stars, and a long blue robe covered with golden owls. His face grew very pale when the King told him that he wanted the moon for his little daughter, and that he expected the Royal Wizard to get it.

'I have worked a great deal of magic for you in my time, Your Majesty,' said the Royal Wizard. 'As a matter of fact, I just happen to have in my pocket a list of the wizardries I have performed for you.' He drew a paper from a deep pocket of his robe. 'It begins: "Dear Royal Wizard: I am returning herewith the so-called philosopher's stone which you claimed" – no, that isn't it.' The Royal Wizard brought a long scroll of parchment from another pocket of his robe. 'Here it is,' he said. 'Now, let's see. I have squeezed blood out of turnips for you, and turnips out of blood. I have produced rabbits out of silk hats, and silk hats out of rabbits. I have conjured up flowers, tambourines and doves out of nowhere, and nowhere out of flowers, tambourines and doves. I have brought you divining rods, magic wands and crystal spheres in which to behold the future. I have compounded philtres, unguents and potions to cure heartbreak, surfeit and ringing in the ears. I have made you my own special mixture of wolfbane, nightshade and eagles' tears to ward off witches, demons and things that go bump in the night. I have given you seven-league boots, the golden touch and a cloak of invisibility –'

168

'It didn't work,' said the King. 'The cloak of invisibility didn't work.'

'Yes, it did,' said the Royal Wizard.

'No, it didn't,' said the King. 'I kept bumping into things, the same as ever.'

'The cloak is supposed to make you invisible,' said the Royal Wizard. 'It is not supposed to keep you from bumping into things.'

'All I know is, I kept bumping into things,' said the King.

The Royal Wizard looked at his list again. 'I got you,' he said, 'horns from Elfland, sand from the Sandman and gold from the rainbow. Also a spool of thread, a paper of needles, and a lump of beeswax – sorry, those are things my wife wrote down for me to get her.'

'What I want you to do now,' said the King, 'is to get me the moon. The Princess Lenore wants the moon, and when she gets it, she will be well again.'

'Nobody can get the moon,' said the Royal Wizard. 'It is a hundred and fifty thousand miles away, and it is made of green cheese, and it is twice as big as this palace.'

The King flew into another rage and sent the Royal Wizard back to his cave. Then he rang a gong and summoned the Royal Mathematician.

The Royal Mathematician was a bald-headed, near-sighted man, with a skull-cap on his head and a pencil behind each ear. He wore a black suit with white numbers on it.

'I don't want to hear a long list of all the things you have figured out for me since 1907,' the King said to him. 'I want you to figure out right now how to get the moon for the Princess Lenore. When she gets the moon, she will be well again.'

'I am glad you mentioned all the things I have figured out for you since 1907,' said the Royal Mathematician. 'It so happens that I have a list of them with me.'

He pulled a long scroll of parchment out of a pocket and looked at it. 'Now, let me see. I have figured out for you the distance between the horns of a dilemma, night and day, and A and Z. I have computed how far is Up, how long it takes to get to Away, and what becomes of Gone. I have discovered the length of the sea serpent, the price of the priceless and the square of the hippopotamus. I know where you are when you are at Sixes and Sevens, how much Is you have to have to make an Are, and how many birds you can catch with the salt in the ocean – 187,796,132, if it would interest you to know.'

'There aren't that many birds,' said the King.

'I didn't say there were,' said the Royal Mathematician. 'I said if there were.'

'I don't want to hear about seven hundred million imaginary birds,' said the King. 'I want you to get the moon for the Princess Lenore.'

'The moon is three hundred thousand miles away,' said the Royal Mathematician. 'It is round and flat like a coin, only it is made of asbestos, and it is half the size of this kingdom. Furthermore, it is pasted on the sky. Nobody can get the moon.'

The King flew into still another rage and sent the Royal Mathematician away. Then he rang for the Court Jester. The Jester came bounding into the throne room in his motley and his cap and bells, and sat at the foot of the throne.

'What can I do for you, Your Majesty?' asked the Court Jester.

'Nobody can do anything for me,' said the King mournfully. 'The Princess Lenore wants the moon, and she cannot be well till she gets it, but nobody can get it for her. Every time I ask anybody for the moon, it gets larger and further away. There is nothing you can do for me except play on your lute. Something sad.'

'How big do they say the moon is,' asked the Court Jester, 'and how far away?'

'The Lord High Chamberlain says it is thirty-five thousand miles away and bigger than the Princess Lenore's room,' said the King. 'The Royal Wizard says it is a hundred and fifty thousand miles away and twice as big as this palace. The Royal Mathematician says it is three hundred thousand miles away and half the size of this kingdom.'

The Court Jester strummed on his lute for a little while. 'They are all wise men,' he said, 'and so they must all be right. If they are all right, then the moon must be just as large and as far away as each person thinks it is. The thing to do is find out how big the Princess Lenore thinks it is, and how far away.'

'I never thought of that,' said the King.

'I will go and ask her, Your Majesty,' said the Court Jester. And he crept softly into the little girl's room.

The Princess Lenore was awake, and she was glad to see the Court Jester, but her face was very pale and her voice very weak.

'Have you brought the moon to me?' she asked.

'Not yet,' said the Court Jester, 'but I will get it for you right away. How big do you think it is?'

'It is just a little smaller than my thumbnail,' she said, 'for when I hold my thumbnail up at the moon, it just covers it.'

'And how far away is it?' asked the Court Jester.

'It is not as high as the big tree outside my window,' said the Princess, 'for sometimes it gets caught in the top branches.'

'It will be very easy to get the moon for you,' said the Court Jester. 'I will climb the tree tonight when it gets caught in the top branches and bring it to you.'

Then he thought of something else. 'What is the moon made of, Princess?' he asked.

'Oh,' she said. 'It's made of gold, of course, silly.'

The Court Jester left the Princess Lenore's room and went to see the Royal Goldsmith. He had the Royal Goldsmith make a tiny round golden moon just a little smaller than the thumbnail of the Princess Lenore. Then he had him string it on a golden chain so the Princess could wear it around her neck.

'What is this thing I have made?' asked the Royal Goldsmith when he had finished it.

'You have made the moon,' said the Court Jester. 'That is the moon.'

'But the moon,' said the Royal Goldsmith, 'is five hundred thousand miles away and is made of bronze and is round like a marble.'

'That's what you think,' said the Court Jester as he went away with the moon.

The Court Jester took the moon to the Princess Lenore, and she was overjoyed. The next day she was well again and could get up and go out in the gardens to play.

But the King's worries were not yet over. He knew that the moon would shine in the sky again that night, and he did not want the Princess Lenore to see it. If she did, she would know that the moon she wore on a chain around her neck was not the real moon.

So the King sent for the Lord High Chamberlain and said, 'We must keep the Princess Lenore from seeing the moon when it shines in the sky tonight. Think of something.'

The Lord High Chamberlain tapped his forehead with his fingers thoughtfully and said, 'I know just the thing. We can make some dark glasses for the Princess Lenore. We can make them so dark that she will not be able to see anything at all through them. Then she will not be able to see the moon when it shines in the sky.'

This made the King very angry, and he shook his head from side to side. 'If she wore dark glasses, she would bump into things,' he said, 'and then she would be ill again.' So he sent the Lord High Chamberlain away and called the Royal Wizard.

'We must hide the moon,' said the King, 'so that the Princess Lenore will not see it when it shines in the sky tonight. How are we going to do that?'

The Royal Wizard stood on his hands and then he stood on his head and then he stood on his feet again. 'I know what we can do,' he said. 'We can stretch some black velvet curtains on poles. The curtains will cover all the palace gardens like a circus tent, and the Princess Lenore will not be able to see through them, so she will not see the moon in the sky.'

The King was so angry at this that he waved his arms around. 'Black velvet curtains would keep out the air,' he said. 'The Princess Lenore would not be able to breathe, and she would be ill again.' So he sent the Royal Wizard away and summoned the Royal Mathematician.

'We must do something,' said the King, 'so that the Princess Lenore will not see the moon when it shines in the sky tonight. If you know so much, figure out a way to do that.'

The Royal Mathematician walked around in a circle, and then he walked around in a square, and then he stood still. 'I have it!' he said. 'We can set off fireworks in the gardens every night. We will make a lot of silver fountains and golden cascades, and when they go off, they will fill the sky with so many sparks that it will be as light as day and the Princess Lenore will not be able to see the moon.'

The King flew into such a rage that he began jumping up and down. 'Fireworks would keep the Princess Lenore awake,' he said. 'She would not get any sleep at all and she would be ill again.' So the King sent the Royal Mathematician away.

When he looked up again, it was dark outside and he saw the bright rim of the moon just peeping over the horizon. He jumped up in a great fright and rang for the Court Jester. The Court Jester came bounding into the room and sat down at the foot of the throne.

'What can I do for you, Your Majesty?' he asked.

'Nobody can do anything for me,' said the King, mournfully. 'The moon is coming up again. It will shine into the Princess Lenore's bedroom, and she will know it is still in the sky and that

she does not wear it on a golden chain around her neck. Play me something on your lute, something very sad, for when the Princess sees the moon, she will be ill again.'

The Court Jester strummed on his lute. 'What do your wise men say?' he asked.

'They can think of no way to hide the moon that will not make the Princess Lenore ill,' said the King.

The Court Jester played another song, very softly. 'Your wise men know everything,' he said, 'and if they cannot hide the moon, then it cannot be hidden.'

The King put his head in his hands again and sighed. Suddenly he jumped up from his throne and pointed to the windows. 'Look!' he cried. 'The moon is already shining into the Princess Lenore's bedroom. Who can explain how the moon can be shining in the sky when it is hanging on a golden chain around her neck?'

The Court Jester stopped playing on his lute. 'Who could explain how to get the moon when your wise men said it was too large and too far away? It was the Princess Lenore. Therefore the Princess Lenore is wiser than your wise men and knows more about the moon than they do. So I will ask *her*.' And before the King could stop him, the Court Jester slipped quietly out of the throne room and up the wide marble staircase to the Princess Lenore's bedroom.

The Princess was lying in bed, but she was wide awake and she was looking out of the window at the moon shining in the sky. Shining in her hand was the moon the Court Jester had got for her. He looked very sad, and there seemed to be tears in his eyes.

'Tell me, Princess Lenore,' he said mournfully, 'how can the moon be shining in the sky when it is hanging on a golden chain around your neck?'

The Princess looked at him and laughed. 'That is easy, silly,' she said. 'When I lose a tooth, a new one grows in its place, doesn't it?'

'Of course,' said the Court Jester. 'And when the unicorn loses his horn in the forest, a new one grows in the middle of his forehead.'

'That is right,' said the Princess. 'And when the Royal Gardener cuts the flowers in the garden, other flowers come to take their place.'

'I should have thought of that,' said the Court Jester, 'for it is the same way with the daylight.'

'And it is the same way with the moon,' said the Princess Lenore. 'I guess it is the same way with everything.' Her voice became very low and faded away, and the Court Jester saw that she was asleep. Gently he tucked the covers in around the sleeping Princess.

But before he left the room, he went over to the window and winked at the moon, for it seemed to the Court Jester that the moon had winked back at him.

JAMES THURBER

THE CATS WHO STAYED FOR DINNER

One evening in spring, a man and a woman moved into a new house.

Just outside their door there was a garden. It was a pretty garden, with flowers and grass and even a tree.

They were very happy, because it isn't easy to find a real garden of your very own, right in the middle of a big city.

The next morning, as soon as they woke up, they ran to the window to admire their garden.

But what do you think they saw? CATS!

They saw so many cats they almost couldn't see the flowers, or the grass, or the tree.

Big cats, black cats, little cats, yellow cats, white cats, grey cats, kittens. Cats with spots, and cats with stripes. And every single cat was skinny, scraggly, scrawny and smudged with the soot of the city. And every cat had fleas.

'Oh, dear!' cried the man and the woman. 'There are so many cats in our garden, there isn't enough room for us.'

They shouted, 'Go away! Shoo! Go home!'

But the cats only sat and stared at the man and woman. They

175

could not go home, because they had no home. The little garden was the only place they had to call their own.

All day the cats played in the pretty garden. They chased the beetles and the butterflies, and smelt the flowers, and climbed the tree, and played a game of tag along the top of the fence.

They had a very good time.

But the man and the woman did not have a good time at all. They wanted to sow flower seeds, and mow the long grass, and dig out the choking weeds, and rest in the sweet spring sun.

But with all those cats in the little garden, there simply wasn't room enough for them too.

That night, the cats disappeared. They went out in search of food.

Every night they had to look for left-overs that had been thrown away, for, since they had no home, they had no one to feed them.

The man and woman went into the garden.

They found a big hole under the fence.

'This is how those cats get in,' they decided. 'We will fill it in, and then we will have the garden to ourselves.' They filled in the hole under the fence.

The next morning they woke up smiling.

They hurried to the window to admire their garden.

But can you guess what they saw?

YES! Cats!

The big cats had climbed over the fence. Then they had dug a new hole under the fence to let in the kittens that were still too little to climb so high.

Every day the cats played in the pretty garden. They would not go away.

The man and woman were the ones who had to stay away. They could only look at the weeds growing stronger and the grass growing longer. They could only look at the sun and their tree. They were most unhappy.

One evening the woman found that there was a bit of milk left over after supper.

'I may as well give it to those skinny, scraggly, scrawny cats,' she decided. She poured it into a pan and put it in the garden. That was on Monday.

On Tuesday, she ordered a whole extra quart of milk from the milkman. By mistake, of course.

Do you know what she did with it?

On Wednesday, she bought too much chopped meat at the butcher's shop – another mistake?

On Thursday, she came upon an extra dozen eggs in her shopping bag. But they did not go to waste, for eggs are fine for cats.

On Friday, the mackerel in the market looked so firm and fresh that the woman completely forgot that they were having supper with friends that evening. She bought some mackerel and brought it home.

Then, of course, she couldn't throw it away – because she knew how cats feel about FISH.

'Now mind you,' the woman warned the cats, 'just because I give you food, you mustn't think I like having you here in our garden. I just happen to have bought this extra food by mistake.'

The cats sat still and stared at her. Then they all CLOSED their big, round, yellow-green eyes.

On Sunday, it rained.

From their window, the man and woman could see the cats huddled together under the weeds.

'I don't have much to do today,' the man announced. 'I think I'll rig up some kind of shelter for those cats – just for something to do.'

He made a tent of striped canvas and stretched it over a corner of the garden so that the cats would have a dry place to sleep.

'But remember,' he scolded, 'just because I've made a shelter for you from the rain, you are not to think I like having you here in our garden. I just happened to have nothing else to do today.'

The cats sat still and stared at him. Then – each one WINKED one big, round, yellow-green eye.

And so summer went slowly by.

The cats began to be not quite so skinny, scraggly, scrawny, because the woman fed them every day. They began to feel good.

And when cats feel good – as you've probably noticed – they begin to wash themselves. They washed and they washed, and they washed away their smudge of city soot. They washed so hard, they even washed away their fleas!

Then one day, winter came. All of a sudden, it snowed and the wind was wild. The man and woman stayed indoors, warm and snug.

The cats huddled together under the icicles in the little garden. The man and woman almost couldn't see them through the thick frost on the window. But they knew they were there. Because now they knew that the cats had no other place to go to.

'I think I'll do a bit of building at my workbench in the basement,' said the man. 'Just to get some practice, you understand.'

He worked all day, hammering and sawing. He worked almost all night, too.

The woman could not sleep for all the racket he was making. Bamm – buzz. Bamm – bang. Bang. Bang.

And she could not sleep in the quiet in between. Because then she could hear the mewing of the cats in the cold quiet of the snow.

In the morning she ran to the window.

What did she see?

Yes! Cats! But look! What else?

A row of tiny houses!

They went into the garden – the man and the woman. This time

he did not shout and stamp. This time she did not scold and swish her apron.

This time they said, 'At first we did not want you here. But now we must admit that we've come to like having you for our very own. We know now that there is room for all of us in this pretty garden.'

The cats sat and stared at them.

But this time their big, round, yellow-green eyes – SMILED!

PHYLLIS ROWAND

BABY SPARROW

When sparrows built a nest up between the pipes outside Paul's bedroom, he was very pleased. He couldn't see the whole nest even when he pressed his face against the window, but he could see bits of straw sticking out from one edge of it.

He couldn't see the mother sparrow sitting on her nest, but he often saw the father sparrow bringing her food. He never saw the eggs, of course, for they were at the bottom of the nest. But when the eggs hatched out, when the baby birds had come out of their shells, he could sometimes *hear* them.

When there wasn't an aeroplane roaring overhead, when there wasn't a car screeching its brakes, when the carpet cleaner wasn't rumbling about in his house, *then* he could hear the baby birds. Often he stood quite still, close by the window, and listened to their high little voices cheeping for food.

The mother bird and the father bird worked hard all day fetching food for their hungry family. The tiny sparrows grew and grew until one day Paul ran to his mother saying, 'I can see little beaks poking over the edge of the nest. The baby birds must be getting big.'

'Let's hope they don't fall out,' said his mother.

'Yes,' said Paul, 'they might get killed if they did.'

180

Paul didn't like to think about that, so he went inside and helped his mother to clean the house. While she used the carpet cleaner, he used the floor mop. He liked the long handle, and he liked the fluffy head of the mop that gathered up the dust. 'Flippy, floppy soft,' he said it was. He liked pushing the floor mop all along the hall. It was like driving some sort of traffic – he wasn't sure what.

That day, when he had finished helping, his mother shook the mop as usual, and then decided to wash it. When it was washed she took it out through the kitchen door and propped it against the coal bunkers, with its flippy, floppy soft top pointing upwards.

She said, 'It'll dry there in the sun. Don't touch it, Paul.'

Paul didn't touch it. He forgot all about it, and so did his mother. In fact, it stayed out all day and all night and all the next morning.

Paul was in his bedroom playing on the floor. Now and again he heard the baby sparrows chirping, but he had got used to them by now, and he didn't listen very hard.

At least he didn't stop playing to listen until the squawking was so loud that it made him stand up and go to the window. They *were* making a noise. He looked up. Only part of the noise came from up there in the nest, and part of the noise seemed to be down below him. How strange! At first he couldn't understand it.

Then he *did* understand it, for a baby sparrow had fallen from the nest. But it had not fallen on the hard ground. It had been lucky. Can you guess where it had landed? On the upturned floor mop that was now quite dry!

Paul wasn't a minute in getting downstairs. As he went he was calling to his mother, 'Hurry, hurry, but don't touch the floor mop. Don't touch it! A baby sparrow's in it!'

His mother opened the kitchen door and looked out. She lifted Paul up so that he could see. There on the flippy, floppy mop, there with its open mouth bigger than its head, squawked the baby sparrow. It was feeling about with its feet. Big feet they were.

Paul's mother said, 'What a shock for the poor little thing, and I don't think it likes our floor mop as a nest.'

'Get him out,' said Paul.

So Paul's mother lifted out the baby bird and held it in both hands. Up above, the mother sparrow flew round and round, not knowing what to do.

181

Paul said, 'Put her baby on the lawn and then she'll feed it.'

But his mother said, 'What about cats? It wouldn't take them long to find a baby bird on a lawn, and remember, it can't fly.'

Paul shuddered. He had forgotten for a moment about cats. 'A cat shan't have it,' he said. 'We'll take it in the house and feed it.'

But the baby bird squawked and squawked. It wanted its mother.

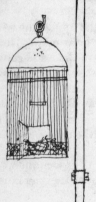

It didn't want to go and live in Paul's house. So what were Paul and his mother to do?

I'll tell you what they did. They borrowed a bird cage from Miss Mabel who lived next door and who once long ago had had a canary. The bird cage was lying empty in her cellar, but Miss Mabel was glad to fetch it up and clean it.

Paul made a bed in the cage for the baby sparrow. He made it out of grass and flower petals and his teddy's old jersey. His mother took down the washing line and hung the cage on the hook there on the house wall, where the mother sparrow would see her baby every time she came to the nest.

Then they opened the cage door wide, and Paul's mother fixed wire across the bottom of its doorway so that the baby sparrow couldn't fall out.

Paul said, 'Are you sure its mother will come to feed it?'

'No,' said his mother, 'I'm not sure. We'll go into the house and watch.'

And that is what they did. The mother sparrow had been watching them anxiously. Now she saw Paul and his mother go inside and shut the kitchen door. They went up to Paul's room and waited behind the curtain. It was a very short wait, luckily. In less than five minutes the mother sparrow flew to the cage with food for her baby. In another minute the father sparrow brought food too. And all day long they fed the babies in the nest and the baby in the cage.

That night Paul was lifted up to put a cover over the cage to keep the sparrow warm and dry in case of rain. For three more days the baby sparrow stayed in the cage, and then can you guess what happened?

It didn't fall out. It flew out. Yes, it had learnt to fly.

MARY COCKETT

NEVER MEDDLE
WITH MAGIC

Old men's socks,
Chicken pox,
Spells and games and jokes.
Rat and bat,
And mice and rice,
Jinx, tricks, hoax.

Uttering the magic words, Professor Molecule sprinkled in the salt, and poured the blue super acid fizz into the pink magic potion.

BANG! The test tubes exploded, the room rocked, the Professor's spectacles fell into the pink potion, and the budgie flung himself

183

on the floor of his cage with shrieks of, 'Don't let the cat in! Don't let the cat in!'

Professor Molecule did not even have a cat, but the budgie always shouted this when in distress. Mrs Rub Tub bustled into the room, choking.

'Botheration,' spluttered the Professor, 'another experiment gone wrong. If that spell had worked, rice pudding growers all over the world would have been rich overnight and I would have been quite famous.'

'That would have been nice,' said Mrs Rub Tub, stepping over a pile of rubble. Mrs Rub Tub was the Professor's housekeeper. It was her job to cook the meals and tidy the house. Tidying the house was a particularly difficult job after one of the Professor's more unsuccessful experiments.

'Making spells is a tricky business,' said the Professor. 'The secret is in the stirring. It has to thicken in the way a plot thickens. Do you understand me, my dear Mrs Rub Tub?' Mrs Rub Tub didn't.

'Let me make it a little clearer,' went on the Professor, putting on his spectacles and wondering why he couldn't see through them. Mrs Rub Tub took them from him and kindly wiped off the pink potion. 'You stir a spell to thicken it as you would stir a soup to thicken it or a gravy or a scrambled egg or custard.'

'Now I understand,' smiled Mrs Rub Tub, 'but spells need hours of cooking. You couldn't possibly stir one all the time, could you?'

'No I couldn't,' said the Professor, 'but I'm sure the children would if I let them off school for the afternoon.'

The children were Alastair, a fine boy of seven with a shock of thick black hair, and a girl called Miriam who was also seven. They were twins.

When they sat down to lunch that day Professor Molecule said, 'I am going out to buy some new test tubes, and I want you two children to stir a magic spell. You must stir it continuously. You must stir and stir, but please remember that magic can be very dangerous indeed if it is handled unwisely. Never, NEVER meddle with magic.'

After lunch the children put the plates into the washing-up machine, a little something the Professor had invented to save Mrs Rub Tub's time. Actually it did not save time at all because the tea cups usually came out minus their handles and Mrs Rub Tub spent all her afternoons gluing them back on again. The Professor put on his wellingtons and his big black cloak, took his walking cane and went out. The children went up to the study to stir the magic potion. They stirred and stirred and the potion grew thicker and thicker.

'This potion looks very magic indeed,' said Alastair, 'I think I will read a spell to go with it.'

'No you mustn't,' said Miriam, shocked. 'Don't you remember? The Professor said we must never, NEVER meddle with magic.'

'Did he?' said Alastair absent-mindedly. 'I didn't hear,' and he took down a heavy spell book entitled, *The Full Works of Dr Boom 1816–1890*. He thumbed through the thick yellow pages.

'After all, Miriam,' he said, 'we couldn't make a worse mess than the Professor often makes. Here's a spell, a nice short one.'

> Goblins, ghosties, goulies, genies,
> Muffling, mumbling, mouldy meanies.

BOOM! The windows flew open, a torrent of wind stormed in and a stout genie fell head over heels into the room and rolled about on the floor, all tangled up in the lace curtains!

'One day,' muttered the strange and struggling genie, 'I will make a graceful and elegant landing, and with something of a smile at the corners of my mouth I will make a long sweeping bow and say, "You called?" '

Alastair helped the genie out of the curtains. Both children were thoroughly alarmed. The budgie lay at the bottom of his cage muttering softly, 'Don't let the cat in. Don't let the cat in,' over and over again.

Once disentangled, the children saw what the genie looked like. He was short and too fat, with a sun tan that suggested he had lived somewhere very hot. On his head there was a blue silk turban, and he wore a pink silk jacket, green silk trousers and blue slippers turned up at the toes. Miriam thought that his clothes were rather like her pyjamas.

'Do you think I could have a cup of tea?' he asked. 'I've just flown all the way from India very fast indeed, and I'm spitting feathers.' There was a distraught squawk from the budgie cage!

Downstairs Mrs Rub Tub was putting on the kettle, setting the best china and opening a packet of Indian tea. She thought the genie would be more used to Indian tea than the blend she usually bought from the corner shop.

'You must be tired after your flight, Mr ... er ... Mr Genie,' said Mrs Rub Tub, trying to engage the genie in polite conversation. The genie meanwhile had his hand firmly jammed in the electric mincer and was cutting his finger nails. There was nothing like it in the Far East.

'Back home,' said the genie, 'all the housework is done by magic. Let me give you a little demonstration, my dear Mrs Rub Tub. How would you like the whole house cleaned from top to bottom?' Mrs Rub Tub looked doubtful, but the genie carefully managed not to notice the look.

'With the aid of a magic spell,' he went on, 'and with nothing up my sleeve I will magic the mop and bucket out of the cupboard and together they will clean the kitchen.' Completely by magic (and there wasn't anything up his sleeve), the bucket jumped into the sink and the hot-water tap filled it up to the top. Unfortunately there were a lot of expensive plates in the sink when the bucket jumped in and every single one of them broke. Then the soap box emptied itself into the hot water. It didn't just empty a thimble full – it emptied out all one and a half pounds of soapy flakes. In a matter of seconds the kitchen was swamped in soapy suds and oozing foam. The mop raced round the kitchen energetically. It mopped the linoleum, it mopped the curtains, and it mopped all the icing off the cake Mrs Rub Tub had just made for tea.

How dreadful!

'Stop!' wailed Mrs Rub Tub.

'Stop, stop!' shouted Alastair and Miriam.

The genie was in the lounge and in the bedrooms and the bathroom and the study. He ran here and there and everywhere waving his arms and chanting magic spells. He didn't seem aware of the chaos he was causing, he was just very pleased that his magic was working. The Hoover rattled quickly down the stairs, dragging yards of flex, and sucked up all the hall carpet and the front door mat and the newspaper. It would have devoured the umbrella rack too, had not Alastair hurriedly unplugged the Hoover.

The watering can flew through the air and watered all the potted plants along the mantelpiece. When it had done this it watered the family photographs, the carpet, the telephone and the back of Mrs Rub Tub's neck. Normally Mrs Rub Tub would have been annoyed at having water poured down the back of her neck but she was busy rescuing gas bills from the electric mincer and she didn't notice.

'HAVE YOU SEEN THE WASHING MACHINE?' yelled Miriam.

'No!' yelled Alastair. He was trying to catch a yellow duster which was polishing the budgie with furniture wax.

'If this spell does not stop immediately,' Mrs Rub Tub was shouting, 'I will ring for the police and I will ... Aaargh!' The washing machine had run past her, and it continued into the garden where it emptied all the clean washing into the vegetable patch and quickly trundled in again. Mrs Rub Tub picked up the telephone receiver and dialled 999 for the police.

187

'Hello,' came a quiet voice. 'Which service do you want, fire, police or ambulance?'

'WOULD YOU SPEAK UP?' shouted Mrs Rub Tub. 'THIS PHONE HAS BEEN WATERED WITH A WATERING CAN AND IT DOESN'T WORK AWFULLY WELL.'

'I SAID, HELLO, WHICH SERVICE DO YOU WANT, FIRE, POLICE OR AMBULANCE,' shouted back the voice obligingly.

'POLICE, PLEASE. COME QUICKLY, IT'S AN EMERGENCY. WOULD YOU LIKE MY ADDRESS?'

'IT WOULD HELP,' came the voice.

'IT'S 64 KENSINGTON PARK ROAD. DID YOU HEAR THAT?'

'YES, THANK YOU!' yelled the voice, '64 KENSINGTON PARK ROAD.'

Realizing that this was an emergency, the police came as fast as they could. In just over one and a half hours, five police cars, seven police motor bikes and a great many policemen on foot raced across London to Kensington Park Road, and up Professor Molecule's garden path. Leading the group was Sergeant Kopwell, who was now squashed up against the front door with a great many police constables breathing heavily down his neck. He rang the bell. Unfortunately, no one heard it. Alastair and Miriam were both shouting very loudly, and Mrs Rub Tub was in the kitchen cupboard tying the sweeping brushes to their hooks in case they got any ideas. The police broke down the door and ran in. They stopped and looked round the house which was by now a lot more chaotic than the London Underground railway in the rush hour two shopping days before Christmas. The police, however, being very bright, knew exactly what to do.

'Er ... what do we do, Serg?' asked the police constables.

'What a stupid question,' said Sergeant Kopwell. 'We find out what is happening and we take notes.'

'What sort of notes, Serg?' asked P.C. Clink.

'Another stupid question,' snorted Sergeant Kopwell. 'We must take notes on ... er ... we must ... er ... What we should be looking for is ... er ... well, dead bodies. Yes, dead bodies and stolen jewellery. And P.C. Clink, how many times have I told you to use your own initiative?'

'Initiative, Serg?' P.C. Clink was more puzzled than ever.

'BRAINS, CLINK. INITIATIVE means BRAINS!' shouted the sergeant, and with that the policemen thundered off in different directions with their pencils and notebooks, peering cautiously into cupboards and looking behind the curtains. P.C. Bonk went into the kitchen and was immediately attacked by a watering can which bonked him on the head several times. P.C. Bonk wrote this down in his notebook.

'At two P.M. precisely,' wrote the constable, 'I came into the kitchen and was immediately attacked by a watering can which bonked me on the head several times.' The watering can, meanwhile, tipped up and watered P.C. Bonk's helmet.

'At precisely two minutes past two,' wrote the constable, 'the very same watering can watered my helmet.' He was just wondering whether this was a very serious crime or not, when there was a strange scuffling sound and it came from inside the kitchen cupboard.

'A burglar,' thought the policeman, suddenly alarmed. The cupboard door was slightly open, but not wide enough for him to see inside. Very stealthily, he crept across the floor, his police boots squeaking gently. Then with one sudden movement, he slammed the door shut and turned the key, locking the burglar in.

'At five past two precisely,' wrote P.C. Bonk. 'I crept stealthily across the floor and locked a dangerous criminal into the kitchen cupboard.' P.C. Bonk was very pleased with himself.

Sergeant Kopwell, meanwhile, had come across the genie in the study. He was sitting cross-legged under the Professor's desk, muttering Indian spells to himself in Indian. 'At ten past two precisely,' wrote Sergeant Kopwell, 'I found a strangely dressed gentleman behaving in a very odd manner. I must ask you, sir,' he said, 'to come with me to the police station.'

'Why,' said the genie rudely, 'have you forgotten where it is?' With this remark, he mumbled a magic spell and Sergeant Kopwell vanished into thin air. It was most astonishing. One minute he was there, and the next minute he just wasn't.

The Professor came home suddenly. He came through the porch and stopped, astonished. He looked at the number on the front door to make sure he was in the right house. He was! 'What on earth ...' he boomed. He didn't get any further because the kitchen door flew open, and out ran the washing machine followed by twenty-eight policemen. They stampeded across the hall and disappeared into the dining-room slamming the door behind them. The Professor was knocked flat on his back in a cloud of dust. He got up crossly.

'What on earth is ...' he began again. The lounge door flew open and the Hoover ran out chased by the genie and thirty-six policemen. They stampeded across the hall and into the kitchen. This time, however, the Professor was a little bit quicker. He caught the last policeman firmly by the ear and dangled him in the air. He was wearing goggles and flippers, the sort one wears to go diving. Together with his policeman's uniform they really did make him look odd.

'And who are you?' growled the Professor.

'Er ... P.C. Nick,' stammered the policeman, trying to salute.

'Well, P.C. Nick,' said the Professor, dropping him with a bump, 'do you think you could explain to me how it is I can leave my house in perfect order and yet return to find it overrun with policemen?'

'Well, sir,' began P.C. Nick, trying to remember everything he had seen and heard, 'it all began with a telephone call with water in it.'

'A telephone call?' said the Professor heavily.

'Yes, sir.'

'With water in it?'

'Yes, sir, and naturally enough we came here looking for a flood, or at least, I did, sir. Then we began looking for dead bodies and stolen jewellery. We found the kitchen full of foam, probably poisonous, and the study simply glumping with pink goo. Then poor P.C. Bonk was attacked by a vicious watering can. You have never seen such a vicious watering can in your life. There's a highly dangerous criminal locked in the kitchen cupboard, and between you and me it is very likely that he has a gun on him. Then stone me if Sergant Kopwell didn't disappear. That was really odd. If you ask me, he was kidnapped. Rushed off to a far-away country bound and gagged. And then there's this really strange little chap wearing a blue hat and a pink jacket. Fancy a chap wearing ...'

'Constable,' interrupted the Professor, 'I can't help thinking that you have this story a little mixed up. Would you be so kind as to tell me where my housekeeper is?'

'No, sir,' said P.C. Nick, 'I don't know where the housekeeper is, but there are two children in the kitchen.'

'Thank you,' said the Professor and he went into the kitchen.

'Hello!' said Alastair and Miriam guiltily.

'You two look very guilty,' said the Professor. 'Perhaps you can tell me what has been going on.'

'It's all my fault,' said Alastair, going very red indeed. 'I used one of your magic spells and now there is a genie in the house causing a lot of trouble and he won't go away.'

The Professor was very cross.

'I am very cross,' he said. 'I have told you over and over again – never, never meddle with magic.' Professor Molecule could have gone on scolding the children for a lot longer, but just at that moment there came a loud banging from inside the kitchen cupboard.

'That's the dangerous criminal,' said P.C. Nick. 'Whatever you do, don't open the cupboard.'

'Dangerous criminal,' snorted the Professor, and he opened the cupboard door. Out fell Mrs Rub Tub, very hot, and furious. Miriam put the kettle on for a cup of tea. It seemed the best thing to do and the Professor went to have a word with the genie.

'I think it's time you went,' he said, in a dangerous sort of voice. The genie noticed the dangerous sort of voice.

'Yes,' he said, 'perhaps it is.' WHOOSH! the windows flew open and the genie flew out. Then there was an explosion of green smoke and pink potion and everything was back to normal. The Hoover was back in the cupboard, the policemen were back in their station, and nicest of all, Mrs Rub Tub's cake was back on the table, complete with icing.

'I think it is time we had our tea,' said Mrs Rub Tub, 'don't you?'

JANE BARRY

DRIBBLE

I will never forget Friday, May tenth. It's the most important day of my life. It didn't start out that way. It started out ordinary. I went to school. I ate my lunch. I had gym. And then I walked home from school with Jimmy Fargo. We planned to meet at our special rock in the park as soon as we changed our clothes.

In the elevator I told Henry I was glad summer was coming. Henry said he was too. When I got out at my floor I walked down the hall and opened the door to my apartment. I took off my jacket and hung it in the closet. I put my books on the hall table next to my mother's purse. I went straight to my room to change my clothes and check Dribble.

The first thing I noticed was my chain latch. It was unhooked. My bedroom door was open. And there was a chair smack in the middle of my doorway. I nearly tumbled over it. I ran to my dresser to check Dribble. He wasn't there! His bowl with the rocks and water was there – but Dribble was gone.

I got really scared. I thought, *Maybe he died while I was at school and I didn't know about it.* So I rushed into the kitchen and hollered, 'Mom . . . where's Dribble?' My mother was baking something. My brother sat on the kitchen floor, banging pots and pans together. 'Be quiet!' I yelled at Fudge. 'I can't hear anything with all that noise.'

'What did you say, Peter?' my mother asked me.

'I said I can't find Dribble. Where is he?'

'You mean he's not in his bowl?' my mother asked.

I shook my head.

'Oh dear!' my mother said. 'I hope he's not crawling around somewhere. You know I don't like the way he smells. I'm going to have a look in the bedrooms. You check in here, Peter.'

My mother hurried off. I looked at my brother. He was smiling. 'Fudge, do you know where Dribble is?' I asked calmly.

Fudge kept smiling.

'Did you take him? Did you, Fudge?' I asked, not so calmly.

Fudge giggled and covered his mouth with his hands.

I yelled. 'Where is he? What did you do with my turtle?'

No answer from Fudge. He banged his pots and pans together again. I yanked the pots out of his hand. I tried to speak softly. 'Now tell me where Dribble is. Just tell me where my turtle is. I won't be mad if you tell me. Come on, Fudge . . . please.'

Fudge looked up at me. 'In tummy,' he said.

'What do you mean, in tummy?' I asked, narrowing my eyes.

'Dribble in tummy!' he repeated.

'What tummy?' I shouted at my brother.

'This one,' Fudge said, rubbing his stomach. 'Dribble in this tummy! Right here!'

I decided to go along with his game. 'Okay. How did he get in there, Fudge?' I asked.

Fudge stood up. He jumped up and down and sang out, 'I ATE HIM . . . ATE HIM . . . ATE HIM!' Then he ran out of the room.

My mother came back into the kitchen. 'Well, I just can't find him anywhere,' she said. 'I looked in all the dresser drawers and the bathroom cabinets and the shower and the tub and . . .'

'Mom,' I said, shaking my head. 'How could you?'

'How could I what, Peter?' Mom asked.

'How could you let him do it?'

'Let who do what, Peter?' Mom asked.

'LET FUDGE EAT DRIBBLE!' I screamed.

My mother started to mix whatever she was baking. 'Don't be silly, Peter,' she said. 'Dribble is a turtle.'

'HE ATE DRIBBLE!' I insisted.

'*Peter Warren Hatcher!* STOP SAYING THAT!' Mom hollered.

'Well, ask him. Go ahead and ask him,' I told her.

Fudge was standing in the kitchen doorway with a big grin on his face. My mother picked him up and patted his head. 'Fudgie,' she said to him, 'tell Mommy where brother's turtle is.'

'In tummy,' Fudge said.

'What tummy?' Mom asked.

'MINE!' Fudge laughed.

My mother put Fudge down on the kitchen counter where he couldn't get away from her. 'Oh, you're fooling Mommy ... right?'

'No fool!' Fudge said.

My mother turned very pale. 'You really ate your brother's turtle?'

Big smile from Fudge.

'You mean that you put him in your mouth and chewed him up ... like this?' Mom made believe she was chewing.

'No,' Fudge said.

A smile of relief crossed my mother's face. 'Of course you didn't. It's just a joke.' She put Fudge down on the floor and gave me a *look.*

Fudge babbled. 'No chew, No chew. Gulp ... gulp ... all gone turtle. Down Fudge's tummy.'

Me and my mother stared at Fudge.

'You didn't!' Mom said.

'Did so!' Fudge said.

'No!' Mom shouted.

'Yes!' Fudge shouted back.

'Yes?' Mom asked weakly, holding onto a chair with both hands.

'Yes!' Fudge beamed.

194

My mother moaned and picked up my brother. 'Oh no! My angel! My precious little baby! OH ... NO....'

My mother didn't stop to think about my turtle. She didn't even give Dribble a thought. She didn't even stop to wonder how my turtle liked being swallowed by my brother. She ran to the phone with Fudge tucked under one arm. I followed. Mom dialled the operator and cried, 'Oh help! This is an emergency. My baby ate a turtle ... STOP THAT LAUGHING,' my mother told the operator. 'Send an ambulance right away; 25 West 68th Street.'

Mom hung up. She didn't look too well. Tears were running down her face. She put Fudge down on the floor. I couldn't understand why she was so upset. Fudge seemed just fine.

'Help me, Peter,' Mom begged. 'Get me blankets.'

I ran into my brother's room. I grabbed two blankets from Fudge's bed. He was following me around with that silly grin on his face. I felt like giving him a pinch. How could he stand there looking so happy when he had my turtle inside him?

I delivered the blankets to my mother. She wrapped Fudge up in them and ran to the front door. I followed and grabbed her purse from the hall table. I figured she'd be glad I thought of that.

Out in the hall I pressed the elevator buzzer. We had to wait a few minutes. Mom paced up and down in front of the elevator. Fudge was cradled in her arms. He sucked his fingers and made that slurping noise I like. But all I could think of was Dribble.

Finally, the elevator got to our floor. There were three people in it besides Henry. 'This is an emergency,' Mom wailed. 'The ambulance is waiting downstairs. Please hurry!'

'Yes, Mrs Hatcher. Of course,' Henry said. 'I'll run her down just as fast as I can. No other stops.'

Someone poked me in the back. I turned around. It was Mrs Rudder. 'What's the matter?' she whispered.

'It's my brother,' I whispered back. 'He ate my turtle.'

Mrs Rudder whispered *that* to the man next to her and *he* whispered it to the lady next to *him* who whispered it to Henry. I faced front and pretended I didn't hear anything.

My mother turned around with Fudge in her arms and said, 'That's not funny. Not funny at all!'

But Fudge said, 'Funny, funny, funny Fudgie!'

Everybody laughed. Everybody except my mother.

The elevator door opened. Two men, dressed in white, were waiting with a stretcher. 'This the baby?' one of them asked.

'Yes. Yes, it is,' Mom sobbed.

'Don't worry, lady. We'll be to the hospital in no time.'

'Come, Peter,' my mother said, tugging at my sleeve. 'We're going to ride in the ambulance with Fudge.'

My mother and I climbed into the back of the blue ambulance. I was never in one before. It was neat. Fudge kneeled on a cot and peered out through the window. He waved at the crowd of people that had gathered on the sidewalk.

One of the attendants sat in the back with us. The other one was driving. 'What seems to be the trouble, lady?' the attendant asked. 'This kid looks pretty healthy to me.'

'He swallowed a turtle,' my mother whispered.

'He did WHAT?' the attendant asked.

'Ate my turtle. That's what!' I told him.

My mother covered her face with her hanky and started to cry again.

'Hey, Joe!' the attendant called to the driver. 'Make it snappy ... *this* one swallowed a turtle!'

'That's not funny!' Mom insisted. I didn't think so either, considering it was my turtle!

We arrived at the back door of the hospital. Fudge was whisked away by two nurses. My mother ran after him. 'You wait here, young man,' another nurse called to me, pointing to a bench.

I sat down on the hard, wooden bench. I didn't have anything to do. There weren't any books or magazines spread out, like when I go to Dr Cone's office. So I watched the clock and read all the signs on the walls. I found out I was in the emergency section of the hospital.

After a while the nurse came back. She gave me some paper and crayons. 'Here you are. Be a good boy and draw some pictures. Your mother will be out soon.'

I wondered if she knew about Dribble and that's why she was trying to be nice to me. I didn't feel like drawing any pictures. I wondered what they were doing to Fudge in there. Maybe he

wasn't such a bad little guy after all. I remembered that Jimmy Fargo's little cousin once swallowed the most valuable rock from Jimmy's collection. And my mother told me that when I was a little kid I swallowed a quarter. Still ... a quarter's not like a turtle!

I watched the clock on the wall for an hour and ten minutes. Then a door opened and my mother stepped out with Dr Cone. I was surprised to see him. I didn't know he worked in the hospital.

'Hello, Peter,' he said.

'Hello, Dr Cone. Did you get my turtle?'

'Not yet, Peter,' he said. 'But I do have something to show you. Here are some X-rays of your brother.'

I studied the X-rays as Dr Cone pointed things out to me.

'You see,' he said. 'There's your turtle ... right there.'

I looked hard. 'Will Dribble be in there for ever?' I asked.

'No. Definitely not! We'll get him out. We gave Fudge some medicine already. That should do the trick nicely.'

'What kind of medicine?' I asked. 'What trick?'

'Castor oil, Peter,' my mother said. 'Fudge took castor oil. And milk of magnesia. And prune juice too. Lots of that. All those things will help to get Dribble out of Fudge's tummy.'

'We just have to wait,' Dr Cone said. 'Probably until tomorrow

197

or the day after. Fudge will have to spend the night here. But I don't think he's going to be swallowing anything that he isn't supposed to be swallowing from now on.'

'How about Dribble?' I asked. 'Will Dribble be all right?' My mother and Dr Cone looked at each other. I knew the answer before he shook his head and said, 'I think you may have to get a new turtle, Peter.'

'I don't want a new turtle!' I said. Tears came to my eyes. I was embarrassed and wiped them away with the back of my hand. Then my nose started to run and I had to sniffle. 'I want Dribble,' I said. 'That's the only turtle I want.'

My mother took me home in a taxi. She told me my father was on his way to the hospital to be with Fudge. When we got home she made me lamb chops for dinner, but I wasn't very hungry. My father came home late that night. I was still up. My father looked gloomy. He whispered to my mother, 'Not yet . . . nothing yet.'

The next day was Saturday. No school. I spent the whole day in the hospital waiting room. There were plenty of people around. And magazines and books too. It wasn't like the hard bench in the emergency hallway. It was more like a living-room. I told everybody that my brother ate my turtle. They looked at me kind of funny. But nobody ever said they were sorry to hear about my turtle. Not once.

My mother joined me for supper in the hospital coffee shop. I ordered a hamburger but I left most of it, because right in the middle of supper my mother told me that if the medicine didn't work soon Fudge might have to have an operation to get Dribble out of him. My mother didn't eat anything.

That night my grandmother came to stay with me. My mother and father stayed at the hospital with Fudge. Things were pretty dreary at home. Every hour the phone rang. It was my mother calling from the hospital with a report.

'Not yet . . . I see,' Grandma repeated. 'Nothing happening yet.'

I was miserable. I was lonely. Grandma didn't notice. I even missed Fudge banging his pots and pans together. In the middle of the night the phone rang again. It woke me up and I crept out into the hallway to hear what was going on.

Grandma shouted, 'Whoopee! It's out! Good news at last.'

She hung up and turned to me. 'The medicine has finally worked, Peter. All that castor oil and milk of magnesia and prune juice finally worked. The turtle is out!'

'Alive or dead?' I asked.

'PETER WARREN HATCHER, WHAT A QUESTION!' Grandma shouted.

So my brother no longer had a turtle inside of him. And I no longer had a turtle! I didn't like Fudge as much as I thought I did before the phone rang.

The next morning Fudge came home from the hospital. My father carried him into the apartment. My mother's arms were loaded with presents. All for Fudge! My mother put the presents down and kissed him. She said, 'Fudgie can have anything he wants. Anything at all. Mommy's so happy her baby's all better!'

It was disgusting. Presents and kisses and attention for Fudge. I couldn't even look at him. He was having fun! He probably wasn't even sorry he ate my turtle.

That night my father came home with the biggest box of all. It wasn't wrapped up or anything but I knew it was another present. I turned away from my father.

'Peter,' he said. 'This box is a surprise for you!'

'Well, I don't want another turtle,' I said. 'Don't think you can make me feel better with another turtle ... because you can't.'

'Who said anything about a turtle, son?' Dad asked.

'You see, Peter, your mother and I think you've been a good sport about the whole situation. After all, Dribble *was* your pet.'

I looked up. Could I be hearing right? Did they really remember about me and Dribble? I put my hand inside the box. I felt something warm and soft and furry. I knew it was a dog, but I pretended to be surprised when he jumped up on my lap and licked me.

Fudge cried, 'Ohhh ... doggie! See ... doggie!' He ran right over and grabbed my dog's tail.

'Fudge,' my father said, taking him away. 'This is your brother's dog. Maybe someday you'll have a dog of your own. But this one belongs to Peter. Do you understand?'

Fudge nodded. 'Pee-tah's dog.'

'That's right,' my father said. 'Peter's dog!' Then he turned to me. 'And just to be sure, son,' he said. 'We got a dog that's going to grow quite big. *Much* too big for your brother to swallow!'

We all laughed. My dog was neat.

I named him Turtle ... to remind me.

JUDY BLUME

EMILY AND THE EGG

Emily was walking through the park one day when she saw something shining under a bush. She went over to the bush and there, to her surprise, she found an enormous egg. It was bigger than the eggs she ate for breakfast. It was even bigger than her brother's football. It was bright and sparkling and green, and Emily thought it was the prettiest egg she'd ever seen. So she decided to take it home and hide it in the garden shed so that her brother wouldn't find it and take it for himself.

She watched over her egg carefully and went to look at it every day, until one morning, when she opened the door of the shed,

she found that the egg had cracked open and the inside of the shell was empty. From the corner of the shed where Daddy kept his lawn-mower came a little curl of smoke. Emily went over to the corner and there, looking at her with round, red eyes, was a little baby dragon. Emily knew it was a dragon because she had seen them in story-books. This one

200

had a green scaly body like a fish, spiky wings and a long, curly tail. When he saw Emily he squeaked and looked frightened, so Emily spoke to him softly:

'Hello, Dragon, I'm Emily. I'll look after you if you like. Are you hungry? I've only got a few chocolate buttons but perhaps you'd like them.'

She popped the chocolate buttons into his mouth where they melted straight away on his hot tongue. The little dragon smiled and licked his lips. He put out his claw for more.

'I'm sorry, I haven't any more,' said Emily.

Just then she heard her brother coming down the garden path so she whispered, 'Sssh! Stay here – I'll be back,' and left the dragon shut up in the shed.

After that Emily visited the dragon whenever no one else was around. She made a bed for him in the lawn-mower bin and fed him on chocolate and crisps which he seemed to like very much. Every night he wriggled out of the shed and drank a lot of water from the pond in Emily's garden. I'm sorry to say he drank the four goldfish in it too.

Every day he grew bigger and filled more of the shed. He made a lot of mess and burned little holes in the shed walls with his fiery breath. He whooshed and puffed like a steam-engine and ate more and more chocolate buttons.

Then one night, as Emily lay asleep, there was a terrible commotion around the shed. Emily was woken by a rushing, flapping noise in the garden. She jumped out of bed and ran to the window. She could see something big and dark moving by the door of the shed. What could it be? Then she heard her baby dragon give a little excited growl and the next moment there was a hissing and a cloud of orange fire came from the black shape and lit up the garden. Emily had such a surprise! There, by the garden shed, was the great glittering body of a huge grown-up dragon. It took Emily's baby dragon gently up in its claws, and with a sudden leap it spread its wings and flapped off into the night. 'Silly cats, fighting again!' she heard her mother say.

But Emily knew better. She never saw her baby dragon again but she still puts a few chocolate buttons out in the shed every so often, just in case.

SARAH MORCOM

THE BIRTHDAY CAKE

Andy's mother made a birthday cake for Great-aunt Connie's eightieth birthday. It was iced with criss-cross hatching and pink roses on top. She wrote 'HAPPY BIRTHDAY' across the top in pink letters.

'I'll take it to her!' Andy offered.

'Very well ... but not on your bicycle!' his mother said. 'You can carry it in my flower basket!' and she put the cake in the flat wicker basket she used for cutting roses.

Andy's mother went out shopping. When Andy picked up the basket with the cake in it a terrible thing happened. The handle of the basket broke off in his hand and the cake rolled away under the kitchen table, landing on its face. The roses were squashed quite flat. The birthday message couldn't be read at all.

Andy was very upset. It wasn't his fault, but that didn't make the cake any better. He decided to re-decorate it himself.

He got a knife and scraped away the roses and the writing. He had to scrape off most of the icing too. Then he got a cookery book and a packet of icing sugar and started all over again.

'Butter icing makes a firmer covering,' said the book, so he put a lot of melted butter into the mixture, and topped it off with peanuts and silver balls. He couldn't write a message, so he just put a big C in the middle. This time he packed it into a tin.

'What have you got there?' asked his friend Carol when he passed her gate. Andy let her peep. 'Yuk!' she said in disgust. 'It's all gone gooey!'

It was a hot day, and the butter icing had slid off the cake into the bottom of the tin.

Andy felt like crying. 'It was all right when I started!' he said.

'I'll do it again for you!' said Carol, 'I know about icing cakes and my mum has lots of sugar!'

They took the cake into Carol's house. Carol scraped off the sugar and iced the cake very proficiently with hot water, that set the icing almost at once. With the forcing tube she wrote: 'Aunt C. 80 yrs.' across the top. It looked almost as good as when the cake began.

'Now leave the lid a little bit open!' Carol told him. 'The air will dry it off.'

Andy hurried on to Great-aunt Connie's. He pushed open the gate and walked very carefully up the garden path.

Great-aunt Connie saw him coming. She opened the door with a welcoming smile on her face, but behind her like a bullet came Micky her dog, who had heard Andy's voice and wanted to welcome him too.

Micky bounded past Great-aunt Connie and hurled himself into the middle of Andy's chest, just where he was holding the birthday cake so carefully between his hands.

The tin flew into the air. The cake shot out of the tin. Over and over it rolled, bounding across the path and into a rose bed. When Andy picked it up the icing was covered in rose leaves and brown earth.

Great-aunt Connie seized Micky by the collar and dragged him indoors. Then she came to inspect the cake which was looking terrible.

'I believe underneath all that earth it is really a very splendid cake!' she said at last, 'And if we scrape off the sugar and re-ice it nobody will ever know what has happened to it!'

Great-aunt Connie iced the cake exactly as Andy described the way his mother had done it.

It looked wonderful on the tea table. Everyone made admiring remarks, and only Andy's mother looked just a little bit surprised. She caught Andy's eye across the table and raised an inquiring eyebrow.

Andy winked at her. He meant to say, and his mother perfectly understood his signal:

'Not now! Just wait till after tea and I'll tell you all about it!'

URSULA MORAY WILLIAMS
Ursula Moray Williams says this is a true story.

SLIPPER-SLOPPER

Mrs Rabbit went to market one fine day, and there she bought a pair of fine brown leather slippers for her son.

'He will be a gentleman, a real gentleman, in these splendid slippers,' she said to herself as she hurried home along the lanes to the little house on the common.

'Here's a pair of slippers for you, Tim,' said she, taking them out of her string bag, which bulged with peas and beans and lettuces. 'You can wear them tomorrow. Always wear a new thing on a new day, my son.'

Tim was delighted with their slipperiness and shininess. He gazed at them whilst he and his mother sat at tea, and he nursed them in his arms all evening. He took them to bed with him, and slept with them hanging on the bedpost.

The next morning he awoke early and put them on his little slim feet. Never had he seen such a slippery pair of shoes! His feet went sliding in and out as he walked carefully downstairs, holding on to the banister lest the slippers should slip downstairs without him. 'Slipper-slopper' they went, as they flapped on each wooden step.

'Do fasten your slippers, Tim,' cried Mrs Rabbit, looking up from the frying-pan in which she was cooking mushrooms and wild sorrel leaves – a tasty rabbit dish.

'They won't stay on, Mother. They are such slippery slippers,' answered Tim, giving them a hitch as they dropped off at the heels.

All day he went slipper-slopper, up and down the fields and across the common. The grass was bruised as he stumbled along, and stones got between his toes. He tumbled down and scrambled to his feet again with a very pink face. The field-mice stopped to look at him, and they laughed up their furry sleeves.

'Look at little Tim Rabbit!' they whispered. 'He thinks he is a fine gentleman, wearing big slippers like that! They are too large for him. All he can do is to go slipper-slopper over the meadows, like Emily Duck.'

Tim was much annoyed, but although he tied his fine slippers with twists of hare grass, and stuffed leaves in the toes, still they flipped and flopped as he walked.

So he sat down, and took them off, and hung them up in a gorse bush! Then he pattered home without them.

Mrs Rabbit went to market again next week, and returned with another pair of slippers for her son. 'He will be like a dainty maiden in these,' she said to herself, as she tripped along the path. 'There never has been such a pretty pair of slippers on our common within living memory.'

'Try these, Tim,' said she, taking them out of her little rush basket, along with apples and onions.

Tim looked with sparkling eyes at the little red slippers. He was sure they would not go slipper-slopper, they were so neat and trim.

He was happy at their brightness and redness, and he took them to bed with him, and slept with them under the pillow.

The next morning he came downstairs, wearing the pretty red slippers. 'Squeak! Squeak! Squeak!' they went.

'Don't make such a noise, Tim. I can't hear myself fry,' exclaimed

Mrs Rabbit, looking up from the pan where the eggs sizzled.

'I can't help it, Mother. They won't be quiet,' said Tim, giving his slippers a tap of annoyance.

All day the little slippers squeaked, out of the burrow, into the wood, across the fields and spinney. 'Squeak!' they went, like a couple of mice.

The ants ran out of his way when they heard Tim coming, and the beetles scurried up the ferns to watch him pass. The squirrels sat in the trees, laughing at him behind their furry paws.

'Oh! Look at Tim Rabbit! He thinks he is a niminy-piminy lady, wearing gay slippers like that, and all he can do is to go Squeak! Squeak! like a flitter-mouse on a summer night!'

Tim was rather cross, and he wrapped cool dock-leaves round his slippers, but still they wouldn't be silent. He soaked them in the stream and rubbed them with dandelion juice, but they squeaked even louder. So he took them off, and hung them in a blackberry bush. Then he ran pitter-patter home.

A week later, Mrs Rabbit went to market again, and on a stall kept by an ancient dame, she found a pair of remarkable slippers. She packed them with her gooseberries and carrots, and carried them home in triumph. 'A fairy might wear these slippers,' she told herself, as she walked through the fields.

'Try these slippers, Tim,' cried she gaily, and she took the tiny pair from her green-leaf parcel. 'These won't squeak or slipper-slopper. I paid a mighty price for them!'

Tim looked at the little white slippers, soft and dainty, and he laughed with glee. They were wonderful! He was sure they wouldn't go 'Squeak! Squeak!' or 'Slipper-slopper'.

He put them on the tablecloth and admired them all evening, and at night he carried them carefully upstairs, and slept with them cuddled to his heart.

The next day at cock-crow he was up, dancing round his room in the little slippers. Then he ran downstairs, and the little white slippers made no sound at all, not a breath or rustle.

'Oh! How you startled me!' cried Mrs Rabbit, jumping up and dropping the toast in the fire. 'How quiet you are, Tim!'

'They don't make any noise, Mother,' answered Tim, stooping down to stroke his little slippers.

He padded out of the house, over the fields, and on to the moor. The bumble-bees and the peacock butterflies didn't hear him coming, till he frightened them with his shadow. The blackbird jumped out of his way with a fluttering heart, and the thrush cried out in terror as he drifted by.

''Pon my word, Tim Rabbit! I thought you were a stoat,' he exclaimed. 'Why don't you walk properly? It isn't manners to startle your friends!'

The hedgehogs sat under the furze, laughing at him from behind their prickles.

'Look at Tim Rabbit!' they cried. 'He thinks he is a fairy, dancing away on those white slippers, and all the time he is only like a shadow, a nothing, a nothing-at-all. Ho! Ho!'

Tim was now very cross indeed, and he picked a peascod from the little wild pea, and popped it in his slippers to make a rattling noise, but the slippers were silent. He tried to sing, to shout, to whistle, but his voice was like the drifting leaves whilst he wore the magic slippers.

So he took them off, and hung them in a hawthorn tree, where they looked like a bunch of may.

When he got home Mrs Rabbit exclaimed, 'Now Tim! Here you

208

are without any slippers again! I shan't get any more for you. You must go out tomorrow and find all the lost pairs, and then I can take them back to the market.'

So Tim sat quietly by the fire, and he wondered where his slippers were.

When he came down next morning, he skipped up to his mother on his little furry toes, and gave her a hug.

'Come along, Tim,' she laughed, and she poured the porridge into the little wooden bowls and put the honey on the table.

'It is nice to have no slippers. I don't want to be a fine gentleman, or a niminy-piminy lady, or even a fairy,' said he, and he rubbed his feet together under the table, and screwed up his happy toes. But he had not forgotten that he had to find all those lost slippers.

He ran to the gorse bush, and the blackberry bush, and the hawthorn tree, but the slipper-slopper slippers, and the squeaking slippers, and the dainty fairy pair had all gone. He scampered up and down, in and out of burrows, in woods and fields and copses, seeking in hedges and ditches, and in nooks and crannies. The other rabbits hunted with him, but no one could find the lost slippers.

Where had they gone? The brown pair had been taken from the gorse bush by little Jenny Wren. The red pair had been taken from the blackberry bramble by Cock Robin. The white pair had been taken from the hawthorn tree by Mr Magpie.

So Tim played hide-and-seek with all the other rabbits, and nobody could run as fast as he. Then he ran home to his mother, hopping and skipping, on his own fleet furry toes, for he vowed that never again would he wear any slippers.

ALISON UTTLEY

THE GHOST WHO
CAME OUT
OF THE BOOK

There was once a very small ghost who lived in a book – a book of ghost stories, of course. Sometimes people caught a glimpse of it and thought it was some sort of bookmark, but mostly people did did not see it at all. When anybody opened the book to read it the ghost slipped out from between the pages and flew around the room, looking at the people and the people's things. Then, when the ghost saw that the person reading the book was growing sleepy or was finishing the story, it slid back into the book and hid between the pages again. There was one page it especially liked with a picture of a haunted house on it.

One evening a child was reading the ghost stories and the ghost slipped out of the book as usual. It flew around the top of the room and looked at spiders' webs in the corners of the ceiling. It tugged at the webs and the spiders came out, thinking they'd caught something. Then the very small ghost shouted 'Boo!' at them,

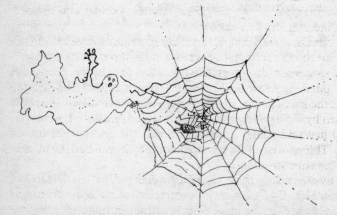

frightening them so that they ran back into their cracks and corners to hide. While the ghost was doing this, the child's mother came in, shut the book, kissed the child and put the light out, all in a second or two. The ghost was shut out of the book and left outside in the world of the house.

'Oh well,' said the ghost, quite pleased, 'a good chance to try some haunting on a larger scale. I'm getting a bit sick of spiders anyway.'

The door was shut with an iron catch so the ghost couldn't get into the rest of the house. It just flew around the bedroom a few times and went to sleep at last in the folds of the curtains, hanging upside-down like a bat.

'What a day to look forward to tomorrow!' it thought happily just before it went to sleep. 'I'll scare everyone in the place. I might not bother to go back to the book again.'

But alas, the next morning the ghost slept in.

The mother of the house came in briskly and flicked the curtain wide. The ghost, taken by surprise, broke into two or three pieces and had to join up again.

'There's a cobweb up there,' the mother of the house said, and before the ghost was properly joined up again she vacuumed it into her vacuum cleaner. Of course, a vacuum cleaner was nothing to a ghost. This ghost just drifted straight out again, but it certainly felt shaken and there was dust all the way through it.

'Now I am getting very angry,' the ghost said to itself, and it followed the mother of the house into the kitchen and hissed a small buzzing hiss into her ear.

'Goodness, there's a fly in the kitchen,' said the mother, and she took out the fly spray and squirted it in the direction of the hiss.

Being a ghost, the ghost didn't breathe, but the fly spray made it get pins and needles all over and it went zigging and zagging about the kitchen, looking like a piece of cobweb blown about the kitchen by a playful breeze. At last it settled on the refrigerator.

'I'll just take things quietly for a bit,' the ghost whispered to itself. 'Things are getting too much for me.' It watched the mother dust the window ledges.

'Why does she do that?' the ghost wondered, for the dust looked like speckles of gold and silver and freckles of rainbow. Some dots of dust were like tiny glass wheels with even tinier glass wheels

spinning inside them. Some specks were whole worlds with strange islands and mysterious oceans on them, but all too small, too small for anyone but a very small ghost to see.

But when the mother began to make a cake the ghost gasped, for she poured in a measure of sugar that looked like thousands of ice diamonds all spangled and sparkling with white and blue and green. 'Let me have a closer look at them,' the ghost murmured to itself, and it flew down into the sugar. At that moment the mother of the house began to beat the cake mixture with her electric egg beater.

'Help!' screamed the ghost as it was whirled into the sugar and butter and got runny egg all over it.

The cake mixture was so sticky that the ghost got rather glued up in it, and before it knew what was happening it was poured into a greased tin and put into the oven. Being a ghost, nothing dangerous could happen to it. In fact the warmth of the oven was soothing and the ghost yawned and decided, as things were so unexpected and alarming outside, to stay where it was. It curled up in the centre of the cake and went to sleep.

It did not wake up until tea time. Then it heard voices.

212

'Oh boy – cake!' it heard the voices say.

'Yes,' said the mother of the house, 'I made it this morning.' And in the next moment a knife came down and cut the ghost in two. It joined up again at once, and when the slice was lifted out of the cake the ghost leaped out too, waving in the air like a cobweb and shouting, 'Boo!'

'Oh!' cried the children. 'A ghost! A ghost! The cake's haunted.'

'Nonsense – just a bit of steam,' said the mother firmly, touching the cake with the back of her hand. 'Funny thing though – it's quite cool.'

'Perhaps it's a sort of volcano cake,' the father suggested. 'Never mind! It tastes lovely.'

'It tastes haunted!' the children told each other, for they were clever enough to taste the ghost taste in between the raisins, a little bit sharp and sour like lemon juice.

The ghost meanwhile flew back to the bedroom where the book lived.

'First the whirlwind and then the desert,' it said to itself, thinking of the vacuum cleaner and the vacuum cleaner's dust bag. 'Then the ray gun and after that the treasure,' (thinking of the fly spray and the sunlit dust). 'Then the moon-mad-merry-go-round and the warm sleeping place,' (that was the electric egg beater and the oven). 'And then the sword!' (that was the knife).

'But I did some real haunting at last – oh yes – real haunting and scared them all. "Boo!" I cried, and *they* all cried, "A ghost! A ghost!"'

That night someone picked up the book of ghost stories and opened it at the very page the ghost loved best – the one with a

picture of a haunted house on it. The ghost flew in at the door of the haunted house and looked out from behind the curtain of the haunted window. 'Home again!' it said. 'That's the best place for a small ghost. Small but dangerous,' it added. 'Quite capable of doing a bit of haunting when it wants to.'

Then the book was closed and the very small ghost went to sleep.

MARGARET MAHY

THE PRINCE AND
THE BEASTS

PART I

There was once upon a time a Prince who had a step-sister. Sometimes the Prince would go to stay in a lodge that stood in a wood full of beasts, and there he would live while his step-sister minded the house.

Each day he would go for long walks into the wood, and his heart was so kind that instead of hunting the wild animals, he watched their habits; and if he found them hurt he healed their wounds, so that he was well loved by them.

Every day when her brother went out, the step-sister used to let a robber into the house, and together they made a plan by which they were going to kill the Prince, and so get his money.

One day, the Prince heard that a Princess was going to be given up to a wicked water-dragon by her father, in order to save his country from being destroyed.

So he told his step-sister that he should go that night to kill the dragon, and save the Princess.

While he was out, the step-sister hid the robber in a cupboard.

The Prince came in early that evening. 'Now,' said his step-sister, 'let me try your strength. See if I cannot tie your hands so that you cannot undo the knots and get them free.'

'Fire away then,' said the Prince, and his step-sister, who was very cunning, tied the knots so that he would take some time to free his hands.

As soon as that was done she opened the cupboard door. Out rushed the robber, waving a broad shining sword. But before he could reach the Prince, a lion had jumped through the open door, his hair bristling with fury, and his tail as straight as a rod. He sprang upon the robber, and killed him before the girl could even scream.

Just behind the lion came a little fox, who ran to the Prince, and bit through the cord that bound his hands.

PART II

'Thank you, my faithful friends,' said the Prince to the lion and the fox, but to his step-sister he said nothing. He could hardly believe even now that she could have done such a thing.

He sat down and made a good supper, before setting out overnight for the place where the Princess was to be given to the dragon.

Then he started to walk to the seashore, which lay a long way off. There he sat on a rock, and waited until the Princess should be brought along.

In a little while he saw a number of people walking towards him, while in the middle of them marched the poor Princess.

'What a beautiful girl,' thought the Prince. 'I must indeed save her.'

Then the people slowly left her, sitting alone upon the shore.

The Prince got ready to fight. The fox, the bear, and the lion had followed him all night, and now they came into view, and very glad the Prince was to see them.

A movement in the sea showed where the dragon was, and soon his nine heads could be seen above the water.

When he was quite near the shore, the fox ran down, and with

his tail splashed water into the dragon's eyes, while the bear and the lion scratched up sand also, so that for a moment he screwed his eyes up tight.

Then, while the dragon's eyes were still shut, the Prince rushed up to his waist in the water and killed him.

The Princess wept with joy, and thanked the Prince for his deed.

Then she said to him:

'Step into this carriage with me, so that I may take you to my father's palace.' She gave him a ring, and half her handkerchief, and they set out for the palace.

PART III

On the way to the palace, the Princess's coachman said to the footman: 'Why should we drive this stranger back? Let us kill him, and we can then tell the King that *we* slew the dragon, and one of us can marry the Princess.'

So while the Prince was sitting with his back to them, they leant over and killed him, leaving him lying upon the road.

But the faithful beasts were following behind, and they sat and wept round his body, wondering what to do.

Just then the Prince's step-sister came along. 'Ah Beasts,' said she, 'what a dreadful thing I did to my brother. I will help him now, to make up for the harm I would have done before.'

Then she told the bear to kill an ox, and when this was done, she told the fox to wait until a bird came to pick at the dead ox, and then to catch it and take it to the lion. This they did, and when the fox brought a crow to the lion, he said:

'We will not kill you, if you will fly to the town where the wells of healing are, and bring back some water in your beak.'

This also the crow did, and the step-sister dropped some water upon the Prince's lips. No sooner was this done than the Prince jumped up, and thanked the faithful beasts, and forgave his step-sister. Then he took her with him to the Princess's palace.

When he came to the palace, he found that a great feast was being made ready, for the marriage of the Princess to the coachman.

'This will never do,' said the Prince, and he made his way to the hall in which the coachman was waiting for his bride, and then he begged that the King might come and hear what he had to say.

PART IV

As soon as the King had come, the Prince pulled from his pocket the ring and the half handkerchief that the Princess had given to him.

He held them out to the King and said, 'These are the tokens by which you may know it is to me, and not to this coachman, that you owe your daughter's life.'

Then the King knew that the Prince was speaking the truth, and indeed the Princess had told him that it was not the coachman who had saved her, only the King thought she was too frightened at the time to know, and was therefore obliged to believe the coachman's story.

So the Prince married the Princess, and they lived very happily together.

He told his father-in-law the tale his beasts had told him, how his step-sister had sent the crow to bring the healing water.

Then the King made much of the step-sister, and she lived in the same palace as the Prince and Princess.

The next day the beasts bade the Prince good-bye, and set off for their own forest.

A few days later, the Prince was surprised to see the lion running up towards him. 'Where are the others?' said he; 'the bear, and the fox?'

'We came to a fire in the wood,' said the lion, 'against which an old woman sat, and she turned my poor friends into stone, by striking them with a rod. Before she could strike me I ran back to get help, for I was afraid she might be poisonous to eat.'

'Show me the way to her,' said the Prince. The lion led him through the wood until night fell, and they saw a fire flickering between the trees.

The Prince, followed by the lion, stepped into the light cast by the fire and asked the witch, who was sitting there, for a night beside it to keep out the cold. 'First you must let me strike your lion with my rod,' said the witch.

'Oh no!' answered the Prince, 'I am his master. Give me the stick, and I will do it. But before I do that, you must bring my bear and my fox to life again, or the lion shall eat you.'

Then the witch threw some ashes over the bear and the fox, and in a moment they came to life again.

The Prince, as he had promised to do, struck the lion with the rod, and said: 'Now bring the lion back to life again or this time the bear shall eat you.'

The witch had to do this too.

Then the Prince bade his beasts good-bye once more, and very grateful they were to him. After they had run off one by one, he walked a safe distance away and threw the stick back to the old witch.

In this way the Prince was able to repay the beasts for their faithfulness to him, and very pleased he felt, as he walked back to his wife to tell her of what he had done.

ANON.

A NIGHT OUT
WITH TOM

It was just an ordinary sort of evening, in an ordinary sort of garden. There was Tom, an ordinary seven-year-old boy, crouching down behind an ordinary bush so that his parents wouldn't see him. He was whispering to his friend, a perfectly ordinary dragon.

'Where are we going, dragon? What are we going to do?'

'We are going to have fun, that's what,' said the dragon. 'Come on. Hold on tight to my tail. Ready for take-off?'

Tom held on tight and nodded.

'Right, then. Off we go!'

Five minutes later: 'Don't stop yet,' pleaded Tom for the third time. 'Can't we go round the Common just once more?'

'No, we jolly well can't,' said the dragon, when he had got his breath back. 'This is the kind of place dragons approach in fear and trembling, let me tell you. It's lucky for us no one saw us gallumphing about all over one of the most sacred sites in dragon history.'

Tom looked around in surprise. 'Sacred? The Common? No one ever told me that before.'

'You can't have been talking to the right dragons. If you had they would have told you that the Common is sacred for all time because it was on this very spot, one dark and misty night billions and trillions of years ago –'

'If it was billions and trillions of years ago,' asked Tom, who liked to get things straight, 'how do you know it was dark and misty?'

The dragon was not pleased. 'It was dark because it was night. It was misty because I say so,' he snapped. 'Don't interrupt. Dragons fall silent in wonder when this story is told.'

'Do they?'

'Yes, they jolly well do.'

Tom thought hard. 'How does anyone ever tell it, then?'

The dragon counted to ten. 'The story-teller doesn't fall silent, you idiot. The audience does. Do you want me to go on or not?'

'Of course I do. I'm sorry.'

'Don't mention it. As I was saying, it was on this very spot, one dark and misty night billions and trillions of years ago, that the Great Egg was first discovered. And when that Egg hatched, what do you think popped out?'

'A chicken?' guessed Tom.

The dragon counted to ten twice. 'A dragon,' he said very gently. 'The founder of our glorious royal family.'

'Gosh!' said Tom, trying to make up for having guessed wrong. 'Did it hatch out right here? By this gorse bush?'

'On this very spot.'

It must have been lucky not to get popped, Tom couldn't help thinking, but he didn't say so. 'How big was it?' he asked instead.

'Big enough.' A small puff of flame shot out from the dragon's mouth.

'Yes, but *how* big exactly? One metre? Two metres?'

'Five metres!' shouted the dragon wildly. 'Twenty metres! What does it matter, for heaven's sake?'

'I don't think it could have been twenty metres. An egg that size would collapse or explode or something.' The dragon let out a funny noise that made Tom look up. 'Can I say something else?'

The dragon sprang onto all fours, landing in the gorse bush, which didn't improve matters. 'No, you cannot say something else. What you can do instead is to sit absolutely still and keep absolutely quiet *without saying a single word*, in utter silence, while I finish my story. O.K.?'

Tom nodded.

Several minutes later, the dragon broke off again. 'What's the matter?' he asked. 'Why are you staring at my shoulder like that?'

'That's what I wanted to say before,' said Tom, pleased. 'And it's not your shoulder, it's your neck. There's a huge spider on it.'

'AAAGGGHHH!' said the dragon, along with a lot of other things Tom didn't catch.

Their journey back from the Common to Tom's home broke all records.

'That was nice, dragon,' said Tom when he was tucked up in bed again. 'It is fun doing things with you.'

'Yes,' said the dragon faintly. But I don't think he really meant it.

KATHRYN CAVE

QUEEN MAGGIE

There was once a Queen called Maggie, who was married to a King named Charlie.

Charlie enjoyed being a King. He liked sitting on his throne; wearing long robes and purple cloaks; nodding ever so slightly when people bowed to him; and counting his bags of gold and silver on a Friday afternoon. He also enjoyed banging on the dinner gong, and when the cook came puffing up the stairs, saying to her, 'I'll have my dinner now, Mrs Pudding.'

Maggie, however, *hated* having to behave like a Queen. She hated sitting on the throne, and refused to do it most times. She hated her purple cloak and would only wear it on the King's birthday. She loathed people bowing to her, and if anyone did she would say to them,

'Get up! You'll make yourself dizzy down there. Silly!'

'My Flower!' complained the King wearily, 'you really must make an effort to behave in a manner more befitting a Queen.'

'What?' said Maggie.

'It's hopeless, isn't it?' said the King to the ceiling.

One Friday afternoon when the King was counting out his money, he let out a great cry of dismay. Maggie came racing into the room.

'What is it, Charlie? Have you sat on a snake?' She knew the King disliked snakes.

'There's a bee on the window, is there?' She flapped the curtains furiously to frighten it away.

'I know! – you've got a tummy ache. It was those dreadful meat-balls Mrs Pudding gave us for lunch.'

'For goodness sake, Maggie!' said the King, when he could get a word in edgeways. 'It's got nothing to do with snakes or bees or meat-balls, it's to do with money. We've only got *one* bag of gold left.'

'Ah, is that all?' said Maggie, wishing it had been something more exciting than that. 'What a fuss about nothing.'

'About nothing! Really, my Petal, how do you suppose I shall pay the servants, or Mrs Pudding?'

'I'll pay Mrs Pudding,' decided the Queen. She liked Mrs Pudding best of all. 'I'll sell my crown.'

'You certainly shan't,' stormed the King indignantly. He knew that Maggie's crown was the only part of the royal regalia his wife *did* like to wear.

'You certainly shan't,' he said again, because he liked saying it.

'O.K.' said Maggie. 'If you don't like that idea, Sausage, I'll organize a jumble sale.'

'You certainly shan't,' said the King for the third time. 'You ...'

But Maggie was half way down the palace corridor, singing, ta ra, ta ra, ta ra, TA RA, because she had the feeling Charlie was trying to say something else.

As soon as she reached the royal bedroom, she bounced up and down on the bed, laughing. 'I'm going to have a jumble sale! A Super Rumble Jumble Sale!'

She rang all the people she knew.
The ones who could knit.
The ones who could sew.
The ones who could make peppermint fudge.
The ones who could draw donkeys for stick-the-tail-on games. And Mr Billy Jolly because he was absolutely marvellous at organizing lucky dips.

They all said, 'yes', of course. No one ever says 'no' to a Queen.

After that Maggie raced downstairs to the kitchen calling, 'Mrs Pudding? Mrs Pudding! I'm going to have a jumble sale because the King hasn't much money left. I want you to make a hundred and ninety-three tarts, sixty-eight éclairs, and a couple of thousand sandwiches – meat paste and eggy ones will do fine.'

'I ...' began Mrs Pudding, turning pasty.

But Maggie had already gone to town to buy tables and garden chairs.

The following afternoon, King Charlie had hardly done three hours throne-sitting-duty (and no one had been in to bow to him) when he heard the most DREADFUL COMMOTION in the garden.

'It's an INVASION!' he gasped. 'It *must* be!'

Then he saw Maggie's jumble sale.

'That Queen is crazy!' he muttered. 'Well, I'm not going out there for a thousand pounds (even though I am short of money). I'm going up to bed and shall put my ears under the pillow until it's all over.'

And he did. Pretty cross he was really.

In the garden everyone was having a lovely time. The shop-keepers in the town wondered why no one was coming into their shops. It was, after all, a Saturday afternoon.

'Haven't you heard?' cried some of the passers-by. 'The Queen is holding a Super Rumble Jumble Sale.'

'Is she?' said the butcher, 'I didn't know.'

'Nor I,' said the baker.

'Nor I,' said the candlestick-maker.

And they drew down their blinds and went to it.

There was a big crowd round the donkey game, because the Vicar was winning over and over again and getting lots of prizes.

'Hem!' coughed Maggie, staring very hard at him until she caught sight of one twinkly eye peeping through a hole in the blindfold.

'Mustn't cheat, must we!' she said, poking the Vicar in the tummy and teasing. 'Tut tut, who's a naughty old Vicar?'

Suddenly the Vicar didn't feel like playing any more and he hurried off towards the tea-tent.

'Oooh! fancy that!' said the crowd, 'and him a vicar!'

Maggie was selling ice-cream now. The queue was getting longer and longer. This was because for every ice-cream Maggie sold, she ate one herself. Some of the people who were at the back of the queue (nearly a mile long now) grew tired and went away to try their fortune in Mr Billy Jolly's lucky dip.

All this time the King could not sleep at all. He kept slipping his ears out of the pillow to hear if the DREADFUL COMMOTION had stopped, but it hadn't.

'It's even *dreadfuller* I think,' moaned the King.

And then he said, 'Well, blow me! I *am* the King after all. And it *is* my garden. I'll go down and stop them. I'll jolly well stop 'em. Cheek!' he said, as he hurried downstairs.

'Where's the Queen?' he bellowed to Mr Billy Jolly.

'Don't know, Your Majesty,' stuttered Mr Billy Jolly.

'And I suppose you don't know either that you're standing on my best pansies? Move, man! Or I'll stuff you into your own bran tub.'

The King wasn't really a violent man. He just felt EXAS-PERATED this particular afternoon. He went stamping round the grounds looking for Maggie. He wouldn't buy a pair of bootees for his grandson, or a stuffed hippopotamus, or even a bag of peppermint fudge, which just proves how cross he was.

Then he came across the ice-cream queue, and Maggie at the top of it.

'THERE you are!' exploded the King, red in the face with crossness.

'Hello love,' said Maggie, giving a little boy an extra big splosh of ice-cream on account of his being only four. 'D'you want an ice-cream?'

'No, I do NOT!' snapped Charlie. 'And I don't think it's fitting for a Queen to be seen licking ice-cream in public.'

'Why not, Dear Heart?' asked the Queen mildly.

'Because ... because, well just BECAUSE!' Charlie couldn't think.

Maggie said, 'Hold the money a minute, will you, whilst I serve the candlestick-maker. He's been waiting simply ages.'

King Charlie took hold of the ice-cream money and it weighed him nearly down to the ground.

'Good heavens!' he thought. 'My whiskers! My best Sunday crown! What a lot of money!'

Maggie finished serving the candlestick-maker and began to take off her apron.

'All right,' she said, 'if my Super Rumble Jumble Sale is really upsetting you I'll tell everyone it's time to go home.'

'No, no!' said Charlie. 'Let us not be hasty. After all, my people are having such a lovely time it would be a shame to send them all home. Do I *look* like an old fuddy-duddy King?'

'Of course you don't look like an old fuddy-duddy King,' cried Maggie, giving her husband a huge hug and an ice-cream. 'You look very handsome. And terribly grand. And most enormously important.'

'Yes,' agreed the King.

'And d'you know what I think?'

'No,' said the King.

'I think everybody would like to shake hands with you – 5p a go.'

'Do you think so, My Petal?'

'I certainly do!' said the Queen.

So King Charlie sent Mr Diggup, the gardener, helter-skeltering into the palace to fetch his throne, and he said to him, 'Put it there, by the pansies, Mr Diggup.'

And he sent Mrs Pudding waddle-waddling into the kitchen to fetch an empty biscuit tin into which he put the money. And he said, 'Put it down here, and *try* not to squash any more pansies.'

Then of course ABSOLUTELY EVERYBODY wanted to shake hands with the King. And they thought 5p was very cheap to do it and excellent value for money. It was nearly dark by the time the VERY LAST PERSON had finished shaking the King's hand, and there were a lot of squashed pansies around the palace gardens, and a lot of half-eaten ice-creams and pieces of sandwiches, and the ear off a stuffed hippopotamus and one knitted bootee someone had dropped ... a month's tidying up for Mr Diggup. But King Charlie was happy. He had lots and lots of money again.

'I *like* Rumble Jumble Sales,' he said sleepily.

'I knew all the time you would,' Queen Maggie said.

And they had six more ice-creams each and then they went to bed.

MARGARET STUART BARRY

THE MAGPIE'S NEST

Once a long time ago, when winter was nearly over and spring had nearly begun, all the birds were busy starting to build their nests. There they all were: the robin and the eagle, the seagull, the blackbird, the duck, the owl and the humming bird, all busy. All, that is, except Magpie. And she didn't feel much like working.

It was a nice day and she was out and about looking for scrips and scraps and bibs and bobs for her collection of old junk – her hoard of bits and pieces she had picked up from behind chimneys or from drain-pipes. Pebbles, beads, buttons and the like, anything bright and interesting or unusual, Magpie was sure to collect. Just as she was flying along on the look-out for a new treasure, she caught sight of Sparrow, her mouth full of bits of straw and twigs.

'What are you doing, what are you doing?' said Magpie.

'Building my nest,' said Sparrow, 'like you'll have to soon.'

'Oh yes?' said Magpie.

'Yes,' said Sparrow, 'put that milk-bottle-top down and come over here and watch. First you have to find a twig, and then another twig, another twig, another twig, another twig...'

'Don't make me laugh,' said Magpie, 'I know, I know, I know all that,' and off she flew. And as she flew on looking for scrips and scraps and bibs and bobs she came up to Duck who was upside down with her mouth full of mud.

'What are you doing, what are you doing?' said Magpie.

'Building my nest,' said Duck, 'like you'll have to soon.'

'Oh yes?' said Magpie.

'Yes,' said Duck, 'throw away that old earwig and watch me. After you've got all your twigs you have to stick them with mud pats like this – pat-pat, pat-pat, pat-pat...'

'Don't make me laugh,' said Magpie, 'I know, I know, I know all that,' and off she flew. And as she flew on looking for scrips and scraps and bibs and bobs she saw Pigeon with a mouthful of feathers.

'What are you doing, what are you doing?' said Magpie.

'Building my nest,' said Pigeon, 'like you'll have to soon.'

'Oh yes?' said Magpie.

'Yes,' said Pigeon, 'put that bus ticket down and come over here and learn how. You have to make yourself warm and cosy – right? Right. So you dig your beak into your chest like this – right? And find one of those very soft, fluffy feathers down there and you lay that out very carefully inside your nest to keep it warm and cosy, warm and cosy, warm and cosy...'

'Don't make me laugh,' said Magpie, 'I know, I know, I know, I know all that,' and off she flew.

Well, not long after that it was time for Magpie to lay her eggs and she looked out from her perch and saw all the other birds sitting in their well-built, warm, cosy nests, laying their eggs. 'Oh no,' said Magpie, 'I haven't got anywhere to lay mine! I'd better hurry.' And she remembered Sparrow saying something about twigs, and Duck about patting them and Pigeon saying something about cosy feathers. So she rushed out and quickly grabbed as many twigs as she could, made a great pile of them, threw a feather on the top – and the milk-bottle-top and the earwig and the bus ticket and she *just* had time to sit herself down and lay her eggs.

And if you look at a magpie's nest you'll see it's always a mess. And she ends up throwing her scrips and scraps and bibs and bobs in it too.

I think she likes it like that.

MICHAEL ROSEN

THE LOST BOAT

Once upon a time there was an old fisherman who lived by the sea with his little grandson Jonathan. Their house was a boat turned upside down, with doors and windows cut in the sides and a little tin chimney fixed on the top. There was green grass round the doorstep and a little path of pebbles going down to the beach. Then there were sand and stones and the tossing, tossing sea.

It was very lonely living there, but it was a good place for catching fish. Grandfather had a small shabby boat and he used to go out fishing in it every night of the week, while Jonathan slept in his warm bed, with the wind howling at the doors or the sea sighing on the stones. In the morning the two of them used to walk to the nearest town and sell the fish in the market-place. Then with the money they earned they would buy oil for the stove and food for the larder.

Now there were two things that worried Grandfather, though he never spoke of them to Jonathan. The first was that he was getting old and the rheumatism in his legs was getting worse and he knew that he would not be able to go fishing very much longer. The second was that the boat was getting old, and though it had been patched and mended a dozen times, it could not possibly last much longer – and if Grandfather could not catch fish to sell, how was he going to feed Jonathan and himself? He worried about it and worried about it. Then one day he had an idea.

'Wood!' he said to himself. 'If I had some wood, I could carve little boats and make little toys to sell in the town' – for as well as being a good fisherman, Grandfather was very clever with his fingers. 'Wood!' he thought to himself. 'If ever I cannot fish, I'll make things out of wood.'

So he stopped worrying about the small shabby boat and the rheumatism getting worse in his legs, and he went on happily catching fish every night of the week and selling it next day in the market-place of the town.

Now one night the sea was very stormy.

232

'It's too stormy to fish tonight,' said Grandfather to Jonathan as he tucked him in bed. 'I shall go to bed myself.' So out he went in the windy night, and he pulled the small shabby boat up near to the house. Then he locked the door, turned out the lamp and went to bed. Grandfather slept well, for he was very old, and Jonathan slept well, for he was very young; and as the night went on, neither of them knew at all what was happening outside.

The storm grew worse and the wind grew high. The waves grew bigger and roared up the beach. The sky was so dark that the moon was covered and the stars were hidden from sight. The wind grew stronger and stronger. It howled at the doors and windows and rattled the little tin chimney. The waves grew wilder and wilder. They began to rush higher up the beach than they had ever rushed before. But Grandfather slept well, for he was very old, and Jonathan slept well, for he was very young, and neither of them knew at all what was happening outside.

The storm grew worse. Thunder rumbled in the distance and lightning flashed across the sky. The wind grew stronger and stronger still. It shrieked at the doors and windows and shook the little tin chimney. The waves grew wilder and wilder. They rushed up the beach over the sand and the stones. They rushed up the little path of pebbles that led to the house. They washed over the green grass that grew round the doorstep, and they pulled and they pulled at the small shabby boat. They pulled and pulled at the small shabby boat, and they carried it out on the water, up on the foam, away and away on the tossing, tossing sea. But Grandfather slept well, for he was very old, and Jonathan slept well, for he was very young, and neither of them knew at all what was happening outside – until the morning came, and then they knew.

By morning the storm had died down, but Grandfather and Jonathan knew at once how wild it had been, for as soon as they looked out of the window they saw that the pebbles of the path were scattered and the grass round the doorstep was white with salt from the sea. Then they saw – oh! – then they saw that the small shabby boat had gone. Gone!

'Oh!' said Grandfather.

'Oh!' said Jonathan, and they put on their coats and went out at once to look for it. They walked along the beach to the east as far as the great craggy cliff, but they could not find the small shabby boat. They walked along the beach to the west as far as the great ragged rocks, but they could not find the small shabby boat.

'It has gone,' said Grandfather.

'Gone,' said Jonathan.

Sadly they walked home again.

'Perhaps the sea will bring the boat back later,' said Jonathan.

'No,' said Grandfather. 'The boat will be battered and broken on the rocks, for it was old and the storm was wild. See, the waves came almost to our very door. Oh dear! Oh dear! Now I can go fishing no more, for we shall never see our small shabby boat again.'

'If we have no fish to sell,' said Jonathan, 'how shall we buy food?'

'Wood!' said Grandfather. 'We must find wood. Then I can carve little boats and make little toys and we can sell those in the market-place instead of fish.'

'What a good idea! What a good idea!' cried Jonathan, thinking that Grandfather had thought of it just at that moment. 'Wood,' he added. 'We must look for wood.'

Now sometimes, but not very often, the sea washed up things on the shore. Sometimes it washed up seaweed and shells, and sometimes, but not very often, it washed up an old box or some broken scraps of wood from somewhere far away.

'Wood!' murmured Grandfather. 'Every morning we must look for wood.' But that day there was none and the next day there was none, and the oil in the stove burned lower and lower and the food in the larder grew less and less.

'Wood!' murmured Grandfather. 'We *must* find wood.'

Every morning they went out to look for some. They walked along the beach to the east as far as the great craggy cliff, but they could not find any wood. They walked along the beach to the west as far as the great ragged rocks, but they could not find any wood. That day there was none and the next day there was none, and the oil in the stove burned out, burned out, and the food in the larder was gone.

The next day was bright and sunny, but when Grandfather tried to get out of bed, a pain shot through his legs and he found that he could hardly move.

'It's rheumatism,' he explained to Jonathan. 'It's been getting worse for some time.' Again he tried to get out of bed, but again the pain shot through his legs and he could hardly move.

'Wood!' he muttered. 'We must find wood. Then I can carve little boats and make little toys and sell them in the market-place. Then we can buy food.'

'You stay in bed, Grandfather,' said Jonathan. 'I'll go out alone and look for wood.'

So Jonathan went out to look for wood. Perhaps the sea would have thrown some on the shore today. Perhaps he would find a lot. He walked along the beach to the east as far as the great craggy cliff, but he could not find any wood. He walked along the beach to the west as far as the great ragged rocks, but he could not find any wood.

Then, just as he was going to turn and walk back, he saw some. He saw a single small piece lying half in a little pool and half out on a rock.

'Wood!' cried Jonathan. 'Wood!'

He clambered out on the rocks and paddled through the pool. He dragged the piece of wood on to the beach and carried it all the way home. 'Wood!' he cried to Grandfather. 'Here's wood at last.'

Grandfather's eyes shone.

'Bring me my tools, please,' he said, and he sat up in bed and cut away the best bits of the wood and sent Jonathan to dry them in the sun. Then in the afternoon he started work. He cut and shaped and smoothed, and he made a little toy boat. Then he cut again with his knife. He cut and shaped and smoothed, and he made a little wooden doll.

'Oh, they are lovely!' cried Jonathan. 'You are clever, Grandfather.'

Grandfather went on cutting and shaping and smoothing, and by evening he had used up all the wood, and he had six little toy boats and six little wooden dolls.

'Tomorrow I will take them to the town,' said Jonathan, 'and sell them in the market-place.'

'It is a long way for you to go alone,' answered Grandfather.

'I do not mind,' said Jonathan.

Next morning he walked alone to the town and he stood in the market-place to sell the little toys.

'Aren't they lovely?' said the people passing by.

'Oh Mother, please buy me a little boat,' begged a boy.

'And please, Mother, buy me a wooden doll,' begged a little girl, and in just a few minutes Jonathan had sold all the little toy boats and all the little wooden dolls. Lots of people were disappointed because he had no more left to sell.

'Will you bring some more next week?' they asked. 'Bring lots and lots. They are so pretty and so beautifully made.'

'I will try,' replied Jonathan. Then he ran to the shops to spend the money on food for the larder and oil for the stove, and he hurried home again.

'The people liked your toys,' he said to Grandfather. 'They want lots more.'

236

'And we want lots more wood,' answered Grandfather with a smile. 'What we want, Jonathan, is so much wood that we can make enough money out of toys to buy food *and* some wood from the town. Perhaps tomorrow my legs will be better and I can help you look for more.'

In the morning Grandfather's legs were not better. They were still so bad that he had to stay in bed, and Jonathan had to go out alone again to look along the shore.

'Wood!' he thought. 'I wish I could find lots and lots of wood, great big pieces of wood.'

He walked along the beach to the east as far as the great craggy cliff, but he could not find any wood. He walked along the beach to the west as far as the great ragged rocks, but he could not find any wood. That day there was none and the next day there was none, and the oil in the stove burned lower and lower and the food in the larder grew less and less.

'Wood!' murmured Grandfather. 'You must find wood. Then I can carve little boats and make little toys to sell in the market-place. Then we can buy food again.'

The next day was bright and sunny, and Grandfather's legs were a little better. He could hobble round the house a bit but still he was not well enough to go out of doors. So Jonathan went out alone again to look for wood. Perhaps the sea would have thrown some more on to the shore today. Perhaps he would find a lot.

He walked along the beach to the east as far as the great craggy cliffs, but he could not find any wood. He walked along the beach to the west as far as the great ragged rocks, and there he saw – not one piece, not two pieces but lots and lots of wood. There were big curved planks of it and small straight chips of it lying scattered over the rocks and in the salt sea pools.

'Wood!' he murmured. 'Lots and lots of it! Just what we want!'

He clambered over the rocks and paddled through the pools. He dragged the wood on to the beach, one or two pieces at a time, until he had stacked it all high on the pebbles out of reach of the sea.

Oh, what a lovely lot there was! He carried some of it home and went back for more. He went back again and again until he had taken it all home and spread it out to dry in the sun in front of the little house.

You can guess how pleased Grandfather was! 'Now we have nothing to worry about any more,' he said; and that afternoon, when part of the wood was dry, he sat in the doorway and sawed away some of the good bits and began his work. He cut and shaped and smoothed. He cut and shaped and smoothed, and he made little toy boats and little wooden dolls, little toy carts and little wooden dogs, little toy houses and little wooden birds. He carved beautiful, beautiful things to sell in the market-place.

When evening came he was very tired but very happy too.

'I've been thinking,' he said to Jonathan.

'What about, Grandfather?'

'All this wood we have,' answered Grandfather. 'I believe it's our own old boat come back to us.'

'Oh!' exclaimed Jonathan. 'I believe it is.'

'It's a strange thing,' went on Grandfather, 'but I think it's going to be much more useful to us as wood than it ever was as a fishing boat.'

'Perhaps it is,' said Jonathan.

PHYLLIS FLOWENDER

DID I EVER TELL YOU ABOUT THE TIME WHEN I WAS BALD?

One day I went with my brother Francis to be minded by Grandma. Our mother was going to a funeral so she was wearing black clothes. She waved good-bye, knowing that Grandma would take good care of us.

Now it was always boring at Grandma's house. We couldn't make a mess and there was hardly anything we were allowed to do except read books or play noughts and crosses. Luckily this time Francis had remembered to bring a pair of scissors with him.

We asked Grandma if she had anything we could cut. We suggested old magazines, old newspapers or old pieces of wallpaper. 'No, no, no!' gasped Grandma with horror. 'That would make far too much mess. Why don't you play a game under the dining room table?'

So that was what we did. We sat under the dining room table and played barbers' shops. I was the first customer. I tucked the hem of my skirt into my collar to make a cloak like the ones in real barbers' shops. Francis cut my hair with his scissors.

Francis snipped and snipped and snipped. The more hair he cut off the more crooked it became. At last he stopped because I only had two tiny wisps of hair left. Then Francis looked frightened.

'We had better tell Grandma,' he said anxiously. 'I think you are almost completely bald.' When we showed my bald head to Grandma she screamed and screamed and screamed.

Then our mother came back from the funeral. When she saw my bald head she burst into tears. You can guess what happened to Francis.

All the way home our mother cried. It was very embarrassing. Francis had stopped crying. He stuck his hands in his pockets and walked along behind us whistling and trying to pretend that he wasn't with us.

When our father saw my bald head he laughed. I asked him if my hair would grow into thick black curls. 'Only if you can keep your fingers crossed behind your back for about six weeks,' he replied. Well, I tried, but my fingers seemed to get uncrossed in the night.

Father helped me to find a hat which I could wear all the time indoors to hide my bald head. The blue and yellow sun-bonnet seemed to be the best so I wore the sun-bonnet all the time.

The following morning I went to school. Even bald children must go to school because they aren't ill. I wore my sun-bonnet beneath my school hood. Mother wrote a note to my teacher Miss White. It said:

Dear Miss White,

I hope you will allow Rosemary to wear her sun-bonnet all the time. She is almost completely bald.

Yours sincerely,
R. Grey

After reading the note Miss White took me into the corridor. She untied my sun-bonnet and looked at my bald head. A tear trickled down her cheek. I hoped she wasn't going to cry like

Mother. She didn't, she just said, 'What a pity. Keep your sun-bonnet on all the time.'

In the hall the whole school stood in rows waiting for the headmistress, Mrs Musselbrook. She strode to the front of the hall. 'Good morning, children,' squawked Mrs Musselbrook.

'Good morning, Mrs Musselbrook,' we chanted back.

The teacher at the piano began to play 'All Things Bright and Beautiful'.

'Stop!' squawked Mrs Musselbrook. 'That girl wearing the fancy-dress hat, take it off at once.'

So I untied my blue and yellow sun-bonnet. A gasp went up from the whole school. 'Fleas!' screamed Mrs Musselbrook. 'Put the fancy-dress hat back on at once!' So I tied my bonnet back on.

We sang 'All Things Bright and Beautiful'. And that was the end of that. After a few weeks my thin, wispy fair hair had grown again. So I stopped wearing my pretty blue and yellow sun-bonnet.

IRIS GRENDER

THE LITTLE CHAP

It was about the time when the papers were full of stories about mysterious flying objects passing across the sky and when even the children were talking about Martians and Moon-men. It was that time when we spent the year at Gran's.

Because she didn't know what to do with us at times Gran would send us on errands. This time it was across the heath and up to the beekeeper's to buy honey for Sunday tea.

All the way there, our Alan played Martians fighting space-monsters, or said, 'What would you do if – ?' without waiting for an answer. Just giving me his ideas and kicking up clouds of the chalky sand whenever a patch occurred across the path, and pretending to fight off strange beasts with the sappy fronds of young bracken.

He was still talking about Beings from Space when we got to the beekeeper's, way out on the heath, under the pine knoll.

He was a very old man, that beekeeper. His hands were twisted and he lifted down our pot of honey with the pads of his fingers, then hooked a little finger under one side of his steel glasses to adjust them so that he could see us better.

Young Alan went on with his space-talk.

'Flying saucers and Beings from another world. That's what they're saying nowadays, is it? Well, I'm not surprised. Not at all,' said the old, old man.

He looked across the heath, where the bees were bumbling in the purple and gold of warm ling and gorse blossoms. 'Don't say it's nonsense, Missy. Say you don't know. Ay, say you don't know.

'There are things you stumble on in the lonely parts. Take what we used to call fairy-rings when I was a lad. Round as a parlour table-top and the harebells laid flat like they had been trod and trod. Out on the heath time and again you'd come upon them. Fairy trod they used to say.' He paused and peered for a moment from under his raggedy white eyebrows. Then, seeing that we children were attentive, he went on in a seemingly irrelevant way, as if caught up in an old memory:

'We never had children of our own,' he said, 'though we should have liked them. Especially Mother, because she came of a large family and the heath is a lonely place for one as is used to company. Still for all that, we once had a dear little chap who gave us a deal of joy – a deal of joy.'

He paused and smiled at us, showing strong old yellow teeth below the fringe of his grey moustache.

'We were passing middle age then, and I was still working as head cowman down at Long's Bottom, and Mother was becoming fretting lonely. It was dull for her then, with me away all day, especially with her legs going sudden like they did. She never moped to me, that wasn't her way; but I knew for all that.

'Well, it were one evening when I was coming home – 'bout this time of year I reckon – that I found this little chap walking all alone in the heather.'

He paused and stared suddenly at my brother who was trapped by his gaze.

'Stark naked he was, with h'eyes like blackberries and brown all over as if clothes had never covered him, and a bare little head with never a hair on it, shining like a h'acorn. There he was, chit-chattering to himself in a foreign sort of language that sounded low and tinkly like a bunch of harebells does when you shakes it close by your ear.'

Alan and I nodded, we knew that sound from past experiment.

'I took his little hard hand in mine, and asked him kind where he had come from, but he only smiled at me. So I looked round for his kin and hollered a bit, thinking at first he might be a tinker's chavvi, but the heath was bare of people. So I took him home to Mother.'

He paused again and I knew our Alan's mind was making pictures like the ones my mind was making – flashes of shiny brown skin and harebells and blackberry eyes.

'I knew we should have given him up to someone,' the old man told us; 'but Mother said "no". The minute she clapped eyes upon his little merry face she knew he was hers for as long as he could be spared to us.

'Mother took him straight indoors and he went happy, holding to the side of her h'apron because she hadn't a hand to spare along

of her sticks. And somehow she managed to bath him in the old wash tub as I filled, and dried him and covered him with one of my h'old nightshirts and fed him, and put him to sleep at last on the ottoman beside our bed.

'That evening she set to work with the sewing machine making oddments of clothes for him.

'"Bill," she said, "we'll watch the papers and we'll keep our ears open, and if he's got worried parents we'll send him back good and honest. But it seems to me," she says, "as no mortal woman on earth would let a little chap like that wander about the heath on his own so disrespectable with no clothes on."

'So we kep' him, for no one ever came inquiring for him and we never heard of such as he being given out lost. As the months went by we came near to forgetting that he wasn't our very own.'

He paused again and we watched the bees in the hardy garden flowers as they dipped and dived, clambered and clung and emerged yellow-dusted and nectar-dizzy!

'He was a queer little fellow was that, but very good and gay. He was keen, too, and quick to show how fond he was by helping us best he could, for all he would never turn his tongue to speak our language. His little nimble fingers were all about the garden pulling weeds for me, and it seemed wherever his fingers fell the flowers have growed the better for it.

'It was the same in the house with Mother. He would fix his bright little eyes on her face, and then do for her the very thing she was just about to do for herself. Many's the morning I'd come down to find him up and about in the chilly first dawn, pulling in firewood with his little thin arms, all the time chuckling to himself as if he was having the time 'of his life.'

Oh, I saw it all – beyond the golden globes of honey-light, beyond the stretches of sun-drenched heath, that strange and happy honey-brown face full of smiles and blessings.

'Mother called him Billy after me and he seemed to know his name, for he would sort of come fluttering down the stairs or across the garden when we called him, quick and pretty as a bird. No one never did know how old he was, but if cleverness was anything he was old as the hills.

'Well, things were very happy for us all. For two years Billy was Mother's own dear little chap. He never once seemed to pine for those he must have known before we took him in. He might have been our very own. And loving! The love in him was so strong it seemed to fill the whole place. Especially towards the end.

'It was in the third summer I noticed a change in the little chap. I never marked its beginning, but his movements became less quick and his smiles less bright, and sometimes, instead of helping us like he'd done before he'd go out into the garden and sit very quiet watching them old spiders making their webs in the currant bushes.

'I didn't like to say anything to Mother, but she noticed all right, for one day she said, "Bill – something funny keeps happening up in Billy's bedroom." We'd given him the little apple-loft under the roof where the martins nested, and hard though it'd been for her, Mother had climbed to keep it sweet for him every day he was with us. "I've been finding long threads of a sort of silky stuff all over the place – like the beginnings of cobwebs – only stronger –

and prettier. I brush them away each morning, but they are back again next day."

'"Some game he's playing with your work-box," I says, though I knew our Billy never played games.

'"Bill," she says, "I've no thread in my work-box as pretty as that. And another thing, Father, Billy's altering. He don't like me bathing him no more. He goes off and hides when he sees me put the big saucepans on the stove. He don't like to be seen naked no more."

'It seemed she was afeared to tell me at first, in case I took against the little chap, but now it all poured out and with the telling came her poor tears.

'"Bill, I think there's something queer growing on his chest. He won't let me look. He laughs, but he won't let me. He's grown different," Mother says.

'And all this time Billy was growing stiller and quieter. Not ill, but quiet as if he had a deal to ponder on, and graver too and somehow powerful. I suppose we had always known he was uncommon. Unchancy really. But we just loved him still and let him be.

'So in a way we were prepared when one Saturday afternoon he turns away from us, and climbs up to his little room, very slow and tired-like, in the little shirt and breeches Mother had sewn for him, with his little bald head bent low as he went. But not as if he had a sickness, mind – but tired – tired out. When Mother gathered her sticks and made to follow him, he turned and shook his head at her and went up alone as if he knew what he had to do.

'"Leave him be," I said to her. "He's tired, the dear chap. Leave him be till the morning," I told her.

'But there was no comfort in Mother. "No, Father," she said (did I tell you we'd started calling each other "Mother" and "Father" since Billy came?). "No, Father, we must just be thankful They let us have him this long. For you know, Bill, he's not of our sort."

'Next morning I helped her up the steps and we went together into Billy's room, timid as children – not knowing what to expect, but somehow knowing that things would be strange.'

The old man paused, and looked deeply, first into my face and then into our Alan's – and I saw that his eyes were full of old man's tears.

'Billy wasn't there. Not our little chap. Not any more. But all across that little room, from ceiling to bed-knob, from quilt to wash-stand, from beam to floorboard, was a great shiny cradle of silky threads, and high up to its middle, rolled up in a bundle of shining silk, still winding and weaving, like I've seen a silkworm wind and weave, was a Creature that must once have been our Billy.

'No, Missy, 'twern't terrible. 'Twere a beautiful and a wonderful sight. We stared as if we were peering through the gate of Paradise, wonderstruck and happy.

'"Come away, Father," says Mother at last, with the tears dropping from her eyes because it was so wonderful and yet so pitiful for her. "We must just wait for what comes of it. But oh, Bill," she says, "I fear that what comes won't be for us."

'So we left it alone until a time came when the threads stopped spinning and the great silky ball lay still in its cradle. Which was the twenty-first day after our Billy had vanished.

'It was late afternoon, and I'd just come in, when we heard a busy sound – like the snapping of bands, and we hurried upstairs together – and as God judges all, Mother went forgetful of her bad legs – without stick or crutch, carried by the wonder of it! And both of us so full of love for our Billy as not to be afraid.

'Just as we were entering that little attic room, the last threads went, and we saw the beautiful shining bundle fall apart. And out of it came a creature of glory. Smaller than ever Billy had been, but shining like a light. It had sort of wings that trembled and shook, and opened and grew, so fast and strange they were like wings on wings.

'It had clusters of eyes opening out on the sides of its head like bubbles of soap, and feelers like the bees have – only longer and curly-looking.

'It was a lovely and lovable thing.

'"Billy," says Mother and puts out her arms to it. But it wasn't Billy no more.

'"We have to let it go," I said, for I saw that those lovely wings were meant for a wider sky than the sky of our poor world. Mother saw that too.

'"Open the window, Father," she said. "But follow him, follow him, Bill. I'd do it myself but for my legs. Follow and see that nothing harms him."

'For to her, even then, he was still in part that little chap she had loved and looked after.

'Then this lovely thing seemed to look at her, with all them bright and shining eyes, and goodness seemed to pour from that looking like the scent comes from the trumpets of lilies.

'Then, it shook out its new wings, and sailed out of the window.

'I hurried downstairs and watched it for a while, hovering over the garden and the hives, and then it bore off gently to the open heath, and although the sun was setting it seemed like the creature held its own light, pure and steady against it.

'I followed after as best I could, until it was lost to sight behind the trees.

'I never saw that lovely thing again. I saw something else though.

'Flying saucers you was saying? Well, I don't know. They may call it that. Anyway I saw it – just above the place where I'd first found him. Mind, it was darkish by then but there was light enough to see it rising, round and flattish and spinning with a noise like an 'umming top makes as it went up and away. Yes, you could say saucerish.

'I stayed there until the moon came up, staring and hoping for more wonders, but all I saw was a round fairy-ring mark in the turf before me where that round thing had been.

'No, I h'aint seen nothing since. And you never hear of fairy-rings being found hereabouts these days so I take it they don't favour these parts no more.'

'What do you think?' whispered our Alan, his eyes popping like blue grapes.

'What do I think Billy was? Well, I thought maybe a fairyman but Mother said he was a Seraphim – like in the Bible – because of his wings on wings and his loving ways. Anyway he wasn't of this world. I suppose nowadays they'd call him a creature from Mars or somesuch.'

I whispered a question.

'The silky threads? Ah yes. Mother gathered them up and joined them, and in the winter evenings before her hands got bad she crocheted them into a great shawl for herself to wear round her poor shoulders.

'She loved it so much, that when she went, I had it put in with her, wrapped round her. It was a lovely sight. In the coffin, as she lay there, you might have fancied she were covered in folded wings.'

And saying this, the old man put the jar of honey into my hands, and forgetting the silver coin on the bench outside his door, turned and went within, and left us to wander, trailing glorious dreams of colour, across the heath and back to our Gran's – with only a pot of honey to show for our afternoon.

DOROTHY EDWARDS

THUNDER AND LIGHTNING

Mr Coombes did not have a tractor on his farm. Instead he had two horses to help with the heavy work. They were black-and-white, huge and handsome, and their names were Thunder and Lightning. In the spring they drew the plough, in the summer they pulled the hay-cart, and in the winter they heaved up tree-stumps with chains and dragged cart-loads of logs back to the farmhouse for firewood.

One fine spring morning, Farmer Coombes was sitting at the breakfast table and looking out of the window as he ate his bacon and eggs. He had already milked the cows and turned them into the meadow, where they were grazing peacefully, but in the paddock, Thunder and Lightning were behaving in a very strange way. They were rampaging. Round and round the field they galloped

until the ground seemed to shake under their heavy hooves. Then suddenly they stopped with a snort, lay down and rolled over and over in the grass. Then they were up and away again.

'Bless me!' said Farmer Coombes. 'What has got into those horses?'

Spring had got into them. Excited by the breeze and the sunshine, they charged at the paddock gate, and as Mr Coombes watched in amazement, first Thunder, then Lightning jumped clear over it into the lane.

The farmer dropped his knife and fork and rushed out across the farmyard, still in his slippers, after the runaway horses. It was a warm morning and he was rather fat, so he soon began to puff and blow.

'Hroo-ha, hroo-ha,' panted Farmer Coombes. Thunder and Lightning galloped on down the lane towards the village, passing the postman on the way. The postman thought he would help to catch the horses, so he ran after the farmer, waving his hat and shouting 'Hoy!'

They passed Granny Crack's cottage, the first in the village.

'Hroo-ha, hroo-ha,' panted Farmer Coombes.

'Hoy! HOY!' shouted the postman.

Granny Crack was hanging her canary's cage in the sunny window and saw the horses charging down the street. She hobbled out to join the chase.

'Come back, oh come back!' piped Granny Crack. But Thunder and Lightning weren't listening. They skidded over the cobbles, past the shop, past the church and past the school. The children were lining up in the playground ready to go in for the first lesson. When they saw Thunder and Lightning flashing past, they all cheered and ran out into the road to follow them.

'Hroo-ha, hroo-ha,' panted Farmer Coombes.

'Hoy! HOY!' shouted the postman.

'Come back, oh come back!' piped Granny Crack.

'Hooray!' yelled the children.

Thunder and Lightning galloped past the last house in the street, where the village policeman was digging in his garden. When he realized what was happening, he dropped his spade and ran after the children.

'Stop, in the name of the Law!' he bellowed. But Thunder and Lightning took no notice. They were going to gallop for ever.

'Hroo-ha, Hroo-ha!' panted Farmer Coombes.

'Hoy! HOY!' shouted the postman.

'Come back, oh come back!' piped Granny Crack.

'Hooray!' yelled the children.

'Stop, in the name of the Law!' bellowed the policeman.

Goodness knows where they would all have ended up, if Thunder and Lightning had not turned a corner and found the road blocked – by a tractor. They slid to a halt, then reared up on their strong hind legs, neighing with disgust. They would have turned and galloped back the way they had come, but Farmer Coombes came puffing round the corner.

'Hroo-ha, hroo-ha!'

He was quickly followed by the postman, still shouting, 'Hoy! HOY!' and Granny Crack, who could hardly whisper, 'Come back, oh come back,' and all the children shouting, 'HOORAY!' at the tops of their voices when they saw Thunder and Lightning held by the farmer.

251

Last of all came the policeman, still bellowing 'Stop, in the name of the ... oh! You have stopped!'

'You've led us a dance,' said the farmer, shaking his fist at the horses. They hung their great heads and whinnied. 'Now we must get back to the farm. There's work to be done.'

'And I must get back to delivering my letters,' said the postman.

'I'm quite worn out,' said Granny Crack.

'We're missing our lessons, ' said the children. 'Hooray!' added the naughty ones.

'I'm supposed to have gone on duty,' said the policeman. 'Suppose there is a burglary while I'm out of the village ... without my helmet, too.'

Farmer Coombes looked at the runaways.

'Thunder and Lightning made us run all this way, so they shall carry us back,' he decided.

So all the children scrambled on to Thunder's broad back while the others climbed on to Lightning. (The policeman lifted up Granny Crack.) They jogged slowly back along the road, the horses looking as if they had never gone faster than a trot in their lives.

The policeman's wife was waiting at the garden gate with his helmet and his jacket. The policeman slid off Lightning's back, grabbed them, kissed his wife and leapt on to his bicycle. At the school,

the children tumbled off Thunder and rushed up to their teacher to tell her all about their exciting ride. Granny Crack was carefully lowered down outside her cottage and went in to make herself a cup of strong, sweet tea. Mr Coombes put the postman down in the lane so that he could finish delivering his letters. Then he led Thunder and Lightning home.

'I suppose you are both too tired now to do any work,' he said to them sternly. 'I think I shall have to buy a tractor after all.' The two big horses shook their heads, neighed softly and nudged the farmer gently with their noses.

'All right,' said Farmer Coombes with a smile. 'Back you go to the paddock for a rest,' and he watched them amble through the gate before he went indoors to finish his breakfast. He had quite worn out his slippers on the road, so he had to buy a new pair – but he didn't buy a tractor.

ALEXA ROMANES

253

THE BLACKSTAIRS
MOUNTAIN

Once upon a time a poor widow and her granddaughter lived in a tiny house on the top of a hill. From the windows of this tiny house you could see down into a green valley, and across the valley to a great mountain called the Blackstairs. Witches lived on the mountain. So every night, before they went to bed, the widow and her granddaughter did four things.

This is what they did: first, they loosed the band that worked the spinning wheel and laid it on the wheel-seat; second, they emptied the washing water into a channel that ran under the house door; third, they covered the burning turf on the hearth with ashes; fourth, they took the broom and pushed the handle of it through the bolt sockets of the house door, where the bolt itself had long ago rusted away. And, having done all that, they went to bed and slept soundly, knowing that the witches could not get in. Because the doing of these things formed a spell to keep the witches out.

But one day the widow and her granddaughter went to market, to sell the linen thread they had spun. It was a wild, wild day, and a wilder night. Coming home, they took shelter from a storm of rain under some trees; and by the time the rain had eased off a bit, it was night; they missed their way in the dark, and didn't get home till very late.

When they did get home, they were so weary that their one thought was to get to bed; and they forgot all about the doing of those four things that they should have done to keep the witches out.

Well, they ate a sup and they drank a sup, and were making to go to their beds when there came four loud bangs on the house door. They were making for the door then, to see who was knocking, when a voice screamed out of the night; and it was such an unholy scream that the widow and her granddaughter stood still in the middle of the kitchen and clutched each other in fear.

254

'Where are you, washing water?' screamed the voice.

And the washing water answered, 'I am here in the tub.'

'Where are you, spinning wheel band?' screamed the voice.

And the wheel band answered, 'I am here, fast round the wheel, as if it were spinning.'

'Broom, where are you?' screamed the voice.

And the broom answered, 'I am here, with my handle in the dustpan.'

'Turf coal, where are *you*?' screamed the voice.

And the burning turf answered, 'I am here, blazing over the ashes.'

Then – *bang, bang, bang, bang* at the door again, and a score of hideous voices howled, 'Washing water, wheel band, broom, and turf coal, let us in!'

The door flew open: in rushed a great company of witches; and in their midst, leaping and yelling, was Old Nick himself, with his red horns and his green tail.

Pandemonium! Witches all round them, whirling about the kitchen, whooping, bawling, yelling with laughter. The grandmother fell down in a faint, and there was the terrified granddaughter standing now in the midst of a throng of jeering, ill-favoured faces and skinny waving arms, with her poor old grandmother lying like a dead thing at her feet.

Old Nick, with the red horns and the green tail, had seated himself on a stool by the fire. He had his hands to his nose, and he was pulling that nose in and out as if it were a trombone, and making the most hideous music with it. The witches began to dance to the music, kicking up their heels, leaping till their heads cracked against the ceiling, upsetting the chairs, the table, the pots and pans, the china and the crocks. *Smash*, went the widow's best china teapot; *smash, smash*, went cups and plates; *clitter, clatter, smash, smash* – everything was tumbling off the dresser. The very dresser itself reeled and swayed and toppled sideways against the window, and the window panes fell out with a crash.

'Oh what shall I do, what *shall* I do?' thought the poor terrified granddaughter. 'Oh, if granny should die! If this goes on till cockcrow granny *will* die – she will never live to see another day! I must do something – but what *can* I do?'

Then an idea came to her. And if a good fairy didn't put that idea into the girl's head, then who did? The music that Old Nick was making with his nose became more and more hideous; the dance of the witches became more and more furious: screaming with laughter they leaped forth and back over the poor old grandmother, stretched on the floor in her faint. But they were taking no notice of the girl. So, holding her breath, and a step at a time, the girl sidled her way towards the house door. The door was still open. The girl slipped through it, and out into the night.

What did she do then? She screamed with all her might, rushed back into the kitchen, and shouted at the top of her voice, 'Granny, Granny, come out! The Blackstairs Mountain and the sky above it is all on fire!'

Instantly the music stopped, and the dancing stopped. Old Nick made one leap through the window; the witches crowded after him, some through the door, some through the window. Out in the night rose a great and terrible cry, as with shrieks and lamentations the witches rose into the air and sped away through the darkness towards their home on the Blackstairs Mountain.

The shrieks and lamentations dwindled away into the distance, but the granddaughter hadn't wasted one moment in listening to them. Directly the last witch was out of the house, she seized up the broom and clapped the handle of it through the sockets where the door-bolt ought to be. Then she dragged the tub of washing water across the kitchen, and emptied the water into the channel under the house door. Then she loosed the band of the spinning wheel and laid it on the wheel-seat; and last, she raked the ashes in the hearth over the burning turf, till not one red ember could be seen. Having done all that, she ran to her granny and brought her to her senses by dashing cold water in her face.

The grandmother sat up. 'Is all quiet at last?' she said.

'Yes, all is quiet,' said the girl.

But no: from out in the night came a distant angry roaring; and the roaring grew nearer and nearer and louder and louder, as the witches came whirling back from their home, furious at the trick the girl had played on them.

The roar ended in sudden silence. Then – *tap, tap, tap, tap*: four quiet little knocks on the door.

'Washing water, let me in!' came a wheedling, whispering voice.

But the washing water answered, 'I can't; I am spilled into the channel under the door. I am trickling away round your feet, and my path is down to the valley.'

'Spinning wheel band, *you* let me in!' came the wheedling voice.

But the wheel band answered, 'I can't; I am lying loose on the wheel-seat.'

'Broom, let me in!' whispered the wheedling voice.

'I can't,' answered the broom. 'I am put here to bolt the door.'

'Turf coal, turf coal, open to me, open!' urged the whispering, wheedling voice.

And the hot turf answered, 'I can't; my head is smothered with ashes.'

Then came such a howling and cursing outside the door as made the widow and her granddaughter fall on their knees and

257

cling together. But, howl and curse as they might, the witches could not get in. They whirled away through the night at last, back to their home on the Blackstairs Mountain.

The widow and her granddaughter had a job of it putting their house to rights. But you may be sure, after that night, never again did they go to their beds until they had loosed the spinning wheel band, emptied the washing water, piled ashes over the hot turf, and pushed the handle of the broom through the bolt sockets on the door.

RUTH MANNING-SANDERS

WHAT MARY JO WANTED

Every time Mary Jo saw a dog, any dog – big or little, black, white, old or young – she wished it belonged to her.

'I would rather have a dog than anything on earth,' she said at least twice a week, usually at the dinner table. She sighed. 'I'd be the happiest person in this town if I had a puppy.' She often read the ads in the classified section under 'Pets for Sale' out loud to her parents.

'Puppies must be trained. It takes a lot of patience,' said her father.

'I'd love to train a puppy!' said Mary Jo. 'I'd do it all myself!'

'Puppies cry at night when you first bring them home,' said her father. 'Nobody gets any sleep.'

'They cry because they're lonesome. I'll be the one to get up in the night and talk to my puppy,' said Mary Jo.

'They must be fed every day. They must have fresh water. They should be brushed. They must be given baths,' said her father.

'I'd do it! I'd do it!' said Mary Jo. 'I *want* to feed and brush and wash a dog.'

'A good dog-owner must take full responsibility for her pet,' said her father.

Responsibility was a word Mary Jo had heard a lot lately – ever since her sister had received a canary for her birthday. She was being responsible for her bird, but she was quite a bit older than Mary Jo. Besides, a bird in a cage was not as great a responsibility as a puppy.

'I would be responsible,' said Mary Jo.

Mary Jo read dog books by the dozen. She drew pictures of dogs. She wrote dog stories and dog poems. One morning she put a two-page theme by her father's plate, 'Why I Want a Dog'.

It looked as if fate were on Mary Jo's side when a new pet store opened downtown.

She showed the big opening-day ad in the newspaper to her parents. She read: 'Special for This Opening. Small, lovable, mixed-breed puppies. Only nineteen dollars while they last!'

'I would like a badger,' said Mary Jo's brother. 'Do they have any badgers?' Jeff had just been looking at a picture of a badger family in a new book from the library.

'Can't we go down to see the new pet store? And the puppies?' Mary Jo begged.

'All right, Mary Jo. I believe you're old enough to take care of a puppy,' said her father.

'Oh,' shouted Mary Jo. 'Get your coats, everybody! Let's go!'

'They *are* cute,' said Mary Jo's mother when they stood gazing down at a little pen full of puppies in the new pet store.

'Cute!' said Mary Jo. 'They're the sweetest creatures ever born in this world!'

Her father laughed. 'Which one do you want?'

Mary Jo barely hesitated. One little furry baby had wobbled over to lick her fingers the minute she knelt beside the pen.

'This one,' she said. 'He came right to me. He's the best, the smartest, the most lovable!'

'Have him wrapped up then,' said her father.

'Wrapped up?' said Mary Jo. Then she saw that her father was joking. He got out his billfold.

The first thing the family did when they got home was to put newspapers all over the kitchen floor. Mary Jo turned her old doll

259

bed sideways in the doorway so that the puppy could not go into the rest of the house.

'It's only until you're housebroken,' she told him when he sniffed inquiringly at the doll bed. He reached playfully for her shoe string and looked up into her face.

'You cute, darling baby!' cooed Mary Jo, picking him up and hugging him.

'Be sure to call the vet this week and make an appointment,' said Mary Jo's father. 'He should have his puppy shots right away.'

Mary Jo and her friend Laurie spent hours deciding on a name for him. They made lists and pored over the section of names at the back of the dictionary.

Jeff suggested 'Mr Pickleponc'. That was the silliest name he could think of.

In the end they decided on 'Teddy' because the puppy looked so much like a small teddy bear, and he even squeaked.

He squeaked and cried – *especially* at night. No matter how cosy Mary Jo made his bed in the kitchen or how many times Teddy yawned at bedtime, he always woke as soon as everyone was in bed and the house was still. He woke and cried as if his heart would break. Mary Jo put a night-light in the kitchen, in case he was afraid of the dark. She gave him a little snack at bedtime, in case he was hungry. She put an old toy dog in bed with him, hoping he would think it was a companion. But he didn't.

Mary Jo staggered sleepily from her warm bed out to the kitchen a dozen times a night. She talked to Teddy and sang to him. As long as she was there, he was happy. He tried to get her to play as if it were the middle of the day instead of the middle of the night, and he licked her with his loving puppy tongue. As tired as she was, Mary Jo could never feel angry with him because he was so joyful each time she appeared at the kitchen door and stepped over the doll bed.

But by the end of the first week she could hardly get up in the mornings. She was almost late for school. Everyone looked tired because although Mary Jo was the one who got up to soothe him, Teddy woke the others with his piercing, sad little cries.

A neighbour told them to wrap a clock in flannel and put that beside Teddy in the bed. 'He'll hear the tick and think it's another puppy,' she told them. But it didn't fool Teddy for one minute.

Finally one morning Mary Jo's mother found her asleep on the paper-covered kitchen floor.

'Is this ever going to end?' Mary Jo's mother asked at the breakfast table. 'I don't ever remember hearing of any puppy crying as many nights as this one has.'

'Some of them get used to being alone faster than others I guess,'

said Mary Jo's father wearily. 'But I'm beginning to wish we had never seen that dog!'

'I'm responsible,' thought Mary Jo. 'I've *got* to think of something to keep Teddy quiet.'

That afternoon when she went to the basement to get some old newspapers for the kitchen floor she saw something that gave her an idea.

After dinner that night Mary Jo said, 'You'll be able to sleep tonight. I've thought of a way to keep Teddy quiet.'

'What is it?' asked her mother.

'You'll see,' said Mary Jo. She went down to the basement.

Her parents heard her lugging something up the stairs. It was an old folding cot.

'I'm going to sleep in the kitchen until Teddy is housebroken and can sleep in my room,' she said.

Her mother and father looked at each other.

'Why not?' said her father. 'That's probably the only thing that will solve the problem.'

And it did. Teddy slept without making one squeak all night with Mary Jo on the old cot just above his basket.

Mary Jo thought it was fun to sleep in the kitchen. It was cosy to hear the refrigerator hum and the faucet over the sink drip now and then. In the glow of the night-light she liked to see the toaster and the coffee-pot gleaming. If she woke at daybreak, it was pleasant to see the new day arriving in the kitchen so early. There was a window to the east, so sunlight came to the kitchen first.

And it was fun to surprise her mother by slipping quietly around early to set the table for breakfast and then hopping back into bed and pretending to be asleep when her mother came to the kitchen.

They both pretended that it was the work of the kitchen elf.

'Mary Jo, wake up!' her mother would say. 'Do you know that the kitchen elf was here again?'

'Was he really?' Mary Jo would say, sitting up. 'I didn't hear a thing!'

And she hugged Teddy and tried not to giggle.

JANICE MAY UDRY

JASON'S RAINBOW

Jason walked home from school every day along the side of a steep grassy valley, where harebells grew and sheep nibbled. As he walked, he always whistled. Jason could whistle more tunes than anybody else at school, and he could remember every tune that he had ever heard. That was because he had been born in a windmill, just at the moment when the wind changed from south to west. He could see the wind, as it blew; and that is a thing not many people can do. He could see patterns in the stars, too, and hear the sea muttering charms as it crept up the beach.

One day, as Jason walked home along the grassy path, he heard the west wind wailing and sighing. 'Oh, woe, woe! Oh, bother and blow! I've forgotten how it goes!'

'What have you forgotten, Wind?' asked Jason, turning to look at the wind. It was all brown and blue and wavery, with splashes of gold.

'My tune! I've forgotten my favourite tune.'

'The one that goes like this?' said Jason, and he whistled.

The wind was delighted. 'That's it! That's the one! Clever Jason!' And it flipped about him, teasing but kindly, turning up his collar, ruffling his hair.

'I'll give you a present,' it sang to the tune Jason had whistled. *'What shall it be? A golden lock and a silver key?'*

Jason couldn't think what use *those* things would be, so he said quickly, 'Oh, please, what I would like would be a rainbow of my very own to keep.' For in the grassy valley, there were often beautiful rainbows to be seen, but they never lasted long enough for Jason.

'A rainbow of your own? That's a hard one,' said the wind. 'A very hard one. You must take a pail and walk up over the moor till you come to Peacock Force. Catch a whole pailful of spray. That will take a long time. But when you have the pail full to the brim, you may find somebody in it who might be willing to give you a rainbow.'

Luckily the next day was Saturday. Jason took a pail, and his lunch, and walked over the moor to the waterfall that was called Peacock Force because the water, as it dashed over the cliff, made a cloud of spray in which wonderful peacock colours shone and glimmered.

All day Jason stood by the fall, getting soaked, catching the spray in his pail. At last, just at sunset, he had the whole pail filled up, right to the brim. And now, in the pail, he saw something that swam swiftly round and round – something that glimmered in brilliant rainbow colours.

It was a small fish.

'Who are you?' said Jason.

'I am the Genius of the waterfall. Put me back and I'll reward you with a gift.'

'Yes,' said Jason quickly, 'yes, I'll put you back, and please may I have a rainbow of my very own, to keep in my pocket?'

'Humph!' said the Genius. 'I'll give you a rainbow, but rainbows are not easy to keep. I'll be surprised if you can even carry it home. However, here you are.'

And it leapt out of Jason's pail, in a high soaring leap, back into its waterfall, and, as it did so, a rainbow poured out of the spray and into Jason's pail.

'Oh, how beautiful!' breathed Jason, and he took the rainbow, holding it in his two hands like a scarf, and gazed at its dazzling colours. Then he rolled it up carefully, and put it in his pocket.

He started walking home.

There was a wood on his way, and in a dark place among the trees he heard somebody crying pitifully. He went to see what was the matter and found a badger in a trap.

'Boy, dear boy,' groaned the badger, 'let me out, or men will come with dogs and kill me.'

'How can I let you out? I'd be glad to, but the trap needs a key.'

'Push in the end of that rainbow I see in your pocket; you'll be able to wedge open the trap.'

Sure enough, when Jason pushed the end of the rainbow between the jaws of the trap, they sprang open, and the badger was able to clamber out. 'Thanks, thanks,' he gasped, and then he was gone down his hole.

Jason rolled up the rainbow and put it back in his pocket; but a large piece had been torn off by the sharp teeth of the trap, and it blew away.

On the edge of the wood was a little house where old Mrs Widdows lived. She had a very sour nature. If children's balls bounced into her garden, she baked them in her oven until they turned to coal. Everything she ate was black – burnt toast, black tea, black olives.

She called to Jason. 'Boy, will you give me a bit of that rainbow I see sticking out of your pocket? I'm very ill. The doctor says I need a rainbow pudding to make me better.'

Jason didn't much want to give Mrs Widdows a bit of his rainbow, but she did look ill, so, rather slowly, he went into her kitchen, where she cut off a large bit of the rainbow with a breadknife.

Then she made a stiff batter, with hot milk and flour, stirred in the piece of rainbow, and cooked it. She let it get cold and cut it into slices and ate them with butter and sugar. Jason had a small slice too. It was delicious.

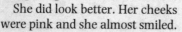

'That's the best thing I've eaten for a year,' said Mrs Widdows. 'I'm tired of black bread. I can feel this pudding doing me good.'

She did look better. Her cheeks were pink and she almost smiled.

As for Jason, after he had eaten his small slice of pudding, he grew three inches.

'You'd better not have any more,' said Mrs Widdows.

Jason put the last piece of rainbow in his pocket.

There wasn't a lot left now.

As he drew near the windmill where he lived, his sister Tilly ran out to meet him. She tripped over a rock and fell, gashing her leg. Blood poured out of it, and Tilly, who was only four, began to wail. 'Oh, my leg! It hurts dreadfully! Oh Jason, please bandage it, *please*!'

Well, what could he do? Jason pulled the rest of the rainbow from his pocket and wrapped it round Tilly's leg. There was just

enough. He tore off a tiny scrap, which he kept in his hand.

Tilly was in rapture with the rainbow round her leg. 'Oh! how beautiful! And it has stopped the bleeding!' She danced away to show everybody.

Jason was left looking rather glumly at the tiny shred of rainbow between his thumb and finger. He heard a whisper in his ear and turned to see the west wind frolicking, all yellow and brown and rose-coloured.

'Well?' said the west wind. 'The Genius of the waterfall did warn you that rainbows are hard to keep! And, even *without* a rainbow, you are a very lucky boy. You can see the pattern of the stars, and hear my song, and you have grown three inches in one day.'

'That's true,' said Jason.

'Hold out your hand,' said the wind.

Jason held out his hand, with the piece of rainbow in it, and the wind blew, as you blow on a fire to make it burn bright. As it blew, the piece of rainbow grew and grew, until it lifted up, arching into the topmost corner of the sky; not just a single rainbow, but a double one, with a second rainbow underneath *that*, the biggest and most brilliant that Jason had ever beheld. Many birds were so astonished at the sight that they stopped flying and fell, or collided with each other in mid air.

Then the rainbow melted and was gone.

'Never mind!' said the west wind. 'There will be another rainbow tomorrow; or if not tomorrow, next week.'

'And I *did* have it in my pocket,' said Jason.

Then he went in for his tea.

JOAN AIKEN

THE STORIES CLASSIFIED

THE STORIES CLASSIFIED

Country

Magical Tales

At Home

Dragons and Monsters

Christmas

Scary Stories

THE STORIES CLASSIFIED

School Stories

Funny Stories

INDEX OF TITLES

INDEX OF AUTHORS

INDEX OF AUTHORS

ACKNOWLEDGEMENTS

The editor and publishers gratefully acknowledge permission to reproduce copyright material in this book:

'Eggs' and 'Jason's Rainbow' by Joan Aiken, reprinted by permission of the author; 'The Dutch Doll' by Ruth Ainsworth, reprinted by permission of the Estate of Ruth Ainsworth; 'Miss Hickory' from *Miss Hickory* by Carolyn Sherwin Bailey, copyright 1946 by Carolyn Sherwin Bailey, copyright renewed © by Rebecca Davies Ryan, 1974. Reprinted by permission of Hodder and Stoughton Ltd and by permission of Viking Penguin Inc.; 'Queen Maggie', copyright © Margaret Stuart Barry, 1974, reprinted by permission of Curtis Brown Ltd, London; 'Never Meddle with Magic' by Jane Barry, reprinted by permission of the author; 'The Paper Palace' from *The Elephant Party and Other Stories* by Paul Biegel (Kestrel Books), reprinted by permission of Penguin Books Ltd; 'Dribble' from *Tales of a Fourth Grade Nothing* by Judy Blume, reprinted by permission of the Bodley Head. Text copyright © 1972 by Judy Blume, reprinted by permission of the publishers, E. P. Dutton, a division of New American Library; 'The Pudding Like a Night on the Sea' from *The Julian Stories* by Ann Cameron, reprinted by permission of Victor Gollancz Ltd; 'A Night Out with Tom' by Kathryn Cave, reprinted by permission of the author; 'What We Need is a New Bus' by Jean Chapman, reprinted by permission of the author; 'Baby Sparrow' by Mary Cockett, reprinted by permission of the author; 'The Little Chap' from *The Magician Who Kept a Pub* by Dorothy Edwards (Kestrel Books), reprinted by permission of Penguin Books Ltd; 'The Seventh Princess' from *The Little Bookroom* by Eleanor Farjeon, reprinted by permission of David Higham Associates Ltd; 'The Lost Boat' by Phyllis Flowender, reprinted by permission of the author; 'A Bunch of Flowers' by René Goscinny, reprinted by permission of Les Editions Denoël Gonthier Planete and of Blackie and Son Ltd; 'Did I Ever Tell You About the Time When I was Bald?' by Iris Grender, reprinted by permission of Century Hutchinson Ltd; 'Quaka Raja' from *Listen to this Story* by Grace Hallworth, reprinted by permission of Methuen Children's Books; 'The Farm Brothers' Band' by Ursula Hourihane from *The Second Read-to-Me Story Book*, reprinted by permission of Methuen Children's Books; 'The Dragon Who Cheated' from *The Dribblesome Teapots* by Norman Hunter, reprinted by permission of the Bodley Head; 'A Fishy Tale' by Gene Kemp, reprinted by permission of the author; 'The Kidnapping of Clarissa Montgomery' copyright © Robin Klein, 1984, reprinted by permission of Curtis Brown Ltd, London; 'The Fiend Next Door' from *The Fiend Next Door* by Sheila Lavelle, reprinted by permission of Hamish Hamilton Ltd; 'The Ghost Who

ACKNOWLEDGEMENTS

Came Out of the Book' from *Nonstop Nonsense* by Margaret Mahy, reprinted by permission of the author and J. M. Dent & Sons Ltd; 'The Blackstairs Mountain' from *A Book of Witches* by Ruth Manning-Sanders, reprinted by permission of Methuen Children's Books; 'The Snowtime Express' copyright © 1962 by Lilian Moore, reprinted by permission of Marian Reiner for Lilian Moore; 'Emily and the Egg' by Sarah Morcom, reprinted by permission of the author; 'In the Middle of the Night' from *What the Neighbours Did and Other Stories* by Philippa Pearce (Kestrel Books), reprinted by permission of Penguin Books Ltd; 'The Castle on Bumbly Hill' by Phyllis Pearce, reprinted by permission of the author; 'The Mice and the Christmas Tree' from *Little Old Mrs Pepperpot* by Alf Prøysen, reprinted by permission of Century Hutchinson Ltd; 'Thunder and Lightning' by Alexa Romanes, reprinted by permission of the author; 'Jack Jackdaw' by Anne Rooke, reprinted by permission of the author; 'The Magpie's Nest' by Michael Rosen, reprinted by permission of the author; 'The Secret of the Stairs' by Lynne Russell, reprinted by permission of the author; 'What Happened to Mustard' from *A Story a Day* by Doris Rust, reprinted by permission of Faber and Faber Ltd; 'Galldora and the Mermaid' from *New Adventures of Galldora* by Modwena Sedgwick, reprinted by permission of Harrap Ltd; 'The Lost Keys' from *Pepper Face and Other Stories* by Ann Standen, reprinted by permission of Faber and Faber Ltd; 'Father Christmas' from *Adventures of Polly and the Wolf* by Catherine Storr, reprinted by permission of Faber and Faber Ltd; 'Many Moons' by James Thurber. Copyright © 1943 James Thurber. Copyright © 1971 Helen W. Thurber and Rosemary A. Thurber, published by Harcourt Brace Jovanovich, Inc. and Hamish Hamilton Ltd; 'The Queen is Coming to Tea' by Hazel Townson, reprinted by permission of the author; 'What Mary Jo Wanted' by Janice May Udry, reprinted by permission of Thomas Crowell Inc.; 'Slipper-Slopper' from *Adventures of No Ordinary Rabbit* by Alison Uttley, reprinted by permission of Faber and Faber Ltd; 'Forgetful Fred' from *The Practical Princess and Other Liberating Fairy Tales* by Jay Williams. Copyright © 1978 by Jay Williams, reprinted by permission of Scholastic Inc.; 'The Birthday Cake' by Ursula Moray Williams, reprinted by permission of the author; 'Mr Antonio' by David Willmot, reprinted by permission of the author; 'The Boring Bear' by Joan Wyatt, reprinted by permission of the author.

Every effort has been made to trace copyright holders, but in a few cases this has proved impossible. The editor and publishers apologize for these unwilling cases of copyright transgression and would like to hear from any copyright holders not acknowledged.

More Puffin collections

THE WILD RIDE AND OTHER SCOTTISH STORIES
ed. Gordon Jarvie

A spirited anthology of modern short stories from Scotland, ranging widely through ghost stories, adventure, drama and humour.

GUARDIAN ANGELS
ed. Stephanie Nettell

An anthology of stories specially written to commemorate the prestigious Guardian Children's Book Award's 20th anniversary.

TALES FOR THE TELLING
Edna O'Brien

A collection of heroic Irish tales to stir the imagination.

THE GNOME FACTORY AND OTHER STORIES
James Reeves

The imagination of James Reeves's stories and the wit of Edward Ardizzone's drawings combine to make this enchanting collection.

Some other books you might enjoy

A TASTE OF BLACKBERRIES
Doris Buchanan Smith

The moving story about a young boy who has to come to terms with the tragic death of his best friend and the guilty feeling that he could somehow have saved him.

BACK HOME
Michelle Magorian

A marvellously gripping story of an irrepressible girl's struggle to adjust to a new life. Twelve-year-old Rusty, who had been evacuated to the United States when she was seven, returns to the grey austerity of post-war Britain.

JELLYBEAN
Tessa Duder

A sensitive modern novel about Geraldine, alias 'Jellybean', who leads a rather solitary life as the only child of a single parent. She's tired of having to fit in with her mother's busy schedule, but a new friend and a performance of 'The Nutcracker Suite' change everything.

THE SEA IS SINGING
Rosalind Kerven

Tess lives right in the north of Scotland, in the Shetland Islands, and when she starts hearing the weird and eerie singing from the sea it is her neighbour, old Jacobina Tait, who helps her understand it. With her strange talk of whales and 'patterns' Jacobina makes Tess realize that she cannot – and must not – ignore what the singing is telling her. But how can Tess decipher the message?